WICKED RAGE

BOOK 3 OF WICKED MAGIC

MINETTE MOREAU

Editor: Amy Briggs
Cover Art: Designrans

CHAPTER
ONE

FEATHER

"C'mon, Feather," Andi begged. "Prom isn't going to be the same without you."

"I don't have a date, remember?" Feather unclipped the last hot roller from her best friend's silky black hair and put it back in the box. "You know Rizan will eat anyone who touches me. Besides, I didn't buy a dress."

"You can be my date." Andi fluffed her hair and pouted, her red-glossed lower lip sticking out. "Just wear the dress you wore to your mom's swearing in."

"Two girls going to prom together isn't going to fly in rural Arizona. Besides, what would Christopher think?"

Letting out a derisive snort, Andi brushed her hair aside to reveal a mating bite on her shoulder. "He might be a mated alpha, but he's a teenage male. You know exactly what he's going to think about having two beautiful dates for prom."

Feather unplugged the hot rollers and set them aside to

cool. "You shouldn't have let him bite you so soon. Aren't you going to miss going to college?"

"That was never my dream," Andi replied, slipping her feet into high-heeled sandals. "I just want to take my place as the alpha's mate and raise a family. Christopher is having enough trouble leading the pack as it is, and it will fall apart unless he has a strong bitch at his side." She paused, her expression going distant and sad. "We lost so many, and it's our duty to make the Arizona wolves strong again."

As if on cue, there was a knock at the door. Andi brushed her cheek against Feather's, an instinctive gesture from wolves to show affection and companionship. "Please, come with us?"

The thought was tempting. Feather sighed in resignation, knowing she was going to spend her prom night alone with Netflix and a few fingers of scotch from the bottle of single malt in her father's office. Even if she wanted to go, which she did not, fates be damned, Rizan would shadow her every step if she got brainless enough to attempt going to prom with or without a date.

The massive diamond rose he'd given her for her eighteenth birthday threw a rainbow on the ceiling of her bedroom, mocking her with its presence. It was a constant reminder of him. She knew the peculiarities of gifts from dragons. It would come back like a bad penny even if she dropped it into a volcano. All she asked for was a little time. She wanted to go to college. There was a whole world beyond Navajo territory, and Feather wanted to explore it. But she wanted Rizan too.

Fates, he was gorgeous. He had that ridge of muscle on his hips that made a smart girl stupid in no time flat, and she wanted to lick it. The part of her that was bear drooled at the idea. His kisses had been so sweet. She could almost taste his essence of cinnamon and vanilla rum on her tongue.

No, bad mage.

Not that Bear ever spoke to her. She was an ephemerally faint presence in Feather's mind, but she'd called her other nature Bear since she was a little girl. It had been almost like having an invisible friend.

Christopher pushed her bedroom door open, his lanky body filling the doorway. As usual, his eyes went soft when he saw Andi. He might be alpha, but the sight of his mate turned him into a puppy.

In an old-fashioned show of manners, Christopher bowed over Andi's hand and kissed her knuckles. Grinning, he said, "Your chariot awaits, my lady."

"Weirdo." Andi tugged on his hand and pulled him into a hug. "I'm trying to convince Feather to come with us. Want to help?"

"No," Christopher straightened, the strength of an alpha wolf blanketing Feather's room making the air thick and hard to breathe. "She's claimed by a dragon, and we won't interfere."

"But—"

"I said no, Andi." Softening, he kissed her cheek. "Let it go."

It was easy to discount Christopher. Barely past his eighteenth birthday, he was all long limbs and bone, with a goofy grin and a cheerful personality. He was a powerful alpha though, and didn't shy away from conflict. His father had been the same way.

"It's okay," Feather said, trying to relieve the tension. "I'm going to binge something on Netflix and steal papa bear's booze. Go on, and have a good time."

"Are you sure?" Andi asked, biting her lip as she glanced at Christopher.

"Yeah, I'm good. Go have fun." Feather ushered the couple to the front door, waving as Christopher's pickup rumbled away. Breathing out a sigh of relief mixed with a little sadness, she shut the door.

"Didn't want to go to prom anyway," she muttered, trudging to the kitchen. She opened the fridge and sighed at the unpalatable offerings her parents favored. Salad with organic veggies for her mother, and enough salmon to choke a bear for her father.

Bleh.

She grabbed her keys off the pegboard by the back door and shoved her bare feet into boots. Kayenta had pizza, and it was only twenty minutes away. Still grumbling, she opened the door and about choked.

Rizan stood on the stoop, his hand lifted to knock. He held a garment bag over one muscular arm. She hadn't seen him in weeks, and not in his human form since he kissed her. He looked... Fates.

"Why are you wearing a tuxedo?" she asked.

The suit fit him like it was made just for his beautiful body. Studs of jet pierced both ears, and ran down the front of his snowy white shirt. He'd tied his thick locs back into a long braid, highlighting a chiseled jaw decorated with rough black stubble.

He stepped through the door, forcing her to move before he touched her. "I'm told this is what one wears to a senior prom."

"I was just headed out for pizza." She grimaced, knowing she sounded like an idiot. What was it about Rizan that made coherent thought disappear from her head?

4

Rizan's eyes flickered with interest at the mention of food. "I'll provide sustenance after we dance." He crowded her, cupping her chin in a warm palm. "My brother told me you wished to attend this event. I will be your escort."

"What?"

Thrusting the bag into her arms, he said, "Get dressed, morsel. I wish for you to dance with me at this prom."

"Aren't you a little old to be going to a high school dance?" she asked. It was a stupid question. Next to Aunt Yan, Rizan was the oldest living thing on the planet.

He shrugged, tightening the seams of his jacket over broad shoulders until she thought they might tear. "I'm sure I'm a little old for many things, but I will be your escort anyway."

Feather glanced down at the garment bag in her hands, trying to decide what to do. He'd brought her a gown, taking away her excuse of having nothing to wear. He'd gone out his way to dress for the event, and boy did he clean up nice.

"You can't eat anyone," she warned. "All my friends are going to be there, male and female, and I'm going to talk to them."

"As long as they don't touch you, I won't eat anyone."

"Lots of them are wolves. They hug each other and people they're close to because wolves do that. You can't eat anyone, period. And you can't threaten it either."

A muscle worked in his jaw and he nodded. "Very well. I'll just roast anyone who touches you. I won't eat them."

"Rizan..."

He cracked a grin, revealing pointed canines. "Don't worry, morsel. Your sire has educated me on what will be expected. I promise to be on my best behavior."

No wonder her parents hadn't insisted on her going to

5

Flagstaff with them. She gritted her teeth, knowing she'd been thoroughly set up. "Fine. Give me fifteen minutes."

Stomping into her bedroom, Feather resisted the urge to slam the door, shutting it quietly instead. She laid the bag on the bed and unzipped it, revealing a stunning dark purple dress beaded with what looked like real diamonds.

She gasped softly, then lifted it from the bag. The heavy silk shimmered, catching the rainbows from the rose on her desk. Strands of diamonds made up the shoulder straps and crossed in the back, leading down to a full, diaphanous skirt. Fates, she'd never seen anything so beautiful. It must have cost a fortune.

She laid it down and pulled boxes from the bottom of the bag. One contained purple stilettos encrusted with yet more bling, and there was a large velvet box she was almost afraid to open. Biting her lip, she lifted the lid to find a choker made of diamonds the size of blueberries, plus earrings and a bracelet to match.

"Holy shit." She'd been born and bred in this desert and didn't have a material bone in her body. Fancy jewelry and clothes had never been her thing, but damn. Rizan sure knew how to tempt a girl.

After stripping down to her panties, she pulled the dress over her head, nearly moaning at the feel of silk against her skin. It fit perfectly, of course, letting her know her mother must have been involved. The bodice dipped low, revealing the upper curves of her breasts. The back fell almost to her ass, making a bra impossible.

She spun in a circle and giggled, letting the skirt flare around her legs. Her smile faded and she took a good look at herself. Diamonds and silk weren't her, but she could fake it until she made it for tonight. Grabbing mascara and a lipstick, she slapped makeup on her face and twisted her hair into an updo with a few strands left out to tickle her shoulders. Although she almost never wore heels, the sandals were surprisingly comfortable, if a bit precarious. She wondered if she ought to leave them off and wear flats.

They matched the dress though, and Rizan wouldn't let her fall. All she had to do was make it out of her bedroom without faceplanting on the carpet.

Her hand hovered over the jewelry box. What if she lost them? They had to be worth a fortune. No dragon would have anything to do with fake gemstones. Shaking her head, she laughed at herself and got the earrings from the box, then pushed the posts through the holes in her ears.

Gifts from dragons didn't get lost. Though passive, it was powerful magic. Even if they were stolen, they'd return to her within a day or two. Morgaine had explained that when Feather mentioned selling the diamond rose so she could donate the money to relief efforts along the coast after Teran's destruction.

The dragons chipped in, dipping into their hoards to fund the cleanup and reconstruction everywhere, not just the United States. Feather was privately convinced Rizan had something to do with it, but the stubborn lizard refused to admit to anything.

That, more than anything, had endeared dragons to humans. They were like rock stars now, especially Rizan. Still elusive and cranky, he was rarely seen, and never in his human form. She doubted there was a teenage girl in the states that didn't have a poster of him on her wall. Even the infants had a fan club numbering in the millions, and a team of lawyers were settling terms to make a movie about them.

Despite seeing beautiful women all over the world go

on social media with offers to let him father their children, Rizan paid no attention to anything except Feather.

The bear inside her growled in jealousy. Although Feather took after her mother and had never developed the ability to shift, a tiny part of her would always be two-natured. It might have been cool to go to Alaska for fishing trips with her dad, but Feather refused to miss something she never had.

She straightened and checked her teeth for lipstick, then opened the door to face her date.

~

RIZAN

When Feather opened her bedroom door, Rizan had to swallow and forcibly push the dragon down. He'd been wise to insist on the dark purple for her garment. It matched the color of her magic perfectly and turned her dusky skin gold like honey. Her heeled shoes made her almost as tall as he was, and she looked like a queen, elegant and too regal for casual contact.

Humans ought to be bowing at her feet, begging to touch the hem of her gown.

Not his mage. Instead of the trappings of power, she preferred rags and boots. She read old books instead of controlling the masses as she ought to. Unlike Davryn, Rizan had no interest in learning to read. Why bother, when one knew all the stories already?

"How do I look?" she asked, biting that plump lower lip.

He bit back a growl, wanting to kiss her more than anything he'd desired in more millennia than he cared to count. Wracking his brain, Rizan tried to remember the appropriate response Morgaine had given him.

I want to strip you naked and devour your sweet pussy until you spill your cum all over my face was not the correct reply, and he'd likely end up with another blast of her magic to his chest. His ribs still ached from the last time she'd done it, and she'd only used a fraction of the power he sensed within her slim body.

Fates, she'd be terrifying with a familiar. When they'd fought together in the battle against Teran, it had taken all his strength to keep up with her. She'd exhausted Myrddin to unconsciousness, yet still poured her magic into his flame, making it hot enough to sear the land to glass.

Although he knew the earth's magic was rebalancing on the thunderbird's wings, Rizan wasn't sure he liked the evolution of mages. Several of his brethren hid in their hoard chambers already, nursing wounds given to them by the disagreeable creatures. He couldn't muster up much sympathy for them though. They'd been warned about what would happen if they tried to take a mage by force.

Yet he couldn't deny the fierce need to carry Feather to his caves and bind her in soft rope, then tease and tempt her until she begged to join her magic with his. Her face would flush pink, and the scent of mage and desert flowers would grow more potent. She would taste like...

"You look beautiful. I knew that color would suit you."

"Thanks." She looked down and opened her hand, revealing the bracelet he'd given her. "I couldn't do the clasp by myself. Will you help me?"

"Of course." He took it from her and wrapped it around her slim wrist, wishing it was rope. When he got it fastened, he lifted her hand and dropped a kiss on her palm. She blinked up at him, her lips parted in a soft smile.

9

She smiled often, but almost never at him and it nearly stopped his heart.

"Are you ready to go?"

"No. I mean, yes. I..." He'd forgotten something and cast about for words to say while he tried to remember what it was.

Disappointment flashed across her face and she took a step backward. "It's okay, really. We don't have to—"

His Feather would never wear that look of sadness again. He would kill anyone who made her sad, and Rizan swore to himself he'd give up his own life to make sure she never felt unhappy.

"I almost forgot your flowers." The white blossoms of Sidhe night orchids filled his hands, their stems twisted into a crown. "A beautiful woman should have flowers, but they aren't as lovely as you."

Blushing a furious pink, Feather lowered her head, allowing him to place the crown on her dark hair. "Who are you, and what have you done with Rizan?" she asked, looking up at him, her dark eyes hooded with thick lashes.

"The day we met, the thunderbird told me to grow some manners. Have I met your expectations?"

Fates knew he'd tried. Morgaine had schooled him for weeks in preparation for this event, and he'd even managed to make Feather's mother nod in approval once.

"Wow. I mean... Yeah." She looked down, still blushing. "We should go now."

Although he had no idea how to drive it, he escorted her outside to show her another present he'd obtained for her. Instead of the rattletrap old pickup truck she called Daisy, he'd purchased something called a 1951 Jaguar, trading it for a handful of rubies of no particular value. She needed something beautiful and elegant.

Feather stopped short, staring at the car. "Awesome, you turned my pumpkin into a carriage for the ball." She laid careful fingers on the hood, petting the glossy blue paint. "We'll have to remember to send it back later."

He held up the keys and put them in her hand. "No, I bought it for you. It's yours."

"Rizan... Fates. I don't know what to say to that."

"You don't need to say anything. Drive it and enjoy it."

She spun around, her dress flaring around her ankles. "You need to stop giving me stuff."

"I like giving you things."

"No." Feather rubbed her forehead. "It's too much. Diamonds, a huge expensive car, this dress. I can't even... And that rose."

Tears welled in her eyes and Rizan understood why his brother went crazy when his mate, Morgaine, cried. It was an awful scent, sickly sweet with bitter salt, and he hated it.

His muscles swelled under the idiotic suit Morgaine had given him, threatening to tear the seams. Flame rose in his belly, an atavistic response to anything that distressed his mage.

Calming himself, he stroked her arms, enjoying the touch of her soft skin. "I don't want to upset you, sweet Feather. My hoard is worthless unless you enjoy it, and I want to share it with you. It makes me happy to give you gifts."

Letting out a breath, she nodded and wiped her eyes. "Okay. Yeah... Okay. I can deal. Just no more presents for a while, please?"

In an effort to cheer her, he said, "But all my gifts were for occasions. You needed a present for your birthday, so I gave you the rose. The dress and jewelry were for your prom, and the car is for graduation."

She cocked her head and burst into laughter. "Okay, you got me there. But no more, please. No more gifts until I graduate from college."

"Except your birthday. I'm going to give you something to celebrate the anniversary of your birth, and maybe also for the anniversary of the date you kicked me in the chest, and every year on this date too."

"What's so special about today?" she asked stroking the leather seat of her car.

Touching her chin, he lifted her face. "It's the day you smiled at me and meant it."

Feather rolled her eyes and got behind the wheel of her new car. "Fair enough. Hop in, cowboy, and I'll take you for a ride."

TWO

FEATHER

I nstead of thinking about how Rizan's words made her feel, Feather caressed the Jag's stick shift, knowing it had some sort of phallic connotation, but totally not caring. It slipped into first like butter, purring to life as she released the clutch.

What was she going to do with a vintage Jaguar? Maybe she could talk her dad into building a carport or something to store it. The Arizona sun would eat her pretty baby alive.

She looked at the dirt road stretching out ahead of her. It wasn't Bonneville, but it was close. "Ready for some speed, Rizan?" she asked.

"I don't understand."

"You will!" She let out a whoop of joy and floored the pedal. She spared a glance at Rizan. He grinned at her, even though his fingers were clenched tightly on the door frame. Downshifting, she floored it, shouting in joy as the Jag leaped forward. She blew past the general store, and left the school in the dust.

Feather never wanted this ride to end. She loved her new car, but she couldn't keep accepting his gifts. Letting out a soft sigh, she slowed down to a speed that wouldn't get her arrested and turned around to head back to the school.

He laid a warm hand on her knee, squeezing gently. "Do you like your gift?" he asked.

"Yes, thank you." She bit her lip, then added, "I'm sorry I was such a bitch about you giving me stuff."

She turned into the school parking lot and eased it into a space in the back, well away from the other cars. Looking out over the football field instead of Rizan, she said, "I'm not a dragon. I feel weird about accepting all these expensive gifts from you. I mean, this car probably cost more than my parents' house. Some of my classmates live on federal assistance, and it's just... I don't know. It's weird to have so many expensive presents when they don't have enough to eat."

"The thunderbird told me you tried to sell the rose to help the humans."

"I'm sorry about that. I didn't mean to offend you."

"You did, at first, but the rose wasn't a gift that made you happy. This vehicle makes you happy, although you and I will have to discuss this need for speed you have."

Rizan got out of the car and rounded the hood. Opening her door, he helped her out. "I will endeavor to give you gifts that bring you joy. I understand you now, I think."

"Oh?" she asked. "What do you think you understand?"

"Objects don't give you pleasure aside from the momentary appreciation of their beauty, do they?"

He cupped her jaw, trailing his hand across her throat and down her collarbone. His lips hovered bare inches above hers, making her want to lean into a kiss. He smelled like musk and something citrusy, tempting her to bury her nose in his chest.

"Yeah, I mean no. I like them and all, but—"

"You value intangibles, sweet mage. Health, happiness, joy. All things that don't come from a dragon's hoard. This car is worth a fraction of the value of the rose, yet you cherish it already."

He took a step back and bowed over her hand. "You'll like my next gift better, I think. Shall we go inside?"

Feather pressed her lips together, resisting the urge to ask him what he planned for her next gift. He took her hand and wrapped it around his arm, the fine wool of his jacket soft under her fingers. She felt like a princess in her beautiful dress and shoes.

Dusty earth and the smell of conflicting perfume mixed with fruit punch met her nose as he opened the gym door. The school hadn't bothered issuing tickets. With only fifty students graduating, what was the point? Instead, they set up a relief fund for the families who had lost children and parents in the fight against Teran. The dark Sidhe had left immense destruction in the wake of his bid for world domination. Millions of lives had been lost, and humanity was still recovering.

Mr. Tully, her physics teacher and one of the chaperones, covered the donation bucket with his hand. "You've already donated enough, Feather. Keep walking."

"I haven't," Rizan replied, opening his hand. Flame rose above his palm, then faded to reveal a perfect sapphire as big as her fist. He dropped it into the bucket and inclined his head. "You may tell my mage if you need further donations."

Leaving Mr. Tully behind, he put his arm around her

waist and moved her further into the gym. "Did that make you happy, morsel?" he asked.

She blinked up at him, the cheap disco ball hanging from the basketball hoop casting shadows over his face. Rizan was so damned confusing. "Why did you do that?" she asked.

"Because I could." He escorted her to the dance floor, pulling her close. "I'm beginning to understand you, Feather Carter. You prefer giving to others, so I shall do the same."

Pop music played from the DJ's laptop in the corner, yet Rizan spun her into a waltz she barely remembered from a dance class she'd taken with her parents ages ago. Had he learned to dance for her? The idea that he'd go to so much trouble for a stupid high school dance almost turned her into a blubbering mess. She'd been horrible to him too. Between blasting him across the desert the first time they'd met and not thanking him for his gifts, she felt like a heel.

She moved her hand from his shoulder to sink her fingers into his locs and pulled him down for a kiss. He growled, yet touched her lips gently, letting her taste cinnamon and vanilla rum. Arousal dripped from her core, dampening her panties and she rubbed against him, desperate for his touch.

Forgetting everything but the need to kiss him, she wrapped both arms around his shoulders, letting him explore her mouth with his tongue. His cock rubbed against her belly, thick and long. Fates, she wanted more, and she resented the barrier of their clothes keeping them apart.

Rizan pulled away, his pupils narrowing to slits in his dark eyes. "Such a tempting morsel. I could take you to my hoard chamber and bring you such pleasure."

"Please," she whimpered. "I—"

Stepping back to put a few inches between them, he said, "But I made a vow to wait five years. You will attend college without my interference."

"I changed my mind," she replied, moving toward him once more.

Chuckling softly, he spun her into the dance. "No, you want to go to college. Your father told me you dreamed of going, and so you shall. Learn, grow, see the world as you wanted."

He was right, damn him. If she went with him now, she'd forever wonder what she'd missed. Five years wasn't so long, really, and he could come visit whenever he wanted. He was a dragon, and could make the trip to Trinity College in the blink of an eye.

"And then what?"

He cupped her chin, the tips of his claws scratching gently across her jaw. "And then you will take your place in my hoard and bond with me. Have your freedom for now, but once that happens, you will never leave my side."

Feather swallowed hard. She could see being bound to him so easily. To have such a close relationship with another being, as Morgaine enjoyed with King Davryn, tempted her. Yet it frightened her almost as much. How could she share her entire being with another creature so much older? They had no shared experiences, nothing in common, and neither of them understood each other, despite Rizan's words to the contrary.

Rizan would consume her, and she had no defense against it.

Dredging up a smile, she said, "We'll see. That's a few years away, and you might find you don't like me so much when I grow up. You might find another mage who interests you more."

Bear sat up and growled at that thought. She didn't like the idea of Rizan with another mage at all.

"Feather!" Andi's shout rang over the music and Feather winced, knowing she'd be the center of attention now.

"Hi, Andi," she said pasting a smile on her face.

Andi and Christopher swept her into a hug, ignoring Rizan's scowl. "I'm so glad you came," Andi said, fingering the diamond strap of her dress. "And you look... Fates, where did you get this gown?"

"Rizan gave it to me."

Andi jerked her hand away. "Damn, girl! If it's from a dragon, you know those are real diamonds, right? This belongs in a safe deposit box, not in a smelly old gym for a high school dance."

"My mage deserved something as beautiful as she is," Rizan replied. "The color suits her."

Cocking her head to the side, Andi inhaled, her nose wrinkling as she bared her teeth. "You look like Rizan, and smell like Rizan, but you sure don't sound like him. Did someone drop you on your head?"

"Enough, Andi," Christopher said, trying to scowl at her. "Behave yourself." The sour expression didn't work on him very well, especially when he hid a grin behind it.

Andi straightened, mortification crossing her face. "I apologize, Rizan. My behavior was unbecoming of an alpha's mate."

Rizan's lips quirked into a smile and he touched the center of his chest. "Your mate is correct, Alpha. The lovely Feather did drop me on my head the day I met her. I still feel it when it rains."

Feather rolled her eyes. "C'mon, Andi. Let's go mingle."

RIZAN

Feather walked away with her friend, leaving Rizan alone with the young wolf.

"I apologize again for my mate's behavior. She knows better," Christopher said.

Rizan turned to face the boy who bore too much responsibility on too-narrow shoulders. All the two-natured had lost many from their ranks, but the battle against Teran had cost the Arizona wolves their alpha, his mate, and dozens of others in the prime of life. "You needn't apologize. Your mate was right, but I'm learning to behave more appropriately."

Christopher nodded. "Thank you." He looked after his mate and Feather as they chatted with a mixed group of two-natured youngsters. "Are you going to take Feather away?" he asked.

"The last time I tried to make Feather go somewhere against her will, she zapped me." Rizan replied, rubbing his chest. "She will go where she wishes."

Letting out a snort, Christopher said, "Yeah, that was pretty funny. She's badass when she's in a mood."

Rizan tried to control his jealousy, knowing the wolf was already mated to a beautiful woman and had no interest in Feather aside from friendship. He wasn't used to having to share attention.

"On the contrary, Feather has a lovely bottom. I'll thank you to keep your eyes on your mate's."

Christopher rolled his eyes and a grin plumped his

angular cheeks. "No, that's not what badass means. It means she's awesome. You know, like sick."

"She's quite well, I assure you. I don't believe mages become ill."

"Damn, dude, how old are you?"

Stroking the stubble on his chin, Rizan considered the question. "I don't know. I wasn't young when the first of the Egyptian pyramids were built. I saw the great floods and volcanoes sweep the land clean for rebirth when the thunderbird last resurrected."

"You're a living fossil. No wonder you don't understand modern English."

The boy was correct, if insulting. Although a few of his brethren had embraced the modern world, Rizan found it too loud and crowded for his tastes. Popular music irritated him, as did the constant barrage of information and stimulus. The vast expanses of uninhabited land were gone, along with most of his favored prey animals.

"I suppose." Rizan focused his attention on Feather. Surrounded by her friends, she looked happy. A small part of him wished he was included, but he had nothing in common with the young people gathered around her.

"What are your plans for the next five years?" Christopher asked, pulling Rizan's attention away from his mage. "Going to school yourself, maybe?"

"I haven't made any."

He jerked sharply and growled when Feather let out a happy squeal, then reached down to embrace a male sitting in a wheeled chair. Still hugging him, she perched on his lap and kissed his cheek.

"That's Justin," Christopher said softly. "He lost his leg and both his parents in the battle. I had to do some fast

20

talking to get the state to agree to let me foster him until he turns eighteen in a few months."

The growl died in Rizan's throat and he swallowed hard. The two-natured had lost so much and his belly twisted with remorse. "What happens after he turns eighteen?"

Christopher shrugged. "He planned on going into the Army to pay for college. That isn't an option for him anymore, so the pack will come up with the money somehow." He went silent and his mouth twitched into a crooked smile. "He wanted to be a doctor."

Holding out a hand, Rizan summoned a treasure from his hoard. "Give Justin this," he said, depositing another sapphire in Christopher's hand. "If it's not enough, tell King Davryn. He'll make up the difference."

Feather might never know of this gift, but he did and it made him feel... good.

CHAPTER

THREE

FEATHER

There was the magic she had inside her, and the enchantment Rizan created with a simple touch on her arm. She couldn't say which was more powerful.

"Are you enjoying yourself?" he asked, pulling her into his arms for a dance.

The words, whispered across the sensitive skin under her ear, made her shiver. "Yes, thank you for bringing me."

"It was my pleasure." He spun her into the waltz, his hand warm against her bare back. "Are you cold?"

"No." She stepped closer and rested her head on his shoulder, wishing she was short enough to rest against his chest like Andi did with Christopher. "How can I be cold if I'm wrapped in my dragon's arms?"

Rizan growled softly and buried his face in her hair. "And you are my mage. My heat is yours, always."

She went silent, allowing him to turn her around the

gymnasium. "What will you do when I'm gone?" she finally asked.

"I will wait for you."

"I'm sure you can think of something better to do with your time."

He tightened his arms around her, then nipped her earlobe, sending a tingling shard of arousal down her spine. "I can't think of anything I'd rather do."

Andi whirled by with Christopher, her laughter filling the air. It was so good to see them happy. There hadn't been enough to smile about in too many months. Couples paired off in corners, their giggled conversation quiet, but no less heartfelt.

The music finally ended and the lights brightened, chasing shadows as quickly as it chased her classmates from their corners. Her eyes burned. This dance was a swan song, but maybe it was the first sign of hope too.

"I guess it's over. The princess turns back into a frog now."

Taking her hand, Rizan walked her outside, following the smiling couples through the double doors and past the elementary school rooms. "You are neither."

"What am I?"

They reached her new car and he cupped her cheeks. "You are a queen."

Lowering his head, he kissed her forehead, his lips lingering for a moment. Pulling away, he cocked his head, then tipped her chin up and kissed her again, his rough stubble rasping against her jaw. The taste of cinnamon and vanilla rum consumed her and she whimpered, wrapping her arms around his thick shoulders.

"Fates help me, I can't resist you," she breathed against his lips before kissing him again.

His lips trailed across her jaw to the sensitive spot under her ear. "You'll make me break my promise, little mage."

"Your promise can start when I leave for London. Kiss me."

His chest rumbled with a low growl and he pulled her against his body, nearly squeezing the breath from her lungs and the desert swirled around them. Never letting his lips leave hers, his flame rose to carry them away.

The sensation of movement was disconcerting, slightly nauseating, and frightening, but she didn't care as long as Rizan kept kissing her. A split second later, they materialized in her bedroom.

"I should have stayed away." He traced a finger across her collarbone and the thin strap over her right shoulder snapped under his claw, scattering tiny diamonds across the floor. His dark eyes glittered almost purple in the reflected light from the pink rose on her dresser. "I promised, but I can't bear to disappoint you." He pulled away, breathing hard. "Send me away, Feather."

She should. Feather knew it. Rizan knew it. Hell, the entire community knew it. But she couldn't. Reaching behind her, she unzipped the dress and let it fall to the floor, then stepped toward him. "I can't."

The seams of Rizan's jacket tore, falling into tatters on the floor. "I can't either," he rasped. "Fates, you're the most beautiful thing I've ever seen."

He looked at her like she supplied the air he breathed. It was heady and intoxicating, even though she wasn't sure she believed him. He was the beautiful one, not her. Five years seemed like forever and much too long to go without his kisses. She wanted this so she could hold the memory close until they could be together again.

"Shh." Feather pulled his hands away from his shirt. "Let me."

Carefully, she popped the studs of his tuxedo shirt away, revealing chiseled muscle, loving how he quivered under her touch. He could have the most beautiful women this world had to offer, yet he trembled for her.

She pushed the fabric aside, then lowered her head to kiss his muscular chest. Her tongue shot out and she traced the ridges of his pecs, just like she'd always wanted to.

"Feather." Her name came out on a low hiss.

"Yes?" She kissed her way down his chest, petting his sleek flanks. The silky hair of his treasure trail sparked tingles in her cheek and she inhaled his musky scent like it was water. "Fates, you smell good."

Fabric tore, and he tossed the shredded shirt away, then picked her up. "You dare tease a dragon?" he growled, his generous mouth twitching into a smile.

"Yes, put me down so I can keep doing it."

He kissed her hard, claiming her mouth with sharp teeth and tongue, then set her down, dropping his hands to his sides. "Do as you will, morsel."

Bear pushed inside her, desperate to set a mating bite to his shoulder, and she felt the sting of fangs erupting. She straightened and closed her mouth, running her tongue over the new dentition.

His expression confused and wary, Rizan took a step back, then picked up the remains of his shirt. "What's wrong?"

She parted her lips, revealing her lengthened canines. "I have fangs."

Blinking, he cocked his head. "Of course, you do. You're partly bear."

"I've never had them before. I didn't know." She crossed her arms over her chest, suddenly unsure. "Is that bad?"

He stalked her, then pulled her arms down. Stroking a big hand down her chest, he leaned close then traced his tongue over her lower lip. "I bet I can make them bigger. You'll need them to give me my mating bite."

Rizan's arms were the only thing keeping her from melting into a puddle at his feet. Although she had many close friends, nobody asked her out. Mages didn't want to date her because of her two-natured heritage, and the two-natured didn't want mage in their bloodlines. They weren't necessarily xenophobic, yet she would never be considered an appropriate mate for anyone simply because the mix of two-natured and mage almost never ended well. It had hurt at first, but she understood it.

Even though her parents made it work, her birth had been an accident combined with a miracle. Babies from such unions sometimes ended up... wrong. The stories told of such creatures were horrifying at best, and would give Hannibal Lecter nightmares at worst.

If Aunt Yan hadn't intervened, she'd have been killed at birth.

Could there be a possibility of a true mating with Rizan beyond taking him as her familiar? Dragons weren't two-natured. They didn't have a human sharing consciousness with an animal. Even in human form, there was no mistaking a dragon for anything else. Bear definitely wanted it, and she'd never once shown interest in another person.

Saliva threatened to drip from the corner of her mouth before she swallowed. "You want a bite *and* a familiar bond?" she asked, her voice quavering.

"Everything," he growled. "In five years, I will demand all you have to give me."

"Greedy."

"I'm also a thief."

In a flash, he tossed her to the bed. She landed and bounced a few times, the breath knocked from her body. Claws bared, he knelt between her knees and grabbed her thighs, spreading them apart.

Hot breath washed across her mons and she let her head fall back. Fates, this was... He was going to do the thing she'd read about, but never expected for herself. The oral sex thing. Her heart pounded, threatening to leap from her chest. The oral sex thing was going to happen to her. Someone was going downtown on Feather Carter.

Are you done?

Bear had never spoken to her, yet the sarcastic voice chased away her spinning thoughts as Rizan touched the tip of his tongue to her core.

"Fates, that feels..."

He licked her, swirling his tongue over the swelling bud of her clit as his claws dug into her inner thighs. The slight pricking pain shot pleasure through her body and her hips bucked against him.

"You smell like wildflower honey, sweet mage. I want to bathe in your perfume and suck your sweet pussy until you come on my face."

Who knew dirty talk was so freaking hot? Letting out a soft moan, she wriggled, desperate to get closer. He tightened his grip on her thighs, keeping her still.

"Please..." She sank her hands into his locs, loosening the tight braid.

"I should tie you," he whispered, taking another swipe at her pussy with his tongue. "Bind you until you can't

27

move and I can feast upon you. Put your hands over your head."

"Fates, yes." She obeyed, the movement making her deliciously vulnerable as her back arched. It was like the filthiest book she'd ever read and she wondered if he'd seen it. He couldn't have. As far as she knew, he hadn't learned to read yet.

He traced a hand down her belly, then circled her opening. "Hold them where they are."

"What happens if I can't?"

"Hmm." He pushed a finger into her tight channel, then curled it up. "I might have to spank you."

RIZAN

Feather's channel gushed perfumed moisture, coating his fingers with her delectable essence. She liked the idea of being restrained and spanked, but that would be a game for another time.

Although he wanted to claim her that very instant and take her bond, he had to make this good for her. This was too important to waste on a hurried rut. Damn his scales for promising her five years. The only option left to him was to ensnare her with passion instead of rope and pray to the fates she remembered him when her time of freedom came to an end.

The thought of her delicate fangs sinking into his shoulder nearly made him spill in the constraining trousers. He hated them, but the flicker of arousal in Feather's dark brown eyes when she first saw him in those ridiculous clothes made him rethink his opinion.

There was little he wouldn't do for his sweet mage.

She spasmed under him, pressing her core against his face. Instead of giving her what she wanted, he let her rub herself against the scruff of beard decorating his chin.

"Rizan! Please, stop teasing me and—"

He sucked her clit into his mouth and rasped his tongue against the little bundle of nerves. Her channel tightened around his fingers, clenching rhythmically, and the thick perfume of her arousal grew stronger. He wanted to roll in that scent until it subsumed his own.

Fingers sinking into his hair, Feather screamed and her channel clamped down, the muscular walls rippling. Although he'd promised to spank her if she moved her hands, he was too happy to give her pleasure to chide her. Then again...

Tracing a hand up her belly, he circled one of her pert pink nipples with a gentle fingertip. "What did I say I'd do if you moved your hands, morsel?"

Her face flushed and damp with passion, she opened glazed eyes. "You said you'd spank me," she slurred. "Worth it. I love your locs."

Resisting the urge to preen, he said, "Turn over."

Shivering, she obeyed, pushing her hips into the air. The sight of her swollen opening made him bite back a groan. There was nothing in the world that could make him truly harm her, but it was impossible to resist the invitation. His hand fell to her round ass with a firm smack.

She let out a sharp gasp, then lifted her hips again. "Fates, Rizan."

A faint pink handprint blossomed on the lower curve of her backside and he couldn't resist giving her a matching one on the other side. "Do you like that?"

"I don't know why, but yes," she breathed, her voice hitching.

He swatted her again, reddening her bottom with carefully placed spanks as he'd watched his brother deliver to Morgaine on occasion. "I'm told the line between pleasure and pain is very thin. Perhaps it is true." He petted her, relishing the heat rising from her skin. "Show me how much you like it."

"How?" she asked, glancing over her shoulder, tousled hair falling over her eyes.

"Touch yourself. Let me see what you like."

Her eyes darkened under thick lashes. "I like it when you touch me."

Rizan wanted to crow like a rooster at her admission, but he calmed himself before he did something unseemly. He slapped her bottom once more. "Let me watch you give yourself pleasure, and perhaps I'll do it again."

With a soft moan, she pushed a hand between her legs. Her slim fingers moved, stroking and petting the silken flesh. Losing interest in spanking her, he knelt and watched avidly, desperate to know what brought her the most joy. His balls aching, he wiped his mouth with the back of his hand, trying to hold himself in place.

Her thighs quivered with strain. "Rizan, please," she whined. "I need more."

Coughing, he cleared his throat, easing the thick lump lodged in his windpipe. "What do you need, morsel?"

"Make love to me, please."

As much as he wanted to draw their time out, he couldn't torment her any longer. Truly, it was torment for them both. "As you wish, sweet. I can't deny you anything."

She turned to sit on the edge of the bed, her plump mouth turning up into a secret smile. "Good to know." Her hands went to the waistband of his trousers and she pulled him close.

"What are you doing?" That smile did strange things to his insides, but he rather liked the sensation. It was fiery and intoxicating like those cocktails his brother loved so much.

"You're wearing too many clothes." She eased the buckle of his belt free and loosened the button, then undid the zipper, the quiet rasp of metal making him shiver. Her eyes widened and she licked her bottom lip, leaving a trail of moisture. "Someone's happy to see me."

"Always."

She looked up at him under the fringe of her lashes and held out a hand. A flat square object appeared in the middle of her palm and she tore it open with her teeth. "I almost forgot something."

"What is that?"

She eased something from the package and held up a translucent circle. "It's a condom. It'll keep me from getting pregnant."

"Would that be so bad?" he asked. He'd never considered offspring of his own, but now the idea was in his head. What was so wrong with him that she wouldn't want his children?

Her voice was soft, but determined. "Ask me again in five years."

"My apologies." He touched her chin, making her meet his eyes. "I forgot our bargain."

"So did I." She turned the pale circle around. "Do you still want to—"

"More than anything." Leaning down, he kissed her, tracing her mouth with the tip of his tongue. Her admission made him want to cuddle her in his arms and tell her everything would be okay.

When she pulled away, her shy smile lit the room. "I wouldn't mind, you know. Just... not yet."

"I know." He stroked a finger down her velvety cheek. "Will you show me how this condom thing works?"

CHAPTER
FOUR

FEATHER

Rizan was the most beautiful male she'd ever seen, and she'd been raised among the two-natured with some of the most gorgeous bodies in the world. After a few months of regular meals, he looked like a fitness model with chiseled muscle under sleek mahogany skin. Veins popped on his forearms, and a thin sheen of sweat made him gleam like a statue.

Rampant and thick, his hard cock jutted up from a nest of black curls guarding his groin. The plush head peeked out from his foreskin and dripped succulent fluid, making her want to taste him.

What was stopping her? Absolutely nothing. She scooted forward and licked his shaft, lifting her hand to pull the delicate skin away from the tip so she could feast. He let out a strangled cough and thrust into her mouth, his hips bucking. Reaching around, she sank her fingertips into the hard muscle of his butt.

"What are you doing?" he asked, his voice low and broken.

"Putting on a condom." She licked the vein on the underside of his thick cock and stroked him. "Fates, you taste wonderful."

"Please." He coughed again and pushed his hands into her hair. "By all the fates, Feather, stop or... I don't believe this is how one uses a condom."

"How would you know?" She sucked his cock into her mouth again, loving how he twitched. It made her feel powerful and sexy.

"Because you dropped it."

Oh, hell. Her cheeks heating, she pulled away. "Can you blame me? Your dick is like candy and I've never—" She shut her mouth before she embarrassed herself any further.

"You've never taken a man?" he asked.

"Only in my fantasies," she muttered, hoping it was too dark for him to see her blush.

"Good." He stepped around her and laid down on her bed, lounging on his back with her pillow tucked under his head. "I like being your first, so I will allow you to do as you will."

"Um—"

"Within reason," he warned. "My patience runs thin, and if you dally too long, I'll be forced to take you and fuck you until you pass out from pleasure."

Yes, please. "That doesn't sound like a deterrent."

At his low growl, she quickly produced another condom, then tore it open. Why the hell was she playing around? Her core ached for him and he was all laid out on her bed like her next greatest meal. Holding the latex between two fingers, she said, "This goes over your cock.

Humans use them to protect themselves from disease and unintended pregnancy."

"Show me, Feather. Now."

She gasped and nearly came again from the effortless dominance in his voice. He might have been a perfect gentleman during prom, but the male she was about to fuck was pure dragon. "Yes, sir. I mean... Fuck. Never mind."

Watching avidly, Rizan let her slide the latex over his pulsing shaft, then pulled her into his arms. "The next time I make love to you, there will be no barrier between us," he warned.

She gazed into his dark eyes, thinking about her answer. Bear encouraged her to rip the condom away and take her due, but everything else screamed at her to wait. Yet she couldn't. His eyes held fathomless need and more than a little pain and she wondered if her expression held the same longing. Feather wanted his babies. She and Bear were in full agreement on that.

"Five years," she promised, straddling his hips.

He fisted his thick cock and positioned it at her entrance, lodging the tip just inside her. "Slowly, love. Not too fast."

Gritting her teeth at the stretch, she eased herself down, using gravity and the slick from her orgasm to ease the way. The hymen was bullshit, but it still felt like he was tearing something and it hurt like a motherfucker.

"Slow down, morsel," Rizan growled, digging his claws into her hips to hold her still. "You're hurting yourself."

"Help me," she whispered, squirming above him. She wanted it over and done, but he was probably right. She'd always been in a hurry to get where she was going, and she really wanted this done so they could go on to the main event.

He pushed his hand between their bodies and thumbed her clit, making her spasm around him. Shards of pleasure shot through her core and she gasped at the surge of delight relaxing her tense muscles. Slowly, she eased her way down until he was fully sheathed inside her. The ache receded, leaving her with nothing but the joy of his ownership of her body.

"Fates, you feel good," she whispered.

"So do you. Like heaven and all my dreams come true as a goddess rising above me."

"I'm no goddess." She leaned down to kiss him, letting the crisp hair on his chest abrade her nipples.

"You are to me." His big hand settled on the back of her head and he put the other on her ass and surged into her. "My goddess who deserves everything I have and ever will be."

The demand and need in his voice made her arousal spike as he thrust into her and all she could do was hang on for the ride of her life. His pubic bone rasped against her clit, sending her ever higher into joy until finally she exploded around him. Her vision went blurry as shards of purple magic careened around the room, shattering the mirror over her dresser, and blowing out a window.

Rolling her to her back, he fucked her hard, driving her into a second orgasm. Flame arched over her head and she reached for it, her muddled senses knowing only that she needed to be closer to him before he left her.

A sharp nip to her jaw brought her back. "No." He grabbed her hands and slammed them to the bed over her head. "Not yet. The next time you reach for my flame, you'll take it."

His jaw tight, he stared down at her, steam flowing

36

from his nose. "You will take my flame, little goddess. And I will take everything you have."

Lowering his head to her shoulder, he bit down. The sharp sting dragged her into another screaming orgasm, magic and flame wrecking her soul along with her bedroom. He stiffened and arched above her, so beautiful it hurt to look at him. His shaft swelled and pulsed inside her and he let out a roar of completion that made her wish there was no barrier between them.

Tears pricked her eyes when he rolled to his back and pulled her against his chest. His soft purr of delighted completion only made it worse and she buried her face into a pillow before he could see her cry. The next thing she knew, she was straddling his lap with her face cupped in his hands.

"Why do you cry?" he demanded. "Are you hurt?"

Feather shook her head, unable to stop the sobs crawling up her throat.

He pulled her to his chest and rocked her, broken growls rattling her body. "I demand you stop crying," he ordered. "It makes me crazed."

"I'm sorry." She choked out another sob and tried to breathe. "I... I don't want you to go, but I was stupid and I made you promise. And I still want to—"

"Shhh," he crooned, his low purr reaching out to touch her soul. "It's five years. A scant moment of our lives. It will be your time of growth and exploration, and I shall do the same."

"But what if—"

"There are no ifs between us, darling goddess. There is only when." He brushed tears off her cheeks and kissed her so gently it made her want to cry again. "I will give you my solemn oath to be there when you need me. I will buy a phone and learn to use it so I can hear the sound of your voice and I will visit for your holidays. I will not leave you."

"I won't leave you either." She settled against his chest, loving his possessive embrace. "Five years isn't so long if I can talk to you."

"Indeed." He settled to his back, still clutching her. "Sleep now, morsel."

RIZAN

He traced a finger down his sleeping mate's shoulder, wishing they could begin their lives together. Why did five years seem so far away? He'd had naps lasting that long. It was a bare blink of time to a dragon.

With a soft grunt, Feather turned over and wrapped a long thigh around his hips. Her core rubbed against him and he let out a quiet groan, wishing he could wake her and start all over, but it was too soon. She would be too sore to play. Although he attached no particular value to a woman's virginity, he was both humbled and delighted to be chosen as her first. It meant no one else had ever touched her. He thanked the fates he'd managed to give her pleasure.

His cock jerked at the thought of watching her give herself joy. Even wearing the condom thing had been stupendously arousing, and the way she slid the thin latex over his shaft...

It had been insulting at first, as if she hadn't wanted his seed to touch her. Yet he understood it. She'd worked very hard to go to college and a baby would take that dream away from her. Aside from that, he didn't want to share her with an infant. With their brood roaming about, Davryn and Morgaine barely had a moment to themselves. Maybe in a few centuries, they could revisit the idea of offspring.

Firmly turning his thoughts away from sinking between her sleek thighs, he considered the young wolf alpha he'd met at Feather's dance, and of his questions. What was he going to do for the next interminable five years?

Educating himself, as his brother was doing, sounded boring. Rizan thanked all the fates he wasn't king. Let Davryn have the headaches. He didn't have the patience to train with the rest of the mages and dragons. Aside from that, he was wary of Grandmother. He didn't know what she was. Not mage, nor two-natured or human, but extremely powerful. Although she seemed benign, she was an unknown and he didn't like it.

The thunderbird was still too new in her current incarnation to give him any sport, and Davryn was too busy. There was nothing to hunt, and even if there was, he wasn't hungry enough to make it worth the effort. The human's food was easier to catch and tasted better. Why bother hunting when there was macaroni and cheese? Building his hoard held little appeal when his future mate had no interest in his treasures.

He considered sleeping, yet it seemed an utter waste of time when he ought to be doing something more productive. He just couldn't decide...

What had Christopher mentioned? An army of sorts? Feather's sire had been in one of those armies. The young wolf in the wheeled chair had also planned to join.

More than anything, he wanted to make Feather proud of him, and he couldn't do that by sleeping the next five years away. It had to be something that would keep his mind and body active enough so he wasn't tempted to roost on the top of her home and wait. Perhaps the army would suit.

He kissed her hair and tried to settle back into sleep, but he wasn't willing to waste these last few precious hours. He didn't trust himself to stay without begging her to free him from his promise.

When dawn pushed silvery tendrils of light through her window, he extricated himself from her embrace, but couldn't resist one last kiss. Her eyes fluttered drowsily and she smiled.

"Good morning," she murmured, her voice husky and thick with desire.

He inhaled, closing his eyes against the perfume of her arousal. "I have to go, morsel."

She pouted, pushing her lower lip out. "No. My parents won't be home for hours. We can stay in bed."

Sitting up, he pulled her into his arms, nestling her in his lap. "I promised you five years, and you shall have it. I'm already tempted to collar you and force your bond, and I won't do that to you."

"I..." She sniffed, then nodded. "I understand." Getting free of his arms, she rose from the bed and dressed. "I'll walk you out."

Although no tears fell, the scent of her distress made him irrationally angry. Scales formed on his skin and it took all his strength to push them back. He kept telling himself it was for the best, but it didn't feel like it. Leaving her felt *wrong*.

His arm wrapped around her waist, they walked outside. She shivered in the chill and gave him a forced smile. "I'll miss you."

Lowering his head, he kissed her forehead, then

touched her jaw. He couldn't leave without tasting her one last time. When he traced her lower lip with his tongue, she whimpered softly and threw both arms around his neck, deepening their kiss.

The points of her canines pricked his tongue, letting a few drops of blood flavor their passion. Growling, she jumped up and entwined her ankles behind his back. Her weight settled against him and he wanted to hold her forever.

He felt the edges of her magic tickle at his. It would be nothing to let her in. Take what they both wanted. Groaning, he pulled away and loosened her hold, then took a step back. "Fates, you tempt me, morsel."

"I wasn't done." She bared her teeth and strode toward him, forcing him to jump over the porch rail to keep his distance.

"Five years. It's but a moment in time."

"I rescind my—"

"No!" He took another step back, then allowed his dragon form to take over. "Keep the rose, sweet one. If you need me, hold it close and whisper my name. I will always come for you."

Stepping back, he gave her a smile, then vanished into mist. The black dragon soared overhead and flew into the rising sun.

"Are you going to let her go?" River, Feather's mother asked. She was as luminously beautiful as her daughter, although not quite so tall. Feather must have gotten her height from her oversized sire.

Rizan stared down at the young people celebrating

their accomplishment. They were dressed in strange black robes with square hats. The attire seemed odd, but he knew nothing about the ceremony aside from it being something Feather wanted.

"I promised her five years. There are four years, eleven months, and fourteen days to go."

And less than a month since he'd had her in his arms. He could still taste her on his lips and the scent of desert wildflowers and rain lifted high on the close air in the gymnasium, making him drool.

"Five years to a dragon as old as you are can't seem like that long."

River never made a secret of her dislike for him, but he didn't take it personally. She was protective of her offspring, like any good mother, and he respected her for it. That didn't mean he was going to give up Feather.

Refusing to take the bait, he said, "It's as good as forever."

"Hmph." River went silent for a moment. "What do you plan to do while she's gone? Sit on the roof of my house and figure out how many cows you can eat?"

He kept his gaze on Feather and her friends, his ears pricking at a metallic squeak coming from their midst. The crowd parted, revealing Christopher, the wolf alpha, pushing Justin in his chair.

"That boy in the moving chair. See that he gets a new one that doesn't make noise. A... I don't know. A good one."

"Wheelchairs are expensive. His pack can't—"

Rizan filed the word away for later use. "I will pay for it. All I ask is that you arrange it, and tell him it came from King Davryn."

She cocked her head, her eyes speculative. "Why?"

"He's Feather's friend. To answer your first question, I'm going to find the army and join them."

Musical laughter filled the air. "What makes you think they'll take you?"

"River, enough," Adam, Feather's sire, said, pulling her to the side. Unfortunately, it wasn't far enough away. Rizan could still hear them. "Feather has already accepted him, and he respects her wishes enough not to force her before she's ready. I'm not sure what else you want from him."

Huffing out a breath, River nodded. "I know, but she's my baby."

"She won't be in five years."

"Shut up, Adam. I'll try to be nice."

"That's my girl." Adam kissed his wife, then brought her back. When they reached Rizan, he said, "Go to Missouri. Fort Leonard Wood is where the two-natured train. I'll call ahead and let them know to expect you."

"All right, thank you."

When he turned to leave, River laid a hand on his shoulder. "Aren't you going to say goodbye to her?"

Everything in him demanded he leap down and claim her before she could escape him. Thigh muscles twitching, he steeled himself against the instinctive drive to get his mate. "No," he finally said. "We've already said our good-byes, and I promised her."

"Do you want us to give her a message?"

Tell her I love her.

"Yes, please. Tell her I... Tell her I'm proud of her, and that I'll miss her."

He left before they could reply, escaping the gymnasium before he did something both he and Feather would regret.

43

CHAPTER
FIVE

FEATHER

Trying to keep her mortarboard in place, Feather craned her neck at the audience sitting in the bleachers. Sweat poured down the back of her polyester graduation gown, making her squirm in her seat.

Damn it. She should have known Rizan wouldn't show up. Letting out a breath, she clutched the notes for the speech she was supposed to give. It wasn't his fault. He wouldn't have known how important this was because she hadn't told him.

If she hadn't been so furious about not being able to see him, she'd admire his strength of will. He was bound and determined to uphold his promise when all she wanted to do was spend the summer in bed with him. It wasn't fair to ask that of him though, and it would have made it that much worse when she left for school in August. Still pissy, Bear snarled and swiped at the back of her head, making her wince in phantom pain.

"Please welcome our valedictorian, Feather Carter.

She'll be leaving us for Trinity College in London in just a few short months."

She flinched at the sound of her name and got to her feet. Mrs. Reyes, the principal, smiled and waved her forward. Feather mounted the stage and stared up at the mostly empty bleachers. There were so few, it was almost as if she could see the holes where people should have been.

Swallowing, she choked around a mouthful of spit. The speech she'd practiced for months fell from nerveless fingers and she forced a smile. "We see graduation as a new beginning, but it's also an end."

Her classmates shifted uncomfortably and she paused before starting again. "It's an end to childhood, but the beginning of adulthood. The end of the small world we know, but the beginning of a bigger life. It's both. It's a line of demarcation between past and future, yet we are the same on both sides of the divide."

Letting her voice rise, she continued. "This is the challenge we will all face in the days to come. I challenge you all to think of this step into the future not as a barrier separating one thing from another, but as a stepping stone on the same path we all tread. I challenge you all, graduates, friends, and family, to step off that stone, but remember and cherish what came before. Celebrate what we've lost."

She looked up, searching for her parents in the front row. Her breath caught at the familiar sight of thick locs between them. "Fates," she breathed. He'd come to see her graduate. A throat cleared, reminding her of what she was supposed to be doing.

"Our parents, children, sisters and brothers, pack and pride who are gone to us now, fought to give us the chance to step off that stone. I challenge you to honor their memory. Succeed beyond their wildest expectations and... Make them proud."

Feather took a step back at the sound of applause and knelt to collect her scattered notes. Rising, she nodded at Mrs. Reyes and said, "Thank you."

She stumbled back to her chair, wishing the whole thing was over. It hurt too much to see all those empty chairs.

By the time the ceremony was over, he was gone again. Shit. She'd wanted to give him her gold honor student cords. Tears welled, but she turned and faced her friends, determined to celebrate with them.

A CHILLY BREEZE blew her hair across her face as she hugged her parents one last time.

"Are you sure you don't want to fly?" her mom asked.

Feather dredged up a smile. "No, I'm good. It's too expensive, and King Davryn can have me there in a few seconds instead of a twelve-hour flight."

She really wished Rizan was taking her. Oh, she liked King Davryn well enough, and Morgaine was almost like an older sister, but she wanted *her* dragon. He wasn't hers yet though, and wouldn't be for another five years.

What the hell had she been thinking to say that all those months ago? The stubborn lizard was giving her exactly what she asked for, so she shouldn't be upset. She tried not to remember her prom night. It always made her cry, but it had been so achingly beautiful between them.

"We're ready when you are, darling," Morgaine murmured, shouldering Feather's bag.

"You don't have to come. I'll be fine."

Morgaine gave her an amused smile, as if she could sense Feather's trepidation. "It's no trouble. Drako promised supper at the pub after we get you settled into your new flat."

"Oh, okay, thank you." Feather tried not to be so relieved by the offer. Although she'd busted her ass for a chance to study in London, she was stupidly nervous. Everything would be fine. Granted, she'd only been to London once, but she spoke the language. For a mage with dragon friends, the trip was just a few seconds. She could be home in a flash.

Taking their hands, she faced her mom and dad. "I'll see you at Christmas!"

Eyes teary, her mom waved as Feather was swept away on dragon flame. She knew what to expect, yet the trip was still a bit nauseating. Morgaine said she thought it was fascinating, but Feather didn't see the appeal. The only good thing about dragon travel was its speed, especially since she wasn't with Rizan.

She blinked and they were there. Wobbling on hard ground, Feather swallowed and tried to keep her breakfast where it belonged. King Davryn had dropped them in a small courtyard with a fountain and several benches. A few people looked at them curiously, then whispered behind their hands as they stole glances at her.

The dormitory looked just like the pictures she'd been sent, including the address mounted on a gatepost set at the end of the courtyard. Soaring several stories, the concrete and glass building housed incoming freshmen and would be her home for the next nine months.

"Thanks for the lift," Feather said, taking her bag from Morgaine. "This is my building, so I'll let you go."

"Are you sure?" Morgaine shared a glance with King Davryn, then added, "We can help you get settled."

This was it. She could continue leaning on Morgaine, or she could grow the hell up, put on big girl panties, and take control. "No, I'm good. I'm supposed to have a meeting when I get in, but I really appreciate the ride."

"Well, if you're sure." Morgaine spared a glance for the people whispering around them. "Call us if you need anything. We can be here in a flash."

"I will." Bending to reach, Feather kissed Morgaine's cheek. "Have a lovely supper, and thanks again for the lift."

"Feather."

Her heart twinged. King Davryn's voice sounded so much like Rizan's. "I'm okay. Promise." She kissed him as well, then waved and let out a tremulous sigh as they vanished.

Big girl panties.

Ignoring the whispers following her, she picked up her bag and strode across the courtyard to the glass double doors, then went inside. Several young people milled around a desk, forming a messy queue as they waited their turn to check in.

She moved to the back of the line, content to wait her turn and get her documents in order. When her turn came, she presented her paperwork and smiled at the man sitting behind the desk. "Hi. I'm Feather Carter."

"Welcome to Trinity." Without looking up, he scanned a printed list of names, then handed her a key attached to a fob. "Room 815. The elevator is to your right. Meeting for incoming first-year students is at three in the student dining hall. Next?"

Picking up her bag, she moved out of the way and checked the time on her phone. She had a couple of hours to kill before the meeting, which would give her time to settle in and hopefully meet her roommate. She wended her way through the crowd in the direction of the elevator, then scowled at the line of people.

There was a stairwell at the end of the corridor, but eight flights of stairs... No, she'd be better off waiting. Eventually, her turn came and she squeezed in behind a girl carrying a box so large she couldn't see over it.

"What floor do you need?"

"Six, please."

Feather pushed the button. "Got it. Do you need help?"

"Thanks. I'm good."

The elevator soon chimed for Feather's floor and she stepped off. Hopefully, it wouldn't be so crowded on normal days. Then again, climbing the stairs would get her step count up. Industrial gray carpet covered the floor, and the walls were painted an uninspiring off-white. Boring, but she wouldn't be living in a hallway.

Following the numbers on the doors, she found her room at the end of the hall. Music blared from several rooms, along with conversations in a multitude of languages and the sound of moving furniture. There were more people on this floor of her dormitory than there were in her entire school. It was exciting and a little terrifying.

She knocked softly, then used her key to open the door. Her roommate, a petite woman with strawberry blonde hair and a mass of freckles scattered over her face, was already there.

Pasting a smile on her face, Feather walked in. The room was decorated with way too much black and white, including frilly comforters and mounds of pillows on both beds. "Hi. I'm—"

Scowling, the woman interrupted her. "You're a freak,

49

is what you are, and I've already requested another flat-mate. Turn yourself around and get out."

"Quit being a twat, Bethany. Nobody cares what a nasty little git like you thinks."

A young human male strode into the room and scowled at the redhead. If she hadn't already tumbled ass over teacup for Rizan, she might have been interested. He looked like a model, right down to the cleft chin and thick dark hair, and that Scottish brogue must have girls falling all over him.

Fates, she missed Rizan. Thinking of his kisses almost made her lose track of the conversation.

"Shut up, Seamus," Bethany snapped. "We don't want the witch at Trinity, and—"

"Who doesn't?" he asked, laying an arm around Feather's shoulders. "You and your equally bigoted friends who share a single brain cell?" He spun Feather around and marched her out, taking her bag from her hands.

Feather put some distance between them. If Rizan caught some strange man with his arm around her, things were going to get ugly. Then again, Rizan wasn't here. "Um, hey, I—"

"No worries, love." Seamus smiled and dropped his arm. "I'm the resident advisor for the floor, and I promise I won't be a jerk. Just wanted to rescue you from the village idiot before you roasted her. I've already got a room for you with someone less stupid."

"Um, I'm not a dragon. I can't actually roast people."

"No, but your incredibly hot boyfriend is. Pity about that."

"Pity about what?"

Seamus let out a dramatic sigh and laid a hand on his forehead. "All the best ones are straight."

She burst out laughing, then tried to keep up as he dragged her down the corridor to another door.

"Oy, Hannah, open up! You've got a new flatmate!" he yelled, pounding on the door.

Feather arched a brow when a low growl echoed through the door. There was a two-natured in there, but she didn't recognize the scent. "Sounds like she isn't interested."

"She's just fussed because Bethany was nasty to her too." Using a passkey, he opened the door. The room was undecorated, containing nothing but the standard institutional desks, beds, and small dressers. No pictures or bedding or anything else that might have given her a clue about her new roommate. Aside from the rangy scent of a two-natured, there was nothing but a tattered green duffle bag on one empty bed.

Still growling, a black and white face peered around the corner of the dresser and bared sharp fangs.

"Fates, you're a badger! That is so awesome!" Feather knelt and stretched out a hand. "I'm Feather Carter. I'm so glad to meet you."

Hannah's growl cut off and she misted into her human form. "Glad to meet a lowly badger?" she asked, crouching to retrieve a T-shirt from the floor.

"Why wouldn't I be?"

"You're a mage." Hannah pulled threadbare jeans over generous thighs then flopped to the empty bed. "Or are you just slumming to see how the other half lives?"

"I'll... um... let you two get acquainted," Seamus said, beating a hasty retreat. The door slammed behind him.

Wow, hammered from both sides. Maybe she should have stayed in Arizona. "Look," she said, dropping her bag on the other bed. "I have no idea what your damage is, but get the fuck over it."

"Did I hurt the high and mighty mage's feewings?" Hannah asked in a singsong voice. "Is she going to call the Council to have me executed?"

Bear sat up as the acrid scent of the badger's fear filled the room, choking and thick.

"I have no idea what you're talking about. Nobody has anyone executed over a schoolyard argument."

Hannah frowned, then cocked her head. "You don't have a Mage's Council in America?"

"No." Feather hung her jacket in the closet. "Never heard of it, but if they're in the habit of executing people for stupid shit, I don't want to."

"Wow." Hannah's shoulders slumped and she sighed. "I'm sorry. I'm just... you must think I'm an awful person."

"No," she replied, softening her voice. "Why are you afraid? I can smell it on you."

"The Council is..." She gave Feather a strange look. "How can you smell that? You're not two-natured."

"My father is a bear. I can't shift, but I have his sense of smell and—"

Paling, Hannah leaped for her and slapped a hand over her mouth. "You can't tell anyone," she whispered. "It's a death sentence for your parents and for you."

"My mother is a United States senator," Feather said, suddenly furious. Fangs itching, she grinned to show her teeth. "My future mate is the brother of King Davryn."

"That won't help you, I'm afraid." Sitting next to her, Hannah drew her knees to her chest. "They've already killed two dragons in Scotland. There aren't enough of the two-natured left in the UK for them to bother with us, but we... Let's just say we keep our heads down and pray we can emigrate to the States."

Wrong.

Feather agreed with Bear, but she didn't know what to do about it.

RIZAN

He circled the place Feather's sire told him to go. Fort Leonard Wood in Misery? No, Missouri. Close enough. Large and spacious, the location was suitable for a dragon of his size and he thought it might be comfortable. Tipping his wings, he descended, meaning to land in a clearing near a fenced compound of low buildings.

As he approached the tree line, something caught him, ensnaring him in a mage spell he couldn't escape. Roaring, he let forth a burst of fire, enraged that someone would attempt to cage him. Yet the flames went no further than his snapping jaws before being snuffed out. His wings itched, receding into his back as he was forced into an unwilling change into his human form.

He dropped from the sky, crashing through the trees. The branches whipped at his naked body, raising welts and bloody cuts on his torso. He landed hard; the wind knocked from his lungs.

"Well, well," a feminine voice said. "Is the dragon too posh to ride the bus like the rest of the recruits?"

He pushed his hair out of his face and opened his eyes, peering angrily at the woman, a tiger if he wasn't mistaken. She was a tiny thing, with blonde hair pulled back into a severe bun and blue eyes like the inside of a glacier. She wore a dusty green uniform and heavy black boots.

"What the bloody hell is a bus?" he asked, climbing laboriously to his feet. He reached for the change, more than ready to regain his dragon form, but something blocked him. "And why can't I shift?"

"Fort Leonard Wood is a no-fly zone," she replied, tossing him a pair of pants like the ones she wore. "You don't get to shift until you're told to. As to your first question, the bus is what you should have arrived in."

Obeying her tacit order, he pulled the ugly green trousers over his hips and buttoned them as a male human hurried to her. "Ma'am, this is Rizan. He's—"

Her expression softened for just a moment. If he hadn't been looking directly at her, he'd have missed it. "I know who he is. We've been expecting you. Get your ass in line with the rest of your class."

Nostrils flaring, he inhaled, taking in the tiger's scent. She wasn't remotely afraid and wore her authority like a mantle. Something about her made him want to test her. "No. Let me shift and I'll consider obeying."

Turning to face him, she smiled, baring glittering fangs. "Make me. If you can take me down, I'll let you shift at will."

Such an easy challenge. It made no sense for the tiger to jump through these hoops, but he obliged her and rushed forward, his arms spread wide. Her booted foot hit his chest and he spun, gasping at the sudden pain. A sharp fist met his jaw, sending him flying into a tree.

He slid to the ground and chuckled, spitting blood to the side. Apparently, Feather wasn't the only one with things to learn. He might have been able to take the tiger if he worked at it, yet he didn't truly want to. "My mate taught me the same lesson when I underestimated her," he said, touching the blossoming bruise over his sternum. "Where is this bus object? I shall pretend I arrived in it."

Rolling her eyes, the tiger held out a hand and hauled him to his feet. "Come on, dragon. You're in the Army now. I'll do a better job teaching you the lessons your mate didn't."

"How?"

"The carrot and the stick. Take the carrot, or I'll beat you black and blue with the stick."

He frowned, following her to a waiting line of more two-natured. "I don't think that's how the cliché goes."

"That's how it goes in the Army." Raising her voice, she shouted, "Line the fuck up, ladies and gentlemen!"

Rizan fell in behind a female Kodiak bear who gave him a sweet smile of encouragement. "Sorry," she whispered. "Colonel Andreyev doesn't believe in manners."

"I heard that! Fifty push-ups for both of you once you're kitted out!"

"What's a push-up?"

Nobody answered Rizan's question. Shrugging, he followed the bear into a building smelling of disinfectant and floor polish. A human male gave him clothes and boots that were strange on his feet, forcing him to dress in underwear, a white shirt, and green trousers.

"Get him a larger shirt," the tiger snapped, walking down the line. "He's a big bastard and will tear the sleeves out."

The human rolled his eyes. "What do you care? Whatever we give them won't last anyway."

Another shirt was handed to him and he changed, thankful for the tiger's interference.

"The one good thing about this is that we don't have to

go through a medical exam," the wolf behind him said. "We can choose on the haircuts too. I'm getting mine shaved."

His feet stalled. Would Feather be upset if he cut his hair? The thought of her chopping off her silky black tresses made him see red, yet it would be five years before he saw her again. He closed his eyes and shivered, remembering her slim fingers easing his locs from the tight braid.

The line moved forward and he stopped at the hair cutter, then sat down in the spinning chair. "Shave it," he muttered.

Grunting in acknowledgement, the human wrapped a sheet of plastic around his shoulders, then turned on a black object, the high whine of an electric motor hurting his ears. Hair fell to the floor and Rizan wondered if he should mourn it.

He would keep it shaved until Feather set her teeth into his flesh and bound her magic with his. He stroked his bald head and walked away. It wasn't bad. It was cooler for one, and he thought he might like not having to mess with it.

Once everyone was through the line to dress them, they waited. And waited.

Then they waited some more until the tiger finally sauntered forward. "All right, recruits, fall in. The government says I have to give you the standard indoctrination shit, so you get to sit on your asses and read for a few hours."

Maybe Davryn had been right about acquiring the skill. He raised his hand to catch her attention. Scowling, she turned to face him, her blue eyes narrowed in irritation. "What do you want, lizard?"

"I am unable to read."

She rolled her eyes and pulled him out of line. "Of

course, you can't. The Fates only know why shit can't be easy with fucking dragons."

"I was unavoidably detained when humans created written language."

His new comrades lowered their heads, refusing to meet his gaze. The humans might not be aware of his time in hell, but most of the two-natured were.

"Shut up before I start feeling sorry for you," she muttered. "Follow me, and don't think I'll forget those push-ups you owe me."

She barked an order at a leopard, sending the rest of the two-natured in another direction before leading him into a cramped office in one of the buildings. "You'll spend two hours a day with me after you finish your training with the rest of your class."

"I—"

"Stow it." She sat behind her desk and typed on a computer then spun the device to face him. "Speaking of which, you need a surname. Pick one out so we have something to call you."

"What's wrong with my name?"

"Humans have two names, and the older supernaturals adopted the practice when it became common. Their given name, plus a family name. My given name is Theodora, and my family name is Andreyev. You have Rizan as your given name, and—"

"I choose Carter. It's my mate's family name." There was no other he would have chosen.

The tiger closed her eyes and rubbed her nose. Her tears didn't make him want to kill something and eat it, unlike Feather's. "Damned dragons. Fucking romantic bastards. That shit makes me want to watch a fucking romcom, so you better knock it off before I turn you into a goddamned pretzel."

"I'm proud to bear my mate's name. You will not disparage her."

She let out a soft growl and lowered her head to hide the moisture glinting in her eyes. "Shut up before I hurt you."

He chuckled, ignoring her ferocious scowl. "You'll find a mate soon, tiger, and I will laugh when they sweep you off your feet."

Stripes blossomed across her face and her fangs lengthened. "Not gonna happen, lizard."

"I'll wager a tenth of my hoard it does."

She held out a hand, black claws sharp on her fingertips. When he clasped it, she said, "You're on. Now, shut the fuck up and pay attention."

CHAPTER
SIX

FEATHER

Keeping her head tucked securely under her umbrella, Feather scurried back to her dorm. Did it never stop raining in this fates-forsaken city? It wasn't even winter break of her first year and she was already tired of it. She missed her friends and family like crazy too, but kept telling herself it was just freshman homesickness.

No, it was more than that. The pressure of her classes, plus living in a place that wasn't welcoming of supernaturals was beginning to weigh on her. The two-natured, well, the few she'd seen, were scared of their own shadows, and the mages were...

Well, the less said about that group of xenophobic assholes, the better. They'd even managed to make her ashamed of her heritage. Bear grumbled softly, less content with their location than Feather was. It wasn't in her to give up, but Trinity sucked big donkey balls.

Ugh. She should have made a site visit instead of

relying on a drive by with her parents during high school. That one fleeting glance at Trinity during her mom's diplomatic tour had been enough to sell her on the place, but she should have looked a lot harder.

Speaking of her mother, Feather needed to tell her what was going on in the UK, but didn't feel comfortable doing it over the phone or in their weekly video chats. Not that there was much her mother could do. As a freshman senator, she didn't have a lot of clout in Congress, and would have even less over a foreign government.

Next year she could move off campus, and she fully intended to beg King Davryn or Morgaine for a lift back and forth to class. She'd just be a commuter student without the need to buy a metro pass. Shaking the water from her umbrella, she pushed open the glass doors.

As usual, no one spoke to her or met her eyes. Some of it was fear, and the rest was bigotry. Her only friends were a couple of humans, like Seamus, who didn't care about supernatural politics. "Hi honey, I'm home," she muttered under her breath, trudging through the lobby to the elevators.

She stepped off on her floor and recoiled at the thick scent of blood wafting through the corridor. Her lips pulled back into a snarl to better taste the odor and she raced down the hall to follow it. As she approached her apartment, the scent grew stronger and mixed with the reek of terror and musk from a...

"Hannah!" The lock refused to open when she shoved her key in and the zap of magic burned her hand.

"Oh, hell no. You do not come into *my* home and fuck up my shit." Her magic rose, a swirl of purple that lifted her hair off her shoulders. The door exploded inward, the frame mangled and hanging drunkenly from its mountings.

Two men and a woman turned to face her, giving her nasty smiles.

"Fates, Hannah!"

Curled into a tiny ball on the floor, clothes shredded until they barely covered her, Hannah's body was a mess of cuts and bruises. Glazed with pain, her eyes fluttered open, then closed again. The woman produced a long thread of pale green magic and struck her, opening a deep wound on her back. Hannah's mouth opened in a scream, but no sound escaped the magical gag around her lips.

"You three picked on the wrong mage," Feather growled, her magic flaring.

"What do you care?" the woman snapped, tossing a blonde ponytail over her shoulder. "It's just a worthless badger. We hunt them all the time."

"Truly, you should thank us for disposing of it. How can you live with the stench?"

Feather scowled at the man who had spoken. Shaggy brown hair hung in his face, and thick brows beetled in confusion. The other man, his hair cut short to reveal a round, slightly pudgy face, nodded in agreement. She'd never considered herself a violent person, but at that moment, she wanted nothing more than to mix her magic with Rizan's flame and turn all three of them into a pile of ash.

"*Her* name is Hannah. *She* studies computer science. *She* is a person." Magic balled in Feather's hands and she sent it out to wrap all three in thick ropes of virulent purple tinged red with her fury. She squeezed, ignoring their gasps of pain as her magic pushed the air from their lungs. Twists of pink, pale green, and orange snapped ineffectively at her and she brushed them off like the annoying mosquitos they were.

"I, on the other hand, am your worst nightmare." Muzzling them, as they'd done to Hannah, she let her magic fly. Although she didn't cut them, the blows she delivered would leave them whining for morphine for days. She kept at it until the woman fell unconscious.

Glaring at the two men, she pulled out her phone and tapped Morgaine's contact. When she answered, Feather said, "Hi Morgaine, I have a favor to ask. Can you and King Davryn—"

She felt a blast of heat and a change in atmospheric pressure, then blinked when Morgaine and King Davryn appeared in front of her.

Gasping, Morgaine fell to her knees next to Hannah. "Poor dear," she murmured, green magic bathing Hannah in healing light. "Let's get you fixed up."

King Davryn growled, a puff of steam jetting from his nostrils as he regarded the three mages. "Is this why you called us?"

"Yes. I need you to take Hannah to Arizona."

Morgaine helped Hannah sit up, then wrapped a sheet around her, but Hannah brushed her hands away and struggled to her feet. "No, please," she begged. "My family is here. They sacrificed everything to send me to uni, and I can't leave them."

"Hannah—"

She shook her head and scrubbed away tears with the back of her hand. "No, Feather," she said, interrupting her. "The Mage Council will go after my family because I defied them."

"Not if I roast these three where they stand," Morgaine muttered. "Rest assured, Myrddin will hear about this."

"Can we evacuate the two-natured? My mother can get them refugee status."

King Davryn glared at the bound mages, then nodded. "Yes, I'll call the dragons in. We'll transport everyone who wants to go."

"Tell them to be careful," Hannah begged, tears streaming down her face. "The Council has already killed two in Scotland, and I heard from my mum that another went missing last week."

"Get the two-natured out," Feather ordered, turning to King Davryn. "Then make sure the dragons know the UK is off limits for a while."

"You can tell them yourself when you get home," Morgaine replied.

"I'm not going home." Feather slapped the female mage awake, then removed the muzzles from all three. She bared her teeth, allowing her fangs to drop. "Your Council needs a come to Jesus moment, and my Bear is spoiling for a fight."

The woman cried out, her face paling in terror.

"Abomination!" The short-haired male's horrified gasp made her smile.

"You have to kill them now," Hannah whispered, covering her face with the corner of her sheet. "It's a death sentence for you and they'll tell."

"No, I don't, but they might wish I had." Purple tongues of magic rose up, surrounding the three. Feather grunted at the strain, wishing she had a familiar. No, she couldn't think of Rizan right now. Although she knew what she was attempting was possible, she'd never done it. Sweat beaded on her brow but she didn't take her attention away from her task long enough to brush it away.

She didn't give up, even when the pressure of concentrated energy made her head ache. When the woman started to shrink, she let out a sigh of relief and kept going.

"Fates, that's a wonderful idea, darling." Green magic

mixed with purple as Morgaine added her strength. "Your mother will be thrilled."

With an inaudible pop, Feather's magic rebounded and she let it fade. In place of three mages, there were now... "Norwegian rats," she pronounced, brushing her hands together. "By the time you three fuckwits figure out how to break the spell, you might have learned something about the two-natured. Oh, and make sure to groom each other. I'd hate for you to be the start of another plague."

"That's bloody brilliant!" Hannah smiled, baring sharp teeth. "Badgers love rats."

Squeaking in terror, the rats raced from her room and down the corridor. She probably shouldn't have used so much magic. It wasn't good for Aunt Yan, but Feather was sure she'd understand. Most likely, she'd laugh her ass off.

"Let's get you and your family to your new home, dear," Morgaine said, wrapping an arm around Hannah's shoulders. "Have you ever been to Arizona?"

Morgaine vanished, taking Hannah with her and leaving Feather alone with King Davryn.

"Are you sure about this? Rizan isn't going to be happy about you staying."

Letting out a sigh, she shook her head. "As much as I'd like to say I'll fix it, I probably can't by myself. I'm too young and I'm American. It's definitely a problem we have to manage, especially if they try to spread their poison to the States."

"Your mother, perhaps?"

"Maybe if she wasn't an elected official, but I'm thinking you and Morgaine, plus Myrddin, Lily, and their husbands." She bared her fangs. "If we're going to terrify them into behaving themselves, we should use real terror."

He chuckled and squeezed her shoulder. "Very well. I'll

arrange things and we'll meet you tomorrow morning." He peered at her, his intense blue eyes seeming to see into her soul. "Keep your phone and Rizan's diamond rose with you at all times, and stay inside. Rizan will never forgive me if you're harmed."

"But—"

"Feather, do as you're told. You're very strong, but you have no allies in this place. That makes you vulnerable." His gaze softened. "We'll deal with this tomorrow."

As much as she hated to admit it, King Davryn was right. She couldn't engage without a posse, especially since she had no idea where to find the Mage Council or how many she'd be dealing with. It occurred to her to call King Omer, but he'd been so busy with Aunt Yan, Feather wasn't sure if he'd know anything. Her shoulders slumped and she nodded.

"Yeah, I'm done with class until Monday, so I guess I'll be calling for pizza delivery and—"

"Just this once, use your magic to summon food. And stay alert."

He kissed her cheek, then disappeared.

RIZAN

"Give me twenty more, ladies and gentlemen. You want to be in the Army? Well, you better prove to me you aren't pussies!"

His arms burning, Rizan did another chin-up, swearing to the fates he would eat that thrice-damned tiger when this was finished. Chin-ups, push-ups, sit-ups, burpees, and endless running. Yet he'd never been fitter or better fed. The ridiculous amount of food his unit was given would turn the head of even the greediest dragon. Six generous meals a day meant he was never hungry, and that was a novel thing for a dragon who had spent thousands of years on the brink of starvation.

Unfortunately, it also meant he would need to molt soon. That was both good and bad. It meant he was growing again for the first time in millennia, but without access to his hoard caves, he would be vulnerable to attack during the first few days. He also needed a body of water big enough to soak. The base pool wasn't half what he'd need.

Maybe the tiger would have an idea. Despite her irascible temperament, she tried her best to meet the needs of all the two-natured, including regular swim time for the Kodiak bear, a shy female with white-blonde hair and whiskey brown eyes who usually turned them all into whimpering babies during hand-to-hand combat training.

He was halfway through twelve weeks in which he was too busy to think of Feather. Between the physical training and the endless classwork, plus his reading lessons, he didn't have time to consider anything except his next task. He hadn't thought of his treasure in days.

The regimented eight hours of rest were a different story. Unlike his classmates, he didn't sleep. Instead, he dreamed of Feather and the scent of desert wildflowers.

The tiger blew a sharp blast on her whistle, then yelled, "Fall in!"

He let go of the chin-up bar, then lowered his arms with a groan of relief before lining up. Mentally, he steeled himself for what would come next. The daily ten-mile runs were his least favorite part of the afternoon regimen. To his surprise, the tiger didn't order them to retrieve the hundred-pound packs they wore. Instead, she strode up and down the line, then stopped, positioning herself in the center of the ranks.

"Listen up. Tomorrow, we begin training with your animal forms." Murmurs rose from his classmates and she held up a hand for quiet. "Don't think it's going to be easier than the last six weeks."

Fates, the thought of taking to the air once more had his muscles twitching and straining against the spell keeping him from changing his form. Too busy anticipating his first flight in weeks, he nearly missed her next words.

"We'll be improving the time it takes you to shift, along with teaching you how to better use your strengths to counteract your weaknesses. Carter, this does not apply to you. You'll be continuing training in your human form."

He growled, the desperation to shift growing. "Why?"

"Dragon," she replied, as if that answered his question. "Really freakishly massive dragon. Honestly, what are we going to teach you when all you need to do is set fire to an enemy before you eat them? The rest of us have to work to be that deadly, lizard."

His classmates burst into laughter and he couldn't help but join them. She had a point, but it didn't solve the problem of his molt. "Ma'am, I wish to speak with you later about that."

"Speak now."

Gritting his teeth, he said, "I need to molt. Soon."

Her smirk of satisfaction irritated him. "It's about goddamned time." She turned to face the rest of his class-mates. "Listen up. We've got a dragon on the verge of molt. Your job is to find him a place where he can take care of business safely and protect him, without letting him get cranky enough to eat you or anyone else."

"I prefer to be alone," Rizan replied, straightening.

"Nope, you get to be an object lesson." The tiger moved closer, her gaze softening as it lit on all of them. "We all have weaknesses. I overheat in my tiger form. So does Sadie," she added, pointing at the Kodiak bear. "Wolves will eventually die if they can't keep a pack connection. Cheetahs are fast, but can't maintain it for more than a mile or so. You have to learn to work together. Support your teammates where they're weak and they'll do the same for you."

Taking a step back, she nodded. "Dismissed."

"My little brother had a corn snake for a pet once. She liked to soak in her water dish before a shed." The young wolf female looked at him, giving him a warm smile. The dark blonde ponytail hanging past her shoulders made her look like a child.

"He's not a snake, Laura," a black bear said, crossing his arms across his chest, brown eyes narrowing.

"Shut up, Ray. I know that." She returned her gaze to Rizan. "What do you need from us?"

"Privacy," he muttered.

She laughed and Sadie joined her. "You're not going to get that, I'm afraid. Tell us what you need, and it can't be privacy."

"Water and rocks to rub against. I... It's been a long time since my last molt. I don't know where to go."

"Colonel Andreyev won't let us go off base," Sadie said, tapping her chin. "We'll have to use the base pool for the water, and maybe some of the concrete buildings instead of rocks."

"It isn't big enough," Rizan replied.

"Fuck. How big are you?" Ray asked. "Can you get at least part of you in the pool? We can use hoses for the rest."

"Maybe my hindquarters if I leave my tail out, and take down the fencing."

His comrades lounged on the grass, surrounding him. Sadie pulled him down, then said, "Okay, we'll make the water situation work. HQ will have to do for something to rub against. It's concrete and pretty big."

"How long are we talking about?" Marina asked. The coyote's button nose wrinkled. "We'll need to set a team to guard the area. We don't want a bunch of humans roaming around to watch the show."

"Overnight if I can stay wet enough to soak off the old hide," Rizan replied. "Then another few days to rest and eat while it hardens."

"Doable," Ray said. "Sadie, you and Gordon take down the fencing around the pool. Marina and I will collect hoses. Cyndi, you go talk Colonel Andreyev into closing the pool."

"The rest of you, go to maintenance and collect push brooms," Laura said. "I have an idea."

He and his team got to their feet and jogged toward the pool. The bears changed their forms and quickly knocked down the fence surrounding the area. Rizan tried to help, pulling the debris out of the way, but they were more than efficient at their work. The rest of his classmates scattered to do their assigned tasks.

"Just out of curiosity," Daniel said, carrying a coiled hose and a broom over one shoulder. "How often do you have to do this?"

"Never if I don't eat. Maybe every few centuries if I can feed well."

"Cool. You'll be able to do it without an audience next time."

"All right," Laura called, hooking her hose to a spigot. "Get scaly, dragon."

He nodded, stepping away from his... friends. When had they become more than classmates? Aside from Feather, he'd never met anyone he'd be willing to tolerate for more than a few hours at a time. Yet this mixed group of two-natured were willing to protect him and help him through the most disagreeable part of being a dragon.

When he thought he had enough room, he shifted, then spread his wings. His hide was crushingly tight, itchy, and painful over his joints. Fates, had he grown that much? Growling, he limped to the pool, folding his wings tightly as he tried to settle into the water. Leaving his tail out, he crouched, then laid his head in the grass a few dozen yards away. He shook, trying to arrange his limbs as well as he could.

Water streamed over his neck, easing the itch, and he turned his head to glare at Sadie. "More," he croaked.

"Soon," she promised. "Get those hoses on his back and tail, folks! When he's good and wet, climb up with those brooms and get busy."

The itch eased and he groaned in pleasure as his friends scrubbed the softening skin. Turning his head to the side, he exposed his throat to Sadie's ministrations, purring softly.

She scrambled up his foreleg and attacked the itchy spot with her broom. "You sound like a kitten. I didn't know dragons purred."

"Keep scratching or I'll eat you," he rumbled, a burst of steam coming from his nostrils. His belly scales tingled, but he couldn't stretch out enough to rub them against the bottom of the pool. With a low grunt, he rolled, sending more water over the side.

"Not cool, dude," Ray said, retrieving his broom as he climbed Rizan's side, soaking wet. "Give us a little warning before you turn over."

"Sorry."

"We've got a seam opening back here!" Daniel called from his perch on Rizan's tail. "Keep after it so we're done in time for supper."

With renewed vigor they swarmed over him, brooms, claws, and even the rough soles of their boots loosening dead scales. He briefly considered keeping his new friends in his hoard for his next shed, but he'd be free to take care of it properly by then.

The scales over his muzzle broke loose and he rubbed his face in the grass, leaving a trail of black hide. When the skin over his belly split, he shot a burst of fire into the sky in warning. "Getting up!"

When his friends cleared out, he hauled himself from the water and shook, sending bits of scale flying. Wings hanging useless, he lumbered to a large building and rubbed against it, desperate to get the last of his old hide off. The rough concrete felt so good and he slammed his tail against the asphalt to break away the toughened scales. A car alarm blared, set off by the impact.

"Hold still," Daniel ordered, his shaven head gleaming in the afternoon sun. "We'll help get the rest of it."

Working together, they tore his old scales off, loosening the hide until he could wriggle free. Panting, he rolled in the grass, delighted with the tickling against his tender new skin.

"He's like rainbows," Sadie murmured, brushing gentle fingers across his shoulder.

"Looks like an oil slick to me," Ray replied.

"It's pretty and it feels like silk," Laura said. "I bet his mate will love it."

"If you're done cataloguing my appearance, someone bring me a cow," he growled, shooting a blast of steam at them. He was ferociously hungry, tired, and still vulnerable until his new skin hardened.

"Cranky bastard." Ray turned to face their team. "Laura, come with me. We'll see what the mess hall has. The rest of you can set up a perimeter to make sure nobody gets too close."

Chewing on a meat stick, something he'd developed a taste for, Colonel Andreyev approached and tilted her head up to meet his half-closed eye. A large satchel fell to the ground next to her. "Loving the new look, Carter."

Something in that bag smelled delicious. "Give me the food you have. I can smell it."

"I have a question first. What have you learned today?"

"This base needs a bigger pool."

"Wrong. Also, you'll be the one cleaning it up in a few days. Try again."

He spat a small ball of fire, irritated by her refusal for a moment until he remembered her words. "Trust my team. Even I have weaknesses."

"Good boy." She gave him a brief smile, then reached into the bag and tossed something at him.

He snapped it out of the air, and a flood of liquid from the broken yolk sack of a hatchling chicken filled his mouth. He stilled, letting the deliciousness trickle down his throat. "More," he growled.

"Figured you'd like them." She threw another into the air. "My best friend is a Harris hawk. They're her favorite."

"I'm not a bird."

Laughing, she gave him another. "No, but you're a

predator. There isn't a single carnivore in the world that doesn't go after eggs or hatchlings."

She fed him the last few chicks, then wiped her hands on the grass before rising to her feet.

Laying a paw down to stop her, he said, "Thanks."

"You're welcome."

CHAPTER
SEVEN

FEATHER

Glaring at the remains of her door, Feather let out a small surge of magic, returning the pieces to their original form. As an afterthought, she added a ward to prevent another magical break-in. Crossing her fingers, she sent up a little prayer to the fates for Hannah's family.

Why were the British mages so awful? It didn't make any sense. The only thing she knew for sure was that her mom hadn't known what was happening. If she had, there was no way she'd have allowed Feather to go to Trinity.

Her phone rang, making her jump. She swiped to accept the call, then said, "Hi, Mom. I was just thinking about you."

"I just spoke with Morgaine, young lady. Were you planning to tell me what was going on over there?"

Feather winced at the fury in her mom's voice. "Um—"

"Pack up your stuff. You're coming home as soon as I can get a dragon to fetch you."

"No, please. I need to see this through."

Her mom let out a sigh. "I'm very proud of you for what you've done, but your father and I need you home. We don't know the situation or who is responsible for this Mage Council, and from what I understand from your roommate, it's not safe for you."

"But Morgaine and King Davryn will be there, and Myrddin—"

"I said no, Feather."

Although she was normally very easygoing, Feather knew better than to argue when her mom took that tone of voice. "Okay, but... Can it wait until tomorrow morning? There's a couple of people I want to say goodbye to."

"No. I don't want you to leave that room for anything."

"They're just humans. I'm sure they're not involved."

"Feather—"

"Please? I promise I won't leave my dorm room."

Her mom went silent for a few seconds, then said, "All right. I'll let you stay tonight on the condition that you stay in your room and ward the door. Use your magic for food if you're hungry, and don't allow anyone in except your friends. Agreed?"

She let out a sigh of relief. Although disappointed she wouldn't be able to give that idiotic Mage Council a piece of her mind, it was comforting to have the support network. "Thanks, Mama. I'll see you tomorrow."

"Tomorrow morning. I'll try to get someone there as early as I can, but keep your phone on you. Love you, baby girl."

"Love you back. And tell Daddy I love him too."

Ending the call, Feather rubbed her face and tried to swallow down her disappointment. Maybe her mom had a point. It would be one thing if she was just a mage, but if

Hannah was right, her mixed heritage put her at terrible risk, even though she'd never been able to change her form.

Part of her understood their autocratic kill order on mixed supernaturals. All the rumors and stories said they were very dangerous, but she wasn't like that, and Hannah was the most peaceful person she'd ever met. It didn't make sense for them to target the two-natured so hard.

The three idiots she'd turned into rats had called Hannah *it*, denying her humanity entirely. Maybe the two-natured weren't entirely human. It didn't make them valueless or dangerous. She choked back a sob, remembering all her friends who died or lost family members in the battle against the dark Sidhe King Teran. Maybe that final battle hadn't happened in the UK. It didn't make their sacrifice any less important.

Desperate for something to take her mind off that damned Mage Council, Feather opened her laptop, then closed it again. What was the point of finishing her term paper for econ if she was going to withdraw from school? Then again, she could recycle it when she took the same class in the States. She wasn't giving up her dream of college for anything—not even a bunch of murderous mages.

By the time she finished her paper, the sky outside was dark and her belly rumbled. The student dining hall was off limits because of her promise to her mom, but she could order from the curry place down the street. No, she couldn't order delivery because she'd have to go downstairs to get it. She hated using her magic for food. It had to come from somewhere and she didn't like not paying for things.

Fingers flying, she messaged her favorite pizza place in Kayenta. It wouldn't be the first time she'd summoned an order instead of picking it up and the owners knew she was good for it. Twenty minutes later, she had a reply. Grinning, she let her magic flare, and a familiar brown box appeared, emanating fragrant steam, along with a paper bag filled with napkins and disposable tableware. There was even a note taped to the box wishing her well.

"Sausage, mushrooms, and pepperoni. Perfect." She lifted a slice and took a bite, wishing Hannah was there to share it with her. She felt dumb eating alone, but it was a normal occurrence. Nobody ever wanted to eat with her.

As she finished her first piece, someone knocked on her door. She got to her feet and bent to look through the peephole, then smiled and opened the door.

"Hey, Seamus. I just ordered pizza. Are you hungry?"

"Thanks, love," he said, following her inside. "I can't stay though."

"Oh, okay." She tried to hide her disappointment with a smile. "I'm glad you stopped by. I wanted to tell you—"

He handed her a box wrapped in brown paper, then looked back at the door. "This came in the mail for you earlier."

She turned it over in her hands, looking for a shipping label. When she saw Aunt Yan's address, she tore it open to reveal a beautiful amethyst necklace.

"Dammit, Rizan. I told you no more presents." A single stone, carved into a rose, hung from a fine gold chain. It was pretty, and wasn't so ferociously valuable she'd feel weird wearing it. Maybe he was catching on to the art of giving gifts. Pulling it from the box, she turned to the mirror and put it on.

Turning back to Seamus, she smiled. "Thanks for delivering it. Are you sure you don't want anything to eat?"

"No." He opened the door, then turned back to face her. "Sorry about this."

"What?" She blinked in surprise as two men filled the doorway, both taller than her and bulky with muscle. "Who are you?"

Magic the color of blood streamed from the dark-haired one to the right and hit her in the chest, catching her unaware. Pain raced through her as another bolt of dark green struck her belly, making her double over and gasp. Lifting her hands, she tried to call her magic, but it wouldn't come.

Grabbing the necklace, she tried to yank it off, but the dark-haired one sent another surge of magic into her, making her scream and convulse with pain. Was this a collar like Morgaine had been forced to wear when she was released from her prison? She couldn't think of what else it might be, and the thought of losing her magic made her scream in fear and rage. Bear roared inside her and Feather wished she could change her form.

"Seamus, help me!"

He shrugged and looked away. "Sorry, love. I needed the money."

"No, you don't." The blond man on the left grabbed Seamus, and with a quick jerk, broke his neck. His magic flared and the body vanished. Sauntering into the room, he grabbed a slice of pizza and ate it.

"We don't have time for that," the brunet snapped. "We need to get our package delivered so we can get paid."

"Let me know how that works out for you," Feather gasped, trying to stand. "Remember the last one you paid off?"

Scowling, he reached down and grabbed her by the throat. "You won't be in a position to care, filthy little half-breed."

"Fuck you," she gritted out, her nails digging deep into the back of his hand.

He squeezed, cutting off her air, then laughed. "Hope I get to be the one to teach you manners." Without another word, he punched her and the world went dark.

WHEN SHE WOKE, her head pounded and she had to struggle to open her eyes. Cracking them, she saw nothing but darkness. Cool stone rested under her cheek and she smelled water and the faint scent of mildew. Thankfully, she still had her jeans and T-shirt, but her shoes and phone were missing.

Something heavy encircled her neck and she reached up to touch it. The amethyst necklace was gone. In its place was a wide metal collar attached to a heavy chain. Nothing happened when she tried to touch her magic. Bear whined, her fear making Feather want to run and hide. Neither of them knew what to do without magic.

Giving up, she tried to stand, but the clank of metal made her still. Bright lights turned on and she narrowed her eyes against the glare.

She was in a cellar of some sort. The walls and floor were dark stone, and the single halogen light cast deep shadows in the corners. There was nothing in the room but a floor drain and a single steel door in the center of one wall. The end of the chain attached to her collar was secured to a heavy eye bolt in the floor, allowing just a few feet of movement.

"You're lovely, for a half-breed," a male voice said. "I think you'll do nicely once we have you trained."

"What are you talking about?" Feather opened her eyes

and blinked to allow her vision to adjust, but didn't see anyone. "Who are you?"

"I've been looking for one like you for years," the male voice replied. "Do you know how rare it is to find a mixed-breed mage?" Without waiting for an answer, he continued. "Usually, the animal is stronger than the mage, and goes crazy when the mage tries to act. But you, my dear, have made peace with your bear."

"We're fine," she snapped. "I'm not going to go crazy or hurt anyone. I can't even shift."

Footsteps sounded behind her and she spun around, nearly tripping over the chain. Staying just out of reach, a man wearing a dark business suit circled her, his pale gray eyes speculative. Thinning blond hair was brushed back over a high forehead. He wasn't ugly, nor was he handsome. Small statured, he looked... soft—like a nondescript businessman on the Tube who would be forgotten as soon as he was seen. His scent was odd too. She couldn't tell what he was. He was probably supernatural, but his personal odor reminded her of a supermarket aisle full of cleaning supplies.

"Ah, well, I hope I can prove you wrong about all those things, lovely Feather."

His smile made the blood chill in her veins.

RIZAN

The cadence announced by the runner at the head of his class was rote by now. He could repeat the nonsensical phrases without concentrating. He still hated running, but it gave him plenty of time to think.

Reading no longer presented such a great challenge, although he struggled with the modern lexicon. He didn't always understand slang or sarcasm very well, yet it wasn't truly required that he do so. He'd even learned to drive, a useless skill for him, but the Army thought it necessary.

The roar of a Jeep sounded behind them. He ignored it, focusing on keeping pace with his comrades. There were only two miles to go before his next meal, and he was starving.

No, not starving. He was familiar with starvation, and being hungry for a forthcoming meal wasn't the same. His recent molt had set his body into a growth spurt and he ate everything in sight, even game when he was in a position to catch it.

The Jeep slowed when it reached him and he cut his eyes toward it. Colonel Andreyev was in the driver's seat, a ferocious scowl on her face. Yet her angry expression was mixed with worry and he smelled a tinge of fear.

"Fall out, Carter. Get in the Jeep," she ordered.

"Yes, ma'am." He stepped out of line and climbed in next to her. "Did I do something wrong? I thought the deer were—"

"Be quiet and let me drive," she growled, pressing the accelerator. They eventually reached the edge of the base, a wooded area with no buildings or other people. Without a word, she got out and gestured at him to follow as she led him several yards away from the vehicle, then stopped and clasped her hands behind her back.

"Why are we out here?" he asked.

"I have something to tell you and I needed to get you as far away from the base as I could." She turned to face him, her eyes darkening. "Feather Carter went missing sometime last night. There were signs of a struggle and all her things are still there."

He burst into his dragon form and roared, sending flame into the Jeep. It exploded into a plume of destruction and smoke that reached the sky.

"Tell me," he said, lowering his head to peer at the tiger. He should never have let Feather go without a mating bond. If he'd mated her, she'd have had his flame and he would have been able to find her anywhere. "Where is she?"

"Her mother and another dragon—"

He growled, incensed that someone dared touch his mate. Flame dripped from his jaws and set the grass at his feet ablaze, then cut off when Colonel Andreyev slapped him across the muzzle.

"Knock it off!" she shouted, the scent of her fear growing. "I'm trying to tell you, but I'm about to piss myself because you're fucking crazy scary."

With no small effort, he forced himself into his human form and reminded himself that eating the messenger wasn't a good idea—especially when she hadn't finished her message. "Sorry. Continue, please."

Nodding, the tiger straightened her spine. "Her mother asked King Davryn for transport to bring Feather home a few hours ago. She says there's some sort of Mage Council in London killing the two-natured and..." She paused and swallowed. "And people like Feather who are mixed species. She intended to bring Feather home while Morgaine and Myrddin dealt with them. Your leave is already approved as a family emergency, and her parents are expecting you in Arizona."

"Very well. Thank you." Intending to leave, he reached for his flame, but a hand on his arm stopped him.

"There's more. I've been authorized to send a squad of elite fighters with you. According to Feather's roommate, the Mage Council has killed two dragons, and a third went missing recently. You're an asset we're not willing to risk."

He considered it for a moment. He needed no assistance in burning London to the ground, yet without a mate bond, he would need help finding Feather. "Who?"

"Two mages, a wolf, a coyote, and... me. We all have specialized skills in espionage and wet work." She squeezed his shoulder, then touched her forehead to his. "We'll get her back, then we'll eat whoever took her. I promise."

Four shadowy forms emerged from the trees. A young woman with short dark hair, tattooed arms and the soft musk of coyote gave him an abrupt nod. "Angel Ramirez, or Vision. I'm the spy."

"Don't let the name fool you," the wolf said in a soft drawl. "She ain't no angel."

"Kiss my Guatemalan ass, Masterson," Angel said cheerfully.

"I'm Dennis Masterson, but call me Techno. I'm your resident geek, gamer, comm specialist, and all-around code monkey."

"Zeke Lohan, Tank if you prefer." the first mage said, his soft brown eyes large in a baby face that looked far too young for the number of weapons he carried. "I specialize in breaking and entering."

"Into what?" Rizan asked.

A female with curly red hair and rosebud lips stepped forward. "Buildings, people, whatever needs broken. I'm Guinevere Warner, AKA Lady Luck. I'm logistics and target extraction."

"The real Guinevere?"

She winked and shrugged. "A gentleman never asks a

lady's age."

"And you?" he asked, glancing at Colonel Andreyev.

"I'm Kali."

"The goddess of destruction and motherhood?" Rizan asked.

"Someone has to ride herd on this lot." She grinned baring long fangs. "We always wanted shock troops. That's you."

"Let's get this done," Dennis said. "I've got a World of Warcraft campaign tonight. Warner, show us what you have."

"Lame-ass nerd," Angel muttered.

"Fuck you, Ramirez."

The words were harsh, yet Rizan sensed deep camaraderie between them. It was the same, yet stronger than the bond growing between him and his classmates. "How long have you been a team?"

"Listen to you, interviewing us and shit," Guinevere said, a smile playing over her lips. "We started working together a little over a century ago during World War One, and we're more than capable of finding your mate."

"Do you have anything for us, Guinevere?" Colonel Andreyev asked.

She nodded. "I know where the Mage Council is holing up. It's an old church just off the M25 north of London."

"Sure you got the right place?" Zeke asked.

"Yeah." She touched her temple and glanced at Rizan. "I can sense concentrated magic from a good distance away. The building is warded heavily enough I can see it from here. Angel will find out for sure when we're boots on the ground. If that's not the right place, Zeke will convince whoever is in there to tell us where it is."

"Good work," Colonel Andreyev said, clapping her

hands. "First stop is Arizona to join up with Feather's parents. Then we go kill shit until we find her. Carter, you're responsible for transport."

Nodding, he held out his arms. "You need to touch me," he murmured, steeling himself for the feel of strangers putting their hands on him. He'd gotten used to touch over the last several weeks, especially after his molt, yet it still seemed odd. When they each had a hand on him, he fixed the image of the thunderbird's metal home in his mind and let his flame surge.

Wavering slightly, Colonel Andreyev stepped to the side and spat, then wiped her mouth with the back of her hand. "Talk about motion sickness," she muttered, glancing around at the people surrounding them.

Feather's parents were there, lines of worry on their faces. Lily, Myrddin, and their husbands stood off to the side, close to each other as usual. Morgaine leaned against Davryn, resting her head on his chest.

King Omer joined them; the thunderbird settled on a falconer's gauntlet covering his left arm. She mantled her wings, then hissed at him irritably.

"Don't yell at me, hatchling," Rizan snapped, ignoring his companions' awed expressions. "I'm already kicking myself for making that fates-damned promise to wait five years. If you want to be helpful, tell me where she is. Otherwise, go chase insects or something."

"She can't," Omer said. "Yanaha can only sense where a lot of magic is being used, and isn't able to find one specific mage."

"Then she can stay home."

"No, we're coming. She says these mages need a lesson in manners, and I've learned better than to argue."

"Enough," he rasped. "I need my mate."

CHAPTER
EIGHT

FEATHER

"What do you want from me?" Feather demanded. Hackles raised, Bear paced in the back of her head, alert, yet wary. The man moved to stand in front of her and she nearly gagged as the scent of chemicals grew stronger. She felt so weak, but didn't know if it was from the smell or from the collar.

"I'm a collector, Miss Carter. I like beautiful things, of course, but they must also be useful." He stepped closer and traced a finger down her arm, then chuckled when she jerked out of reach. "But I am curious about how strong the bear is in you."

"That can't be any possible use to you. I can't shift. I've never been able to."

He made a noise of acknowledgement, but didn't attempt to touch her again. "Indeed. That's probably what saved your life when you were born. Good for both of us, is it not?"

"Are you going to get to the point sometime today?"

His face darkened and faster than thought, he back-handed her. She flew backward, but the chain jerked up short and dragged her to the floor. His foot connected with her ribs, rolling her to her back as she tried to get her lungs working again.

"It would behoove you to learn a little respect, Miss Carter. You'll stay healthy longer."

She spat blood at his shoes, making him grimace and step back. "Are you going to get to the point, *sir*?"

"That's acceptable for now." He snapped his fingers, and the door opened to reveal the dark-haired man who had taken her. He carried a heavy wooden chair and put it down a few feet from the end of her chain. Sitting down, the odd-smelling male crossed an ankle over his knee. "You're a unique specimen. As far as I can tell, you're the only mixed-breed supernatural in the world, and I'm curious to see what I can do with you."

"I have no idea what you're talking about. I'm just a mage." She absolutely refused to mention Lily Archer and her babies. Lily was a dragon with light Sidhe ancestry, and her children... At least one of them was Myrddin's. She didn't trust this crazy man not to go after them.

More than anything, she wanted Rizan and wished she'd never extracted that stupid promise from him. She could have mated him and still gone to school.

"Does she not even speak to you?" he asked, leaning forward in his chair.

"No," she lied. "My bear is... I don't think she's awake."

"Hmm." A thread of smoky gray magic lifted from his outstretched hand, then wafted toward her.

Feather tried to scrabble out of the way, but the cloud grew, enveloping her in crushing pain that squeezed the very thought from her head. Bear roared, desperate to escape, adding cacophony to the shards of agony cutting through her body. As quickly as it started, he pulled the magic away, leaving her biting back tears.

She knew what he was now. The knowledge made her stomach clench and she took a deep breath to force down the nausea crawling up her throat. "What would a dark Sidhe want with me? Why am I so special?"

"You're an experiment, my dear. As a mage, you're immediately recognized by any supernatural." He rested his elbows on his knees, his eyes glittering. "But as a bear in a mage's body... Will people know what you are? If, as I expect, you become invisible to another supernatural, I can use you in so many wonderful ways."

"I don't see how that will gain you anything."

He scowled and she steeled herself against another blast of his magic. "I was told you were intelligent, but you're completely missing the point. Do you not see how far you could go? You could walk in your human form, your bear hiding you from mages, the two-natured, and even other Sidhe. You could appear as a mere human."

Feather chewed on that idea for a moment. She'd never had the desire to appear as anything but a mage until she came to England, but there were times she wished she wasn't so immediately recognizable. Another thought occurred to her.

"Are you the one who has made the mages here go crazy and harm the two-natured?"

Shrugging, he gave her a twisted grin. "No, but I reap the benefits. As I said, I like to acquire things, and I've just added three dragons to my collection. I have them in magical stasis in my trophy room."

"That's revolting. I won't have anything to do with capturing other creatures."

"It doesn't matter." He stood and another cloud of magic built in his palm. "All you need to understand is that I want you to. You'll eventually learn that my opinion is the only one you should care about."

Blowing on it, he sent the roiling magic toward her, then turned away. "Let me know if she passes out, or if she manages to do what I want."

Feather yanked on the chain, desperate to get out of the way of the vaporous cloud. "No! Let me go!"

Ignoring her, they walked out and slammed the door. Moving slowly, the ball of magic stalked her like it was sentient, leaving her no escape.

Razor blades filled her mouth and lungs, cutting off her gurgling scream. Although they weren't physically cutting her, the pain was unimaginable. It felt like she was being torn to ribbons from the inside out. Her bear yowled, a high-pitched screech that hurt her head even more than the dark Sidhe magic.

Curling into a ball, Feather sobbed. She didn't have enough bear to shift.

"I can't do it!" she screamed. "I can't shift. Why are you doing this?"

A speaker from above the door crackled to life. "I think you can," the man said. "If you can't, then I suppose we'll see how long it takes a mage to die from pain."

FEATHER'S VOICE was broken from screaming by the time they came back. She'd almost grown used to the tearing agony that made even the beat of her heart painful. Her jeans were cold and wet between her legs. She'd pissed herself at some point, but didn't have the strength of will to care.

"It showed up a few hours ago," the dark-haired man said. Feather didn't know their names, so he was Tweedle Dum. She called the dark Sidhe Tweedle Dee.

Dee and Dum for short.

"Interesting." Dee kicked at an object on the floor and she heard it roll away. "How can I use this to my advantage?"

Opening bleary eyes, her breath caught at the sight of the pink rose on the floor a few feet away. Gifts from dragons always returned to their owners. Could Rizan track her with it?

"It must be worth a fortune. How did it get here? She didn't have it in her pockets."

Dee knelt next to her. "Tell me, my dear. Are you fucking a dragon?"

"She's been seen on the television with one of them, sir. The brother to the current King."

"Fascinating." He stood and walked away. The heavy surge of his magic filled the room and coalesced into a shimmery gray cage around the rose resting several feet out of reach. "Poor dear," he murmured, crouching in front of her once more. "I'll wager you were thinking he'd track that bauble to you. My spell will eventually make him forget the diamond and you entirely. It must be such a disappointment."

"What do we do with it?" Dum asked.

"Nothing. Let her look at it as a reminder of how forgettable she is." Another cloud of magic formed in his palm and he sent it wafting to her. "Alas, I'm growing impatient. You'll either shift or die."

RIZAN

Rizan itched to change his form. He could almost feel scales growing, but he forced himself to wait. Morphing into a dragon in the middle of Cheshunt wasn't going to work, and Colonel Andreyev would have his hide for it. Logically, he knew a tiger was no match for a dragon, yet he respected her. She was intelligent and well-versed in urban combat, while he'd have been just as happy to burn the city to the ground.

River Carter wasn't any happier to be restrained. Flares of her angry dark blue magic sparked, held in check by Myrddin and Morgaine.

The setting sun cast everything in shadow as streetlights flickered to life. Humans crossed the street when they approached the small cut stone church, wise enough to get out of the way. "Is this the place?" he asked.

Guinevere stared up at the spires, then closed her eyes and nodded. "Fifteen strong mages, and a dozen more who can barely light a candle."

"They're arguing," Feather's sire, Adam, said. His face darkened and he opened his mouth over long fangs. "They want to go to the States and eradicate the two-natured there."

"Is my baby in there?" River asked, wringing her hands.

"We won't know until we get inside," Myrddin replied. He wrapped a large hand around the back of Lily's neck and squeezed gently. "That's why we can't bring the building down yet."

Yanaha was silent on Omer's arm, her feathers smooth against her body.

"Angel, I need recon. Find us a way in," Colonel Andreyev ordered.

"One back door Santa coming right up," she replied, misting into her coyote. She trotted around the corner, then disappeared into the shrubbery surrounding the church.

Zeke played with a piece of clay, a wicked grin lighting his face as he pushed it around the handle on the large wooden front door.

Colonel Andreyev rolled her eyes. "Take that shit off, Lohan. We're not blowing the door off a church."

"What will a lump of clay do?" Rizan asked.

"It's not clay. It's C4, and the most wonderful toy," he replied, putting the substance back in his pocket.

Angel returned and yipped softly before returning to her human form. "You realize we have a dragon and a bear who can just knock the door down, right?"

Zeke nodded. "Your point?"

"Never mind. There's an unlocked entrance on the other side. Looks like it leads into the rectory."

"Any targets?" Colonel Andreyev asked.

"No, but I heard voices. They're closer to the front of the building, so I couldn't make out the conversation."

"Perfect." Guinevere brushed her hands on her trousers. "Shall we go knock some heads together?"

Silently, they trooped to the rear entrance. Rizan inhaled, desperate for the perfume of desert wildflowers, but found nothing save the scent of his companions and the smell of aged stone. Angel cracked the door open and held a finger to her lips.

As they slipped inside, the peppery odor of mage filled his nose, but not the right mage. A puff of steam escaped, making Colonel Andreyev flick the back of his head with hard fingernails. Scowling, he rubbed the sore spot, then nodded.

She was right. He had to keep himself under control. Six weeks ago, it wouldn't have been possible, but her guidance had taught him wisdom and patience. Well, some, at least.

"Through there," she said, pointing at a darkened corridor.

"My daughter isn't here," Adam suddenly growled. "I can't smell her, meaning she's never been in this building at all."

Rizan resisted the urge to turn Feather's sire into a mid-evening snack. "Be silent," he hissed. "They'll know where she is."

Acrid tears filling her eyes, River let out a silent sob. The smell didn't make him need to kill something, but it was similar enough to Feather's that he didn't want it to continue.

"Enough, people." Colonel Andreyev eased her way to the front. "We'll find her, but we have to get these mages secured first."

Scales burst across Rizan's face and his claws lengthened. With no small effort, he pushed them back. This place was much too small for him. Gathering his composure, he followed the tiger into a large room with tall ceilings. Stained glass lit by the setting sun colored everything in shades of blue and pink, and long benches rested in orderly lines on either side of a central aisle.

An ornate cross was hung on the wall in a circular area over the heads of several mages who were paying too much attention to their vociferous argument to notice what was about to descend upon them.

"All right, everyone. Focus and let's see if we can get rid

of that filthy half-breed's spell," a female in a yellow cardigan and tweed skirt said.

Magic surged from the group, a muddled current of color that struck the center of their circle. Three youngsters appeared, naked and shaking with fright.

"Are you all right?" she asked, passing them robes.

Still trembling, they nodded. One of them, a blonde female, said, "She turned us into rats, Mistress. I've never felt magic so powerful."

Arching a brow, the woman said, "Why do you think you were told not to approach her? We had a plan in place, but you've spoiled it and we have to start over."

"Sorry, Mistress. We thought if we—"

A blast of light pink magic struck the girl in the chest, throwing her backward. "You've alerted her now. What do you think will happen when she goes home and bonds with that dragon of hers?"

"Let's go," Colonel Andreyev whispered. "We're wasting our time. They don't know where she is."

Perched on Omer's arm, the thunderbird cooed softly.

"Are you sure, Yan?" he asked. When she clicked her beak, he nodded then strode across the room.

"Fates..."

The soft whisper echoed and the woman in yellow spun around, a nervous smile replacing her angry scowl. "Your Majesty," she murmured, bowing low. "You honor us with your presence. How may we assist you?"

"You're Prudence Daniels, right?"

"Yes, I'm so pleased you remember me. I last saw you—"

"Yeah, anyway," Omer interrupted. "My wife wanted to discuss your behavior, I think."

"How delightful!" Her smile widened until she was

beaming. "It's truly welcome news to hear you've taken a new queen. That... creature you had was simply awful. May we meet her majesty?"

Omer shrugged, a boyish grin crossing his face. "Oh, Yan and I settled our differences. Lover's spat and all. We kissed and made up."

"Oh, I see." The woman's smile faded slightly. "What can we do for you?"

"I have no idea. I'm just the messenger boy." He tossed Yanaha into the air, and cawing softly, she circled the room. Shards of lightning descended from her wingtips and settled on the gathered mages.

Screams erupted, filling the air as the mages tried to brush away the sparks. Colored magic flared, rising from them in a glittering rainbow to coalesce around the thunderbird, and Rizan closed his eyes against the glare.

"Fates... My magic." A young male fell to his knees sobbing. "It's gone!"

Easily twice her former size, Yanaha landed and perched on the lectern below the cross. Bright light flared around her and she stepped forward in her human form wearing battered jeans and a black tank top bearing the logo of a football team. Raking her hands through thick dark hair, she smirked down at them.

"I'm back, bitches! Miss me?"

"Your language is appalling, Yan." Omer pulled her into his arms, then kissed her soundly. "But fates, it's good to see you again."

She smiled and traced a finger down his jaw. "Hey, lover boy. Kiss me like you mean it."

Omer caught her as she jumped up and wrapped her long legs around his hips. A tall sconce crashed to the floor as he pushed her against a wall, still kissing her.

"You took our magic!" Prudence shouted, her arms wrapped protectively around her midsection. "How dare you?"

Giving Omer one last kiss, Yan let go of him, then turned to face the powerless mage and shrugged. "Honestly, I'm not sure what you expected. Y'all were fucking up my chi when you started killing the two-natured. Anyway, we have to run. My husband owes me a few dozen orgasms."

"You can't leave us like this!" a man cried. "How will we survive?"

Lightning sparking from her fingertips, Yan jumped from the pulpit and strode toward him. "I can, and I will. You have all caused harm to the two-natured, and to me personally. You could have used your gift to help all creatures, but you turned it into something ugly and mean. You will live out the rest of your very short, miserable lives as humans."

"I repent!" the young blonde woman shouted. "I promise, I—"

"Don't bother." Yan turned on her heel and wrapped an arm around Omer's shoulders. "Pray the fates have mercy on you because I won't."

Pushing her way through, River approached, balls of blue magic filling her hands. "That filthy half-breed is my daughter," she hissed. "And Mama Bear has come to call."

"Abomination," one whispered, attempting to call magic that was no longer there.

"You think the thunderbird is a bitch, asshole?" Reaching down, she grabbed his collar and pulled him to his feet. "You have no idea who you're fucking with. Where. Is. My. Daughter?"

"They don't know," Rizan said, losing patience. "The lot

of them are useless to me." He inhaled, allowing flame to blossom between his jaws.

Spinning around, Colonel Andreyev kicked his feet out from under him. Hissing out blue fire, he got to his feet. "Don't cross me, tiger."

Claws bared, she gripped his chin. "Grow the fuck up, Carter. They're worthless, but I will not allow you to kill humans in a church. Am I clear?"

Grudgingly, he nodded.

Relaxing her grip, she let her hand fall. "We're going to find her. I promise."

CHAPTER
NINE

FEATHER

A blink of time.

One scant moment.

What was five years, but a collection of seconds stretching into minutes, hours, days...

Bear howled, desperate to be free of the crushing pain smothering her under the weight of dark Sidhe magic. Yet it was almost a comfort now.

Feather hovered, aware of her body, but detached. Something was broken inside her. A thread stretched too far snaps, rebounding back on itself without a care for what it damages on the way. The butterfly effect, chaos theory. Strings and quarks and dark matter, coalescing into one single point of perfect destruction like a star approaching supernova.

The existential big bang of a soul separating from consciousness. She laughed hoarsely at Bear's distress. Fuck reality. Dissonance rocked her socks.

"Her fangs are growing," a male voice said.

His name was Dum. Like the cheap lollipops. Well, that was what she called him.

"Good. Let's see what she does with additional stress."

Why was five years important? The pressure grew, separating her further from Bear's roars of agony. Someone wanted her to wait for that long, but she didn't know who it was or what significance it had. Must not have been that important.

The pain stopped and Bear was gone.

Big. Fucking. Bang.

BEAR

"Just as I expected, see?"

She stood, wobbling on two strange feet without claw or sensitive pads. Still smelling of unpleasant chemicals, the male had too many words she didn't care to understand.

If it wasn't feed, fight, or mate, what use did a bear have for words?

"Get dressed, darling," the male said, tossing a pile of fabric at her.

"Fuck you." The words were strange and it was hard to speak, but she liked the taste of them.

Fear rising from the second male made her salivate and she licked her lips. He smelled delicious, like something juicy and meaty. She stepped forward, but something hampered her movements. Pulling harder, she jerked forward and metal snapped behind her.

The male fell screaming under her claws and teeth. His blood was spicy hot and seasoned with fear, the meat a succulent treat. The odd smelling male touched her and she snapped at the offending hand.

"That's my girl," he crooned, his voice soft. "I'm proud of you."

A stream of blood tickled its way down her hairless chest and she snarled. "Go. Away."

"Do you want more good meat?"

Fangs bared, she leapt at him, but a whip cut of agony drove her back and she crouched over the remains of her meal. Parting her jaws, she roared.

"Shhh," he said, backing away. "Finish your food and we'll talk."

"You talk too much." She pulled a chunk of fragrant liver away and slurped up the strands of viscous tissue. He provided meat and the absence of pain as long as she didn't attack him.

Strange, but she had meat right now and could wait to kill him.

"My words are valuable to you."

"You are meat."

"I can give you more. All you have to do is listen."

The faint voice of the mage who had once occupied her body drew her attention, but she brushed the irritant away. Listening to that voice brought nothing but pain.

Her hairless ears pricked and she devoured the last of Dum's liver. "Speak."

FEATHER

Was this how Bear felt?

Locked away, her voice a faint whisper in the ear of

someone who wasn't listening, Feather pounded against the spectral walls enclosing her in Bear's consciousness.

"There are certain people I wish to have killed. You do that, and I will give you all the meat you want."

Bear nodded her agreement and ate another chunk of Dum, making Feather's stomach turn.

"You need to get dressed."

"Fuck you."

Dee cocked his head, a smile ghosting across his lips as he formed a ball of magic between his palms and sent it into her body.

Pain is an all-encompassing thing.

Until it isn't.

Pain means nothing to a creature who can't feel it, but Feather could. Her soundless shrieks went unheard as if she was no more than an ant under the boot of a hiker.

Bear ignored her screams and finished her meal, then wiped bloodstained hands on Dum's shredded clothes. "Stop it. The she is loud."

"Hmm. Let's try something else."

The debilitating agony flared again and Bear grunted, then pushed her aside in a vain attempt to get the pain to stop. "I listen," she growled, giving up.

"Get dressed, half-breed."

Bear pulled a black cocktail dress over her head, tearing it. "Speak, meat."

"Good girl," he crooned, stroking a hand down her back. "All you have to do is obey. The pain will stop and you'll have all the meat you want."

"Who do I kill first?"

Dee produced a photo. "He'll be at the theatre tonight. Work with your mage to find him."

Feather's scream of denial went unheard.

CHAPTER
TEN

RIZAN

The aircraft stalked him, afterburners flaring as it tried to keep up with his sharp ascent. Paint pellets burst in the air around him, a few even hitting their target when a second pilot joined their little dogfight. Rizan coughed out a laugh, sending a plume of flame into the sky.

"Two against one is hardly fair," he said, knowing they couldn't hear him.

When he reached the apex of his flight, he took a moment to enjoy the sight below him. The upper atmosphere was clear and unpolluted, and the curve of the earth below shimmered with sunlight. Beautiful, and a sight he never tired of seeing. He wondered if Feather would like it.

There was so little to smile about, and he relished the opportunity to have some fun. It didn't make up for four years, nine months, and twenty-four days of missing her. She was gone and presumed dead.

Alas, he was too high for his playmates to follow. They circled below him, looking like tiny dragonflies. Giving the curved horizon one last fond look, he tilted his wings and descended into a spiraling freefall. Fates, he'd missed this.

The planes chased, jets roaring as they tried to catch him. He spun and darted upward again, slowing to give them a better chance. Who knew humans could be so entertaining?

Aside from their wonderful food, which he still thought was a defense against predation, they'd become more than a rabble of superstitious cretins. Humans were clever, with a wit he hadn't expected. Some had even become friends.

Rizan slowed, his thoughts turning to Feather as they always did when he wasn't doing something else. She smelled like desert wildflowers after a rain. Sweet and fecund, mixed with the peppery perfume of mage. He missed her scent. Missed her.

His thoughts of Feather cost him. A paint pellet hit him between the eyes, spraying red across his face.

"Challenge accepted," he murmured. Spinning in place, he dove into a sharp spiral, the planes close on his tail. More paint burst in the air around him, covering him with viscous color.

The ground loomed in his vision, and at the last minute, he darted up, followed by one of the planes. The other hit the dirt, its pilot safely ejected away from the fireball.

Snorting out a laugh, Rizan landed, followed by the surviving plane.

"You know, those Raptors cost a fortune."

He lowered his head, peering at Feather's sire. The bear tried to look stern, yet a grin twitched the corners of his mouth.

"They should have thought of that before trying to outfly a dragon."

Adam hadn't aged well. The loss of Feather had hit him hard. His sable hair was almost completely gray and dark shadows creased the skin under his eyes. Her mother looked no better, and had given up her seat in Congress to focus on the search for her missing daughter. Sadly, they were both losing hope of finding closure.

He misted into his human form and climbed into his car. Everyone called her defective. Imperfect. Mage mixed with two-natured, destined to go mad. A ticking bomb just waiting for a chance to explode. They used her disappearance as evidence of her insanity.

His Feather was not the creature they described. Did they not remember her attempting to sell a dragon's gift to help her community? Or her endless patience when she babysat the orphaned hatchlings?

No. Filled with judgment, they called her monster, denigrating her memory.

Unlike everyone else, he knew she was alive. There had been times he could have sworn he smelled her. Once in Paris in a café down the street from Opéra Bastille, then again in Mogadishu. Both times, her wildflower and rain perfume faded before he could chase it down.

There was also the diamond rose. He had no idea where it was, meaning someone had used powerful magic to hide it. If Feather was truly lost to him, it would have returned to his hoard, regardless of the magic binding it.

"Call Kali," he said after docking his phone. He'd resisted learning to drive, but saw the attraction now. His Viper roared and spat gravel as he raced away from the flight line and he smiled wistfully, remembering the vintage Jag he'd given Feather. She'd loved that little car. The call connected as he sped past the guard shack.

"It's about time, asshole. I've been trying to get in touch with you for a week."

"Piss off," he replied, downshifting into a turn. "I'm supposed to be on leave."

"Cancel it. I need you to do a flyover in Bangkok. There's been rumors of some asshole picking on little girls and I'd like you to remind him it isn't a good idea."

"Do I get to eat anyone this time?"

She gave him a name, then said, "Yeah, but keep it on the down low. He's the son of a diplomat."

"So? I'll roast him in private, but make sure everybody can hear him scream."

"Look at you, my baby boy all grown up and shit," she replied. "Got something else for you after that."

"Talk to me."

"This goes no further, understand?"

"Got it."

He waited for her to speak. It wouldn't be the first time he'd gone after sensitive targets. There was a reason he was called Reaper.

"We've got an assassin active in western Europe. She's centered around London, but doesn't seem to have a home base."

"Why do I care?"

"Our intel says her next target is..." Kali went silent and his ears pricked.

"Speak, tiger."

"Adam and River Carter."

He worked that through his mind as he reached Route 58 and turned east. "Why? They're both retired."

"Unknown. Our sources also say someone has been asking after you too."

He barked out a laugh and shook his head. "That won't end well for our little assassin."

"This one is different," Kali said. "She's... I don't know. We find bodies, but they aren't whole. It's like she... Rizan, I don't think she's human. I think she's two-natured."

"Whatever. I'll take care of it after I deal with the fuckwit in Thailand. Do you know what she is?"

"Angel thinks she's a bear, judging by the state of the bodies, but she isn't leaving a scent trail. It's almost like she's invisible."

"How do you know she's female then?"

"We don't. Not for sure, anyway. I just have a feeling about it."

Kali didn't get those feelings often, but they almost always bore fruit. "Tell me about her targets."

"That's the funny thing. There isn't a pattern with them. We've found humans, Sidhe, mages, other two-natured. It's like she picks them at random."

"Money?" he asked. A siren blared behind him and he grimaced at the triple digit number on his speedometer. "Hold that thought. I'm about to get pulled over again."

Slowing down, he muted the tiger's snorting laughter and eased to a stop on the shoulder, angling the vehicle to protect the approaching state trooper. He recognized the familiar sway of her hips almost immediately.

Leaning down to peer in his window, Officer Abby Lutz shook her head, sending wisps of pale blonde hair flying in her face. "We have to stop meeting like this, Your Highness."

He hid a grimace at the address, but it wasn't worth the effort to convince the few humans he encountered that he wasn't royalty. "I can't pass up the chance to see my favorite cop." He passed her his license and registration, along with a handful of hundred-dollar bills to pay the ticket. "You stop my heart with your beauty."

"My husband's going to use that bald head of yours as a cue ball if he catches you hitting on me."

Rizan had no interest in Abby, aside from teasing her. She was a lovely woman, but his heart already belonged to Feather.

"He's a lucky male to have such a kind and beautiful mate," he replied, signing the ticket. Her scent washed over him, a pleasant mix of musk and apples he usually found appealing, yet it seemed off today. "Are you well?"

She grimaced and took the clipboard. "I've been nauseous all day. How did you know?"

"You smell strange, but I don't know much about humans."

"Gee thanks," she muttered. "Just what a woman always wants to hear."

"Hmm." Reaching out, he laid a hand on her stomach, meaning to give her a bit of magic to ease her discomfort. The minute he touched her, he chuckled and drew his arm back. The second heartbeat under her ribs was unmistakable.

Opening his palm, he produced a platinum baby rattle that had once belonged to Peter the Great, then passed it to her.

"What's this?" She scowled and tried to give it back. "You know we can't accept bribes."

"It's a gift for your new son, Abby. Congratulations on your blessing."

Her mouth fell open and she backed away. "How did you—"

He touched the tip of his nose, then said, "Dragon. You really shouldn't stand in the middle of the road like that."

Blinking, she returned to the relative safety of the shoulder. "Are you serious?"

"Yes. Humans don't usually survive being hit by cars. Also, tell your husband I'll eat him if he doesn't take better care of you. He's let you get too thin."

Abby laid a hand on her abdomen and a glorious smile bloomed on her face. "A baby," she whispered, spinning around to return to her vehicle. "Gotta go, Rizan!"

He waited until she was safely in her car before unmuting his call and driving away. "Sorry about that."

Uncontrolled giggles filled the speakers. "Fates, Rizan, just wait until I tell the team you've gone soft on a human cop. What did you give her?"

"A rattle given to Peter the Great in 1672. It's platinum, so she should be able to clean baby spit off it."

"Damn, go big or go home on the baby gifts." She paused and the laughter left her voice. "You asked about money. We haven't been able to find a definitive answer on that. A few of her targets have been wealthy, but not enough to warrant a professional hit."

"What do they all have in common?" he asked, talking more to himself than to Kali.

"If we knew that, we might have better luck tracking her down."

He grunted in acknowledgement. "Email me a list of her kills with dates and locations, then put a team on River and Adam."

"Sending it right now. I already have people moving in on Adam and River as well, but I have another question for you."

"What?"

"Would you be willing to stash the Carters in your hoard caves? I mean, nobody knows where they are, and—"

"Yes, but not right away. We'll use River and Adam as bait until I get back from Thailand. Also, I just left Adam at Edwards. Have someone make sure he gets back to Arizona."

"Harsh, Rizan, even for you."

"Expedient," he retorted. "Besides, if the assassin can get past the thunderbird, we have a much bigger problem."

CHAPTER
ELEVEN

BEAR

She caught the rabbit out of the air and bit down, ignoring its shrill cry. Hot blood filled her mouth and she crunched greedily. Lumbering forward, she grunted for more. Dee laughed, the sound grating on her sensitive ears, then pulled another from a cage at his feet.

"One more, then playtime is over."

The male had a name. If she focused, she could sometimes remember it. But that meant listening to the she locked in the back of her head. Although the screaming faded many winters ago, Bear could hear her maddening weeping, especially after a kill.

Bear liked to kill. A lot.

The second rabbit twisted, making her miss the killing bite. Growling, she swiped at it, her paw catching its hindquarters. It spun through the air and slammed into a pine tree, leaving a thick smear of blood on the bark as it fell to the ground. It wasn't alive anymore, but she ate it anyway.

Full of misplaced arrogance, Dee laid a hand on her foreleg. She shook him away, smoothing her fur into place, then snapped at his face.

Immediate pressure settled in the back of her head and on her shoulders, forcing her to the ground. The she inside her screamed and pounded against the walls of her cage, sending shards of sickly purple magic ricocheting around her skull.

Disobedience made her remember things when all she wanted was a photo and a scent trail leading her to her next target. Bear hated it and often thought of killing Dee, but he was the source of prey. Obedience made things simple and pleasurable.

"Change your form, darling. It's time to get to work."

Grunting, she obeyed. Fur receded and she shrunk into the hated human form. "Will I get to kill many?"

She was unused to speaking and her voice didn't work like she thought it should. Humans had smooth, fast voices. Hers was rough and hoarse, and she stuttered. It didn't matter though. She didn't need speech.

Dee tossed her a piece of cloth and she pulled it over her head, obeying his unspoken order to cover her unsightly body. Grimacing, she followed him into his wooden cave. She hated the walls surrounding her with their reeking stench of chemicals and mold.

She especially hated the shiny pink thing in a gray cage sitting on his desk. The she produced too much noise when she saw it, and her piteous sobs made Bear's head ache. Worse, it made her remember the spicy sweet scent of a male she didn't want to know.

If she found him, she'd kill him whether Dee liked it or not. That would make the she in the back of her head go away.

FEATHER

She understood why half-breed mages were killed at birth. It was a harsh reality Feather had never been forced to face, but Bear was chewing on the carpet crazy.

They both were.

Bodiless, voiceless, powerless, she huddled in the darkened prison of her own head, helpless to stop Bear's murder spree. She killed without mercy, targeting humans and supernaturals alike.

She understood a few of them, like the human male who won an auction against her captor, Vyron Muir. He was too greedy and spiteful to allow such an insult.

Most made no sense though. The young falcon in Paris who gave him a smile and held a café door for him died not two hours after that innocent encounter. Pretty and kind, she was no match for Bear. Neither was the aged street vendor in Amsterdam, or any of the dozens of lost souls sacrificed for no good end.

Bear had a taste for blood now, and she liked it. Feather stretched in the tiny space, once more prodding for weaknesses. Was Vyron teaching her to hunt with live prey? The idea chilled her. If that was true, who was his ultimate target?

"I have a special treat for you, darling," Vyron said, holding up a picture. "You can have two this time. A male bear and his mate."

Bear took it and Feather's breath caught. It was an old photo, taken at her high school graduation. Her parents stood on either side of her, smiling into the camera.

"Where?" Bear asked.

"South of Kayenta, Arizona." Chuckling softly, he added, "You might remember it."

"All places are the same. Is it close or far?"

"Very far. You'll fly on a plane again."

"No. Make it close."

Feather leaped at the barrier, slamming her fists against it. "No, you sick fuck! Don't you touch my parents!"

Grunting, Bear swiped at her, sending her reeling, but she got back up and tried again, her weak magic looking for cracks.

"The she in my head is bothersome. Make her stop and I will go on the plane to kill the bear and his mate."

Feather felt the horrifying itch of his building magic. Steeling herself, she stared at the diamond rose and a silent scream rose in her throat as her soul caught fire. Vyron had gotten very good at sending his nasty spells at Feather instead of Bear, and took every opportunity to punish her if Bear complained.

"Better?" Vyron asked.

"Yes."

"Good." Veyron looked into Bear's eyes and smirked. "We can't have the she disturbing you, can we? After you get rid of the bear and his mate, I have one more task that should solve your little problem with her once and for all."

"I will do that first."

"Patience, darling." He sat down and pushed a plate full of raw salmon toward her. "That final task will require all your strength and concentration."

"Do that first," Bear repeated, gnawing on the fish.

"I said no," he snapped. "When you kill the bear and his mate, a dragon will come. You will take control of the she and force her to entice the location of his hoard from him, then lure him back here."

"Then I kill him?"

"Yes. After that, you will have all the prey you want."

Stunned into silence, Feather wept, balled up against the torturous pain. Still crying, she lifted her head. Maybe she couldn't save herself, but she'd be damned by the fates before she let Bear touch Rizan or her parents.

As Bear ate her salmon, Feather quietly started digging. There might not be a hole now, but she'd fucking make one.

RIZAN

"Get the children out," Rizan said softly, making an effort not to frighten the small ones as they trooped outside. "I need to have a few words with the pimp."

"Guinevere and Angel are on it," Zeke replied. "We have foster homes in the States lined up already, along with medic-trained mages. It smells like about half of them are positive for HIV."

"Good. Leave now." He inhaled, smelling piss. The sick little fucker had wet himself.

"Nope." Zeke's normally sunny expression was absent and his eyes hardened. "We also found three clouded leopards. They say they're sisters, and he had them locked in a pit out back. The oldest is twelve."

"Oh my." The Thai rolled off his tongue as he turned to face the pimp. He might not read well, but he'd always had a facility for human language. It was very useful in his current line of work. "You've been a very naughty boy, haven't you?"

Parasites like the one cowering on the floor looked for two-natured children because it was impossible for them to carry human disease. It also meant their parents were probably dead. It might be common for humans to sell their children into prostitution, but no two-natured would ever do so willingly.

"Please," the man said, holding out his hands. "It's just business. You understand, yes? I get you a girl, pretty and clean, and—"

Rizan inhaled and let out a concentrated stream of blue flame, but went slowly, starting at his feet. He wanted screams to echo across downtown Bangkok as a warning to the next asshole who decided exploiting babies was a good idea.

Zeke's red magic flared, twisting itself with his flame. The man burst into a cloud of ash, cutting off his cries for mercy.

"I wasn't done," he growled, resisting the urge to punch his teammate.

"I was," Zeke snapped, pulling out a block of C4, his favorite toy. "I'm blowing this place off the map. Either help or get out of the way."

Cocking his head, Rizan studied his friend. "Why?"

Zeke set charges around the room, linking them with det cord. "My best friend when I was a kid was named Rebecca. She was a year or two older than me and human, but I loved her more than my life. When she was fourteen, her parents sold her to a nobleman as his wife."

"Seems young, but such things happened—"

"He killed her before their first anniversary. I returned

the favor. Got myself transported to Australia for it. I'd have been hung if I'd been an adult."

Nodding, Rizan said nothing and helped Zeke set charges. He knew so little about his teammates, but they all had histories, stories of their own to share. He wasn't the only one with a past he preferred to forget.

The Army was good for helping people do that. He wondered what Feather was doing and prayed to the fates she wasn't learning things that would make her unhappy later.

Two months and four days were left until his promise was fulfilled. When he found her, there would be no more waiting. A dragon had only so much patience. His time in the Army would be done and he would tear the world apart to find her. Although his team tried to help and gave him information he wouldn't have had otherwise, there were some things they wouldn't do—like destroy a city to find one missing woman.

Following Zeke outside, he found Guinevere and Angel surrounded by crying little girls. Three, bedraggled and skinny, raced to him and climbed his legs like monkeys, then wrapped thin arms around his shoulders. Under the dirt, he smelled the dusty musk of cat. Cuddling them gently, he watched the brothel explode.

Leaving his teammates to clean up, he sent out a burst of flame and let it carry him to Arizona. Morgaine would be the best mother for the orphaned leopards.

The desiccated desert wind struck his face with the scent of familiarity as he strode toward Yan's double wide trailer. Hands shoved into her pockets, she met him at the bottom of her porch steps.

"What do we have here?"

"Clouded leopards," he replied, setting the girls down. They clutched at his legs; their eyes wide.

"I know what they are. Why are they here?"

"We rescued them from a brothel in Bangkok. I'm giving them to Morgaine to raise."

"No." She knelt and held out her arms. "Come here, little ones," she said in perfect Thai. "Are you hungry?"

She took them inside and a sharp pang shot through his chest. He shuddered in a vain attempt to dislodge the sensation and misted into his dragon form for the short trip to River and Adam's house. To his surprise, a pearlescent hide glinted in the sunlight, revealing Lily Archer sprawled on the ground in front of the house.

For a moment, Rizan thought she was his sire, come back from the dead—or wherever he was hiding. The resemblance was uncanny.

Although she was still very small, she'd grown quite a bit since he'd last seen her dragon form. Instead of being the size of a pony, she was about the length and breadth of a tour bus. It would be interesting to see how large she became. After being stunted by Morgaine's magic for so long, he'd wondered if she would ever achieve proper growth.

Standing, she stretched like a cat and shot a ball of flame at him. "It's about fucking time you showed up."

"I hadn't realized you'd be waiting, but I was unavoidably detained."

"You sound like a damned lawyer." Turning her back on him, she rolled and scratched her sides against the rough ground, then stood and shook herself. "My husbands threw me out until I stop being a bitch."

"Molting?" He hid a smile. Lily could be cranky at times,

and as much as her husbands loved her, he was certain they weren't up to the dragon princess during a molt.

"You have no fucking idea." Spitting out another ball of fire, she rubbed her muzzle with a delicate paw. "I've been praying that asshat assassin shows up so I can eat her. I'm ridiculously hungry."

"The Gulf of California is a two-hour flight south. Soak overnight and the old hide will peel right off."

"What's wrong with Lake Mead? It's closer."

"Salt water is better than fresh. I'll put in a call to The Rio in Vegas for afterward. That's the best place to go for a post-molt feast."

"Dragons aren't allowed in Las Vegas."

"Trust me. I know people."

"Asshole." She flared her wings, bright scales blinding in the sunlight. "I'm out of here."

Chuckling, he made the call and charged her feast to Davryn's account. It was only fair, since he was the reason dragons weren't allowed in Vegas anymore. Closing an entire buffet for one dragon was ferociously expensive, but it was the easiest way to get fed in relative comfort without getting arrested.

A curtain twitched at the front window, revealing Feather's parents, looking drawn and tired. River lifted a hand in a silent wave, the mage ward preventing anything more. Taking Lily's spot in front, he wrapped his tail around the house and watched the setting sun paint the desert red.

CHAPTER
THIRTEEN

FEATHER

Feather dug furiously at the tiny hole she'd managed to open, but she had to be careful. Bear would sense her efforts if she got too aggressive. All she needed was a gap big enough to get free for just a few moments.

A blink of time. Scant seconds in the life of an immortal.

She bit back a laugh and scratched harder. The conversation would go so fucking well.

Hey Rizan, remember how I promised to mate you? Yeah, no. I need you to kill me instead.

The plane landed with a sharp bump, making Feather still. Bear hated to fly and her instincts were on high alert. When the door opened, she stepped off, nose working as she walked to a waiting limo. At least she hadn't argued about clothes this time and wore a pair of yoga pants and a T-shirt. As usual, the driver didn't show his face or ask any questions. Vyron would have paid him a fortune for his silence.

Bear had a preferred time for her kills. She liked predawn hours, but she didn't fuss too much as long as it was dark. When her attention turned to the road and her upcoming meal, Feather got back to work.

She barely noticed when the vehicle sped through Kayenta. They were too close to home and she hadn't made nearly enough progress. Trying to control her panic, Feather prodded the opening and dug deeper, desperate to widen it.

"Stop it," Bear growled, swatting at her.

"Suck my lady dick." Thankfully, Vyron wasn't around. Bear's complaints brought immediate retribution, but she wouldn't remember Feather talking back for more than a few minutes.

The car stopped a few miles from her parent's house. Bear got out and walked into the darkness, her bare feet silent on the hard-packed sand. Picking up speed, Bear was soon flying through the desert scrub and too quickly, her parents' house came into view.

"Shit shit shit!" Now was not the time to make mistakes, but she had to do something before Bear reached her parents. "Hey, furball!" she shouted, pounding against the barrier keeping her confined. "How long do you think Vyron will let you hunt after you've given him what he wants?"

Bear's mental punch knocked her backward and she reeled from the pain. Pulling herself together, she tried again, the barrier wavering under her blows. "I think he's going to get tired of your shit and put you down like a rabid dog."

Her footsteps slowed, but Bear shook her head and kept running. "No."

"Yes," Feather replied. "You're going to end up as a rug on his trophy room floor."

"I will tell him what you said."

"You do that, stupid furry bitch," she muttered, but Bear had already tuned her out. Feather hadn't even been lying about Vyron, but Bear lived in the now and didn't perceive future events. To her, he would always be the provider of hunting and food, yet if his goal was the theft of a dragon's hoard, he'd have no need for Bear afterward. At least not alive.

Something moved ahead of them and Bear stilled. Feather tried to see what it was, but Bear's night vision was shit. A breeze lifted, carrying a familiar scent toward her.

"Fates." She slammed against the barrier, desperate to break free. "Rizan!"

She kept shouting his name, louder and louder over Bear's roar of confusion. "Remember that diamond rose, bitch?" she hissed, knowing Bear could hear her. "That dragon is my mate, and he gave it to me. You'll never—"

Bear's angry swipe knocked her senseless, but it was too late.

"Come out, little bear. I can smell you." Eyes glittering in the faint sliver of moon, he lowered his head. "Strange, though. You smell almost human, but I don't think you are."

Bear growled softly and stalked forward. Feather rolled her eyes. "Seriously? You think you're going to get past a dragon? Are you really that dumb?"

"Kill the two inside, then the dragon. Then I eat."

No, she wasn't dumb, she was a bear, and that meant stubborn to the point of idiocy. "You forgot Vyron's orders," she said softly, easing herself through the tiny crack she'd made in the barrier. Bear was too intent on her prize to notice the movement. "He told you to let me out so he can find the dragon's hoard."

"I don't need you."

"The feeling is mutual." Gathering her strength, she pushed Bear aside and broke free, taking control of her own body for the first time in years. "Rizan!"

She nearly cried with joy as his strong claws closed around her body and lifted her into the air. Bear fought back, rending and tearing in a desperate attempt to regain control.

"Feather?" He inhaled, bringing her close to his face. "It can't be."

"Listen!" she cried, desperate for just a few seconds before Bear overpowered her. "Dark Sidhe, Vyron Muir. He separated me from Bear and is using her. Kill us, please!"

"You don't smell like my Feather. What magic is this?"

Bear slammed her against the walls of her prison, forcing her back inside. "I will remember," she growled. "And Vyron will punish you."

"No!" She threw herself against her prison walls, but Bear had her locked up tighter than ever.

"Who is Vyron Muir?" Rizan asked.

"Give me the two inside, then tell me where you keep your hoard. After that I will kill you and eat you."

His laughter boomed across the desert and she saw her parents' faces pressed against the front window. She prayed to the heavens for them to stay inside. They would be safe behind the mage ward around the house, she hoped.

"How can I resist such a bargain?" he asked, the scales on his muzzle crinkling into a toothy grin. "But first, you'll tell me why you look like my missing mate."

"I am no one's mate," Bear growled. "The she is locked away and will stay there forever."

"Unfortunately, the bear is right," a familiar voice called out. Leaning heavily on a cane she didn't need, Grandmother approached, her face sad but stern.

"What are you talking about, old woman?" Rizan asked, lowering his head to peer at her.

"Feather is gone," she said gently. "The bear has control and has lost her mind."

"I'll get her back."

"It doesn't work that way." Sighing softly, Grandmother settled into the porch swing, pushing it into movement with a bare foot. "If the animal takes control, they always go mad."

"I refuse to accept that." He tightened his claws around her, but she didn't struggle.

It was time to let go, and Rizan would make it okay. She didn't want to die, but didn't see a way around it. Bear couldn't be allowed to live.

Bear was silent. Maybe she finally realized something bigger and meaner was in control. Steeling herself, Feather slammed against the barrier and broke free, ignoring the whips of dark Sidhe magic cutting into her being.

"Grandmother is right, Rizan. Kill me, please. Find Vyron and kill him too before he hurts anyone else. Just... protect my parents until it's done."

"I will not."

Lowering her head, she kissed the shimmering scale above his knuckle. "I love you, Rizan. I always have. If I didn't have you, I wouldn't have made it through the last five years. Bear would have gotten her wish, but every time I saw that pink rose, I thought of you and it gave me enough strength to go on until I could see you one last time." Tears pricked her eyes, but she forced herself to continue. "Please, give me this last gift and let me go."

"Do as she asks," Grandmother urged. "Let her make the decision while she has the clarity of mind to do so." Her eyes seemed to bore into Feather's soul, and she added, "I'm very sorry, Feather. I didn't want this for you. You were always my favorite."

~

RIZAN

"I will not," he hissed, sending a plume of steam over the old woman's head. Aside from a few lines under her eyes and a crease between her brows that hadn't been there before, Feather looked exactly like he remembered, with long black hair and golden skin. She felt the same in his arms, yet her scent was very wrong

Every few seconds, it would shift between the metallic scent of old blood and her wildflower and rain perfume. He squeezed her tighter, desperate to hold on. There was no way he was letting her go now that he'd finally found her.

"Can't you smell it on her?" Grandmother snapped. "She has to fight her bear for every second of lucidity. Are you so selfish you won't give her the peace she begged for?"

His throat seized on a reply as he realized why her scent was changing. "I—"

Her voice softening, she touched his side. "Let her say goodbye and do as she asked. It's the only way."

The mage ward faded around Feather's parent's house and they rushed outside.

"Feather!" Tears flowing unchecked down sallow

cheeks, River hugged herself and looked up at her daughter. "I'm so sorry, I shouldn't have let you out of my sight."

Adam pulled her close and lowered his head into her hair, but said nothing at first. Straightening, he gave Feather a weak smile. "We love you, baby. Our miracle little girl."

"My prey." The words came out of Feather's mouth, but it wasn't her voice. This was rough and deep stuttering speech, as if she was trying to communicate through unfamiliar vocal cords. The scent of old blood surged for a moment, then was replaced by wildflowers.

In her own familiar voice, Feather said, "Mama, it's okay. I should have listened to you. I love you both so, so much, but it's time for me to...I'm sorry."

She let out a short scream, and an instant later, his claws were filled with wriggling bear emitting the stench of copper pennies.

Still sobbing, River turned away, burying her face in Adam's chest.

"Do us a favor and..." Adam shook his head, wetness glittering on his cheeks. "Take her into the desert so her mother doesn't have to see it."

Grandmother rose to her feet, then helped them inside. When the door closed behind them, she turned. "I am sorry, Rizan, but it's for the best. I'll prepare the community for her memorial."

"No."

Her face darkening with irritation, she said, "Feather begged you, dragon. I know for a fact she's never asked you for a fates-damned thing, and you refuse?"

"I don't care if she's a bear. I'll—"

"You'll do this or I will."

"Who are you to have so much power?" He didn't

dispute her words. He'd always known she was something to be wary of, but he didn't know what she was.

"You can call me a caretaker. The thunderbird manages this world's magic and I deal with everything else." She jerked her chin at Feather. "Feather is no longer the woman you fell in love with. As much as I care for her, she's become an abomination. She cannot be allowed freedom again."

"Don't call her that!" He lowered his head and growled. "You call me selfish, but you allowed her to grow to adulthood like this, knowing you'd have to—"

"I took a risk and hoped," she interrupted, her expression softening. "But she's beyond that now."

Rizan covered Feather's squirming body with his free paw, and got himself a nasty bite for his trouble. Feather's teeth were quite sharp, it seemed. "A bargain, old woman. Give me two months and four days to bring her back."

"No. She's too dangerous."

"I'll take her to my hoard. It's six hundred nautical miles from the nearest land mass, so she won't be able to escape unless she can fly. Give me time to try. Please."

"You would sentence her to suffer longer?" Grandmother rolled her eyes. "Sadistic bastard."

"If there's even a slim chance of saving her, yes."

She let out a breath, then nodded. "Fine. Two months and four days. You will present her to me upon that day, prove she's well, and I will consider letting her live."

"And if I don't?"

"Your hoard isn't hidden from me, dragon. I'll take care of matters myself."

The bear bit him again, her desperate struggles breaking his heart. His Feather was inside that creature, fighting for every moment of clarity. Maybe he was cruel as the old woman called him, but he couldn't give up without trying to help her back to herself. "One more question and I'll go. Can I bond with her as her familiar?"

"If you try and fail to bring her back, you'll die when she does." She leaned on her cane and turned away. "Think about it before you do something stupid, and make sure you're in your human form first."

"Why?"

"You'll be easier to bury."

"Charming," he muttered under his breath, scowling when she vanished into the darkness. He wondered if Yanaha got her caustic personality from Grandmother or if it had been the other way around.

He held the bear up, gazing into her unfamiliar face. "Neither of us are going to die, morsel. I'm going to make this right for you, and then I'll never let you out of my sight again."

Snarling, she snapped at him. He tapped her nose gently and she let out a questioning grunt of surprise.

"No more biting," he admonished. "You'll never get what you want that way, and you're much too small to harm me."

She growled and tried to lunge at him again, making him bare his teeth. "In fact, you're hardly a mouthful, but I understand bear is delicious. I suggest you remember that."

It was an empty threat, of course, but he didn't think the bear was fully aware of how far he would go to keep her safe. Still, she quieted in his claws and stopped struggling.

As his flame rose to take them to his hoard, her mother appeared in the window, her hands flat on the glass. "Thank you," she mouthed.

At his nod, she turned away and a second later, he stood on the windswept cliffs above his home in the Southern Ocean. Barely a mile across, the island was desolate and barren. No vegetation grew here, other than a bit of lichen in protected crevices, and there was no beach. Aside from that and the distance from the nearest land, the water never warmed above forty degrees. He let her free, watching with amusement as she raced to the cliff edge and looked down.

"Take your time and explore," he said, keeping his voice calm and soothing. "The cave opening is just behind you when you're ready to come in."

Misting into her human form, she immediately began shivering, her dusky skin turning blue with cold. "Let me go," she gritted out. "I have to obey Vyron and return to him."

"Why?" He opened his paw, producing a sable cape from his hoard, then tossed it to her.

Never letting her eyes leave his, she crouched to pick it up and wrapped it around her shoulders. "He gives me prey and quiets the she, but he makes pain when I disobey."

"You won't have to worry about him here, I promise."

"You lie."

"Sometimes," he agreed. "But not to you. Anyway, explore to your heart's content and come in when you're ready. Perhaps consider changing your form before you freeze to death, yes?"

He brought forth his human form, smirking when he felt the rush of her magic signaling her shift. Darting to the side, he let her slam face first into the rock next to the opening to his caves.

When she snarled and lunged at him again, he puffed a little ball of flame at her, making her grunt and back away. "Be a good girl and run along. I have some calls to make, but I'll provide food when you're ready to come in. Oh, and watch your step. The water is barely above freezing, and I believe there are sharks."

The last bit was a tiny white lie, but he doubted she'd recognize it. No sharks came this far south.

She lowered her head, moving it side to side. He wondered if she would try to attack again, but she lumbered off, picking her way down the gravel-strewn path. He wasn't surprised Vyron used pain and its absence to force her obedience. As distasteful as it was, it was an effective way to control a dangerous animal with limited reasoning.

He would do the same thing, after a fashion, but his response for good choices would be a true reward instead of the absence of punishment. If his hypothesis was correct, Feather's consciousness had been forcibly split. As long as he could convince the bear to listen, he might be able to bring them back together.

A clinical psychiatrist would have a field day with her. Thankfully, he had plenty of information at his disposal. He also had Morgaine, who had proven herself to be a gifted researcher.

Pulling out his satellite phone, he tapped Kali's contact, and she answered almost immediately.

"I have the assassin," he said.

"Good. Where's the body? We need to identify her and find her handler."

"Well, that's a rub now, isn't it? It's Feather Carter, and she's with me on my hoard island."

"After all these years." She let out an audible hiss. "Where has she been? How did this happen?"

"Vyron Muir happened."

"Never heard of him. Who is he?"

"Feather says he's dark Sidhe. He's managed to... I'm

not sure how, but he's separated Feather from her bear, and somehow the bear has taken control."

"Can she escape?"

"Not unless she can swim with icebergs for six hundred miles. I told her there were sharks, so I doubt she'll try."

"Fates! Where the fuck are you?"

"You know better than to ask me that. Suffice to say, I have her. I need everything you can learn about Muir within the next day or two."

"We'll get right on him," she promised. "What else do you need?"

"Nothing for me, but keep a team on Feather's parents. Until we have Muir neutralized, I'm concerned he'll go after them out of spite for losing his toy."

"I have people on their way already. They should be arriving shortly, but I'll let you know when."

"Thanks." He paused for a moment, then said, "Kali, I need you to put everything on this. Feather doesn't have much time."

"How so?"

"Let's just say she has a stay of execution for the next few months, but I'm afraid I'm going to lose her. I need to find out what Muir did before the bear takes over completely."

CHAPTER
FOURTEEN

BEAR

The she inside Bear wanted to jump into the water. She even tried to take control when they reached the edge. Bear hated to be confined, and didn't understand why so many creatures wanted her to die.

Except the big dragon. He gave her warmth, and hadn't harmed her. If she attacked Vyron, he would have...

Vyron would have hurt her, and she'd have gone hungry for many days. The dragon had offered her food and not pain. It was very confusing.

"Rizan isn't an asshole," the she said waspishly. "He's trying to help us, and it's your fault we're stuck here."

She grunted, then changed her form and tried to find a way down to the water, hoping to put as much distance as she could between her and the dragon.

"I wish Vyron was here to make you quiet."

"He's not. Guess what else?"

"What?"

The she screamed loud and long, then cackled out a bitter laugh. "You can't shut me up, you stupid furry bitch."

"Be quiet!"

"Make me."

Bear tried to hit her like Vyron said to do, but couldn't catch her. She'd gotten very small and sneaky, and as hard as she tried, Bear couldn't force the she back into her cage.

"You're like a tick," Bear said. "Blood sucking annoyance."

"My name is Feather, idiot. You've only lived with it for twenty-three years.

"Why must you speak?" Bear sat and slumped against the rock. "I don't like it."

"I don't like being forced to kill people. I hate being kept from my mate. I hate when Vyron hurts us," She went silent, giving Bear a few seconds of peace before speaking again. "I hate that he's divided us. You used to be my friend."

"You never listened to me!" Bear shouted. "You never let me change my form or hunt or do anything else!"

"You never asked. You never fucking asked me, and now we're going to die."

Her voice lifted in song, an off-key, tuneless dirge that made Bear's ears hurt. Asking the creature to be quiet wasn't working, but maybe if Bear let her make her awful noise, she would be silent later. Curling up, Bear laid a paw over her ears and tried to go to sleep.

～

FEATHER

Thank fuck. Feather crept from her hiding spot and took control, changing her form back to her human body. The frigid wind bit at her, but she wouldn't be cold for long. Although it was only a few feet to the edge, she had to be careful not to wake Bear or attract Rizan's attention.

She shuffled forward, the stone cutting her feet, then looked down into the wind-tossed sea below. "Fates, it's a long way down," she muttered softly. Her bare toes gripped the edge and she took a deep breath, steeling herself for what she was about to do.

"C'mon Feather. It's one stupid step."

"I'd rather you didn't."

Screeching in fright, she stumbled and fell, but something hard and muscular caught her around the waist and dragged her back before she went off the cliff. Air tearing in her throat, she looked up into Rizan's warm brown eyes.

Fates, she'd missed him so damned much. Without a word she threw her arms around his neck and kissed him. His lips were every bit as soft as she remembered and his cinnamon and vanilla scent tangled around her. Images of their first and only night together raced through her head and she bit back a moan, unwilling to wake Bear.

"No, morsel," he said softly, pulling away. "Judging by your aborted attempt at flying, I assume I'm talking to Feather instead of her passenger."

Still trying to catch her breath, she nodded and rested her head against his chest, letting his scent comfort her. He was right. She might be able to have a conversation with him, but sex and kissing was sure to wake Bear eventually. "Yeah, but I don't know for how long."

Narrowing her eyes, she looked up and drew in a sharp breath. "Where the fuck is your hair?"

Chuckling softly, he wrapped the fur around her, then picked her up. "I cut it off almost five years ago when I went into the Army, but I'll let it grow now that I have you back. Let's get you inside before you try to jump off my cliff again."

Fates, she'd missed so much, and the bald look was good on him. "Why did you stop me?"

"Because I think I can bring you back. We'll try operant conditioning, and—"

"Someone's gotten an education along with a haircut," she muttered, letting him carry her into a surprisingly warm cavern. She hadn't managed to finish her first semester, but tried not to feel too jealous. In truth, she was stupidly proud of him. "That's what Vyron did. I'll pass, thanks."

His entry cave was comfortable and spacious, and looked more like the inside of a posh ski lodge than what she remembered from King Davryn's hoard. Tapestries picked out in shades of blue and purple covered the walls, complementing thick rugs strewn across a polished floor. Couches and comfortable chairs made up a conversation area surrounding a massive television complete with gaming systems. One wall boasted a large painting of a desert landscape, reaching almost to the ceiling.

A tiny puff of steam flowed from his nostrils. "He used the absence of pain to reward your bear, I assume. That isn't what I intend, but I need your help."

"I can barely help myself." Grimacing, she added, "You saw how my attempt at suicide went. I couldn't even do that right."

He kissed the tip of her nose and settled into an overstuffed recliner, still holding her. "This is easy, especially for one who I'm sure has spent the last five years cataloging her opponent's weaknesses. Tell me what she wants."

"She wants to kill, eat, and sleep. That's pretty much it. What are you planning?"

"As I said, operant conditioning. Whenever she agrees to work with you instead of against you, she'll get a reward. A live animal, perhaps. If she fails, she gets nothing."

"I don't think it will work," Feather replied. "She doesn't reason or react like a human."

"No, she reacts like a bear." He settled her more firmly against his chest, then pushed her head down on his shoulder. "I think you'll have to give up a little control too."

"Absolutely not." The thought was horrifying. She'd seen firsthand what Bear was capable of. "If it's alive and she can catch it, she kills. That's all she thinks about, and I will not—"

"Think about it," he urged. "She's out now, and aside from ending your life, we're not going to go back to the way things were. Is it not worth an attempt to make peace with her?"

Instead of considering it, Feather let herself enjoy these few moments of relative peace in the lap of the man she loved more than her own life. The thought of Bear harming him was... No, she couldn't allow it. But maybe he was right. She'd spent five years fighting against both Vyron and Bear. What would happen if she tried to give Bear what she wanted? Could they come to an agreement and live amicably? She didn't think it was likely, and worse, Bear might harm Rizan.

He was invulnerable in his dragon form, but not as a human. Then again, Bear hadn't managed to touch him, much less hurt him.

"Maybe," she finally said. "I could try, but I'd rather take a swan dive off that cliff than let her hurt you. What are you going to do about sleep? She's not going to call détente for a nap."

"That's easy enough. I'll just sleep in my dragon form. She can wear her teeth to nubs on my scales without waking me up."

She laughed softly and shook her head. "You've thought of everything, I see."

"Not everything." He sobered and tipped up her chin. "We need a... safeword? Is that what people call it? Something you can do or say to tell me she's coming back."

She kissed his jaw and snuggled closer. "I wish we could do fun things with a safeword, but..."

Bear chose that exact moment to wake up. She roared and took a swipe at Feather, driving her away.

"Shit!"

RIZAN

He supposed that was as good a safeword as any. Although he wished for more time with Feather, he let her go when she scrabbled from his lap and changed her form.

"You've had her for almost five years," he murmured. "Could you not allow us time to chat?"

Opening her jaws, she bared her teeth and snarled, then tore the hell out of his favorite napping couch. She ripped his television from the wall and broke it before she went after the carpeting. Rolling his eyes, he let his flame surge, repairing the damage almost as fast as she could make it.

She finally stopped and panted softly, her tongue lolling over her lower jaw. Hunkering down on her hindquarters, she glared at him balefully before her eyes caught on something behind him.

Turning to look, he allowed himself a small smile at the sight of the diamond rose resting on the sideboard. "Wonder if Muir is missing that yet."

With a huge leap, she crossed the chamber and snatched it between her jaws, then swallowed it, looking very pleased with herself.

He burst into laughter and held his sides. "Oh, morsel," he gasped. "You can't get rid of it. Gifts from dragons never leave their owner." He laughed again, shaking his head. "Well, this one will leave you, but I doubt you're going to like it."

To his surprise, she didn't attack him, even though he supposed he must look very vulnerable still seated in his favorite recliner. Instead, she cocked her head and peered at him, her muzzle wrinkling. She was finally thinking instead of reacting, and he wished he knew what was going on in that furry head.

"Now that you're calm and listening, would you like a treat? There's a wild goat outside. Go have fun, and we'll talk when you come back."

She misted into her human form. The diamond she'd swallowed rolled away and she blinked in surprise. "You are a strange male. I don't understand," she said, her voice still rough, but he could almost hear Feather behind it.

He wanted nothing more than to pull her into his arms and tell her how much he loved her, but now wasn't the time. "Why are you confused?"

"You offer food instead of punishment."

"Punishment is unnecessary. You are a bear, doing

what bears do. As you saw, it's nothing to repair what you damage."

"The goat will make me sick if I eat it."

"No, it's a perfectly ordinary mountain goat, although you'll have to work to catch it."

"Why do you do these things?"

"I want you to think about—"

"I only want to kill. Thinking is too hard."

Feather had a point about the intellect of her bear, but he could work with it. "I'm not asking you to think a lot. I want you to think about something very simple."

"Nothing is simple anymore," she said in a small voice.

He hoped Feather was listening and wouldn't fight against what he was about to suggest. "It can be if you let it." Leaning forward, he rested his elbows on his knees. "After you find your goat and have a good meal, think about what would happen if you and Feather came to an agreement and started working together."

"No. The she is greedy and will put me in a cage forever."

"Have you asked her? Have you given her reason to trust you?" He leaned back and crossed an ankle over his knee. "I remember when she had fangs for the first time. She was so pleased. Think about why she isn't happy anymore."

She stared at him pensively for several seconds, then morphed back into her bear form. Her paws thudded against the floor as she escaped.

"That went well," he muttered, going to the sidebar. He needed a fucking drink. His phone chimed with an incoming call from Kali and he tapped to accept it.

"You're in the fucking Southern Ocean?" she asked. "What the hell, Rizan?"

"Tell everyone on the planet," he muttered, cursing his addiction to gadgets. She'd have never found him if not for that damned phone, but it was necessary to keep in contact with his team.

"You know I won't, but you might want to consider pulling the chip out of your phone."

"I will," he promised. "What can I do for you?"

"So far, we're not coming up with a ping on Vyron Muir. Does Feather know where she was held? I'd like to try to narrow the search down."

He put Kali on speaker and poured a few fingers of scotch into a glass. "She probably does, but she's out hunting right now, and I didn't think to ask her earlier."

"How are things going with her?"

"I don't know yet. She's completely separated from her bear and it's... May I ask you something?"

"If I can answer, I will."

"Do you and your tiger disagree? Does she ever try to force her way in and take control?"

"No. There are times she wants to hunt, and I give it to her because it's something we both enjoy. Sometimes she gets irritable if we have to sit still too long, but aside from that, we get along. Why do you ask?"

"They're fighting each other for control. Neither one of them is willing to give an inch. The bear wants to hunt, and Feather wants her dead. I just wondered how it was with other two-natured."

"We're all born knowing we share a consciousness and we grow up learning to live with each other. Feather didn't get that. Also, it probably has a lot to do with what she's been forced to hunt," Kali replied. "If she can't convince her bear to take game animals instead of people... Are you prepared to do what's necessary?"

"No. Not yet, at least. I have two months, and one more trick up my sleeve if it doesn't work."

"Don't do anything stupid, Rizan. Put her down and get out. There are other mages out there who aren't quite so damaged."

"Thanks for the support," he muttered. "Call me back when you have something useful to tell me."

After ending the call, he turned his phone off and pulled the chip as Kali suggested. Although he'd had this hoard for millennia, maybe it was time to find another. Right now, the remote and inaccessible location suited his purposes.

Ending Feather's life was not on his agenda. He had no intention of taking that final step with her. If his attempt at retraining her bear's instincts didn't work, he'd bond with her as her familiar, forcibly if necessary, and confine her to the island. Reaching into his pocket, he pulled out the collar he'd stolen from Morgaine. She'd been compelled to wear the gem encrusted bauble to control her magic after her release from prison. It was a last resort. He didn't want to force Feather, but if it meant she would live, he'd lock the collar around her graceful neck himself.

CHAPTER
FIFTEEN

BEAR

"It's right there, dumbass. Meat on the hoof."

Feather was annoying, but she was right. The furry creature ascended the cliff, seeking the safety of higher ground. Yet it didn't interest her and Bear couldn't understand why.

"Why aren't you killing it?" Feather asked.

Bear sat on her haunches, then laid down, resting her muzzle on her paws. "I don't know."

That damned male challenged her to think, but Bear didn't know what to do with all the unfamiliar things. Large game, free for the taking. No punishment. It was all too strange. She didn't know if the mountain goat was bait. Would the dragon hurt her if she took it?

"Fuck, you're mental," Feather snapped. "Rizan is the last male in the world who wants to harm us."

"How do you know that?" Bear sat up, wishing she could silence Feather. "He's confined us, and we're too far away from Vyron."

"Because he's our mate. Go hunt the goat, and shut the fuck up."

"I don't believe you. You never want to hunt."

"It's a fates-damned goat. Eat it."

It felt good to irritate Feather. "No. Not until you tell me why I can hunt this and not other creatures."

"Because the goat isn't a person. It doesn't have a mate or young to care for. It doesn't have someone who will miss it when it's gone, or a goal to achieve, or anything else. It's just a goat."

"The dragon told me to think," Bear replied. "I don't know what to think, so you will do it for me. Tell me what I should do to make the dragon let us go back to Vyron."

Feather shifted inside her and stretched, prodding for weaknesses. "Sure," she said in a silky voice. "Walk to the edge of that cliff and jump off. You won't have to worry about thinking after that."

"You're not helpful." Losing interest in the goat, Bear got up and lumbered to a sheltered spot away from the frigid wind. "I'm asking just like the dragon said."

"You're not asking the right questions."

"Why do you have to be so confusing?"

"Why do you have to be so obtuse?" Feather poked hard at her cage and Bear flinched at the sharp pain. "Ask yourself what Vyron gives you that Rizan hasn't."

Bear could do that. It wasn't thinking. Vyron gave her prey, but so had the dragon. He gave punishment, and the dragon... hadn't. Aside from that, there was a faint memory of pleasure and happiness when she thought about the dragon, but not when she thought about Vyron.

The dragon smelled delicious and wonderful, like something she wanted to rub against so she could carry the intoxicating scent forever. Vyron smelled unpleasantly of sharp chemicals. "I don't understand this."

"Rizan loves us," Feather said softly. "He brought us here to try to save us. That is the difference between him and Vyron."

"I don't need love." Bear snorted, then added, "It's stupid."

FEATHER

If she had control of her body, Feather would rip her hair out. Trying to reason with Bear was like talking to a toddler. A very stubborn, homicidal toddler.

"You'd rather go back to letting Vyron torture us?"

Bear grunted and turned over. "I don't know."

Maybe she was going about this the wrong way. Feather was asking her to have human emotions and adhere to the mores of a society she didn't understand. She'd also had almost five years of relative freedom in which she could do what bears do, according to Rizan.

Taking another approach, Feather said, "Rizan wants us to work together."

"No. I don't want to."

Do not shout at the stupid bear. "Okay. You don't have to."

"That's it? You'll give up and go away?"

"I can't go away. This is my body too, remember? But yeah, I'm giving up."

"Good. Can we go back to Vyron now?"

"You can try it." She crossed her fingers, praying something would penetrate Bear's thick head.

Bear got to her feet and lumbered to the edge. "I don't know how to get there."

"There is that," Feather agreed.

"You will help me."

"Nope. I said I was giving you what you wanted, remember? You're on your own." Feather pressed her lips together before she said anything else, but smiled at Bear's growl of frustration.

"Tell me what to do," Bear demanded.

Go back to your little corner of my head, never speak again, and let me bond with my mate. Feather kept her thoughts to herself. None of that was going to happen.

"You want me to go away. You wish I wasn't here."

"Sometimes," Feather admitted, unwilling to lie.

"You never wanted me."

There was something in Bear's voice that sounded like hurt.

"I used to wish you could come out. I wanted to go fishing with our sire in Alaska, and play with the other two-natured. I wanted to be like them. I was so happy when we grew fangs because it meant we'd be able to give Rizan our mating bite."

Bear went silent for several seconds, then said, "I will give him a mating bite. Will that make you let me go?"

"No. He won't accept it now."

"Why not?"

"Because he has to kill us in two months. You see everything as prey, even our parents. I don't think you can stop murdering people. But that's okay, because I want him to. I'm tired of fighting the inevitable."

"What will you give me if I agree to stop killing?"

"It doesn't matter," Feather replied, trying to goad Bear

into thinking just a little harder. "You can't do it, and I don't trust you enough to bargain."

"I'll prove to you I can. Then you will agree to my terms."

Rolling her eyes, Feather gave up. "What about my terms?"

"I already know your terms. You want me to go away forever."

"Nope."

Bear flinched with surprise, her furry butt hitting the rough ground a little too close to the edge of the cliff for comfort. "I don't believe you."

"I know."

"Tell me what you want."

Feather's patience was almost at its end. Rizan was wrong about Bear. She wasn't listening worth a fuck, and having a conversation with her was like pulling teeth.

"Shared time. I always wanted to hunt feral hogs with you. I want to eat wild berries and find mushrooms. I want to be with our mate and go back to school to finish my education, and I want people not to be afraid of us."

"I will not share. I like people being afraid."

"Yeah. That's why we're going to die in two months."

"No. I will go back to Vyron."

"Let me know how that works out for you," Feather muttered. "Even if you manage to escape, Rizan knows your scent now and he will track you. Aside from that, you're exposed, and everyone knows what you are. If Rizan doesn't catch you first, Vyron will kill you because your usefulness as an assassin is over."

"Lies!"

"Do us both a favor and let Rizan do it. He'll be humane, which is more than you'll get from Vyron."

RIZAN

Feather shambled into the cave, growling softly when she saw him. Although he wondered why she hadn't killed the goat he'd left for her, he refrained from asking and splashed another measure of scotch into his glass.

Tipping his drink toward her, he said, "Welcome back. Did you enjoy yourself?"

Still growling, she stalked him, then changed her form. "Feather says Vyron will kill me. I think she lies."

Cocking his head, he lifted the glass to his lips. It was very strange. Although she was as beautiful as he remembered, her scent reminded him she wasn't his Feather and he felt no attraction. "Well, she knows him better than I do, but I think it's very likely he'll want to."

"He needs me. I will be safe with him and he will make her be quiet."

"No, he might have gotten use out of you when nobody knew about you, but that is no longer true. Even if I let you go, you'll be hunted down by someone else."

"Feather wants us to die."

"Did she say that?"

"Yes." Bear frowned and shook her head. "No. She said we needed to die, but that is the same."

It wasn't, but Bear probably didn't understand the difference between want and need. "What else did she say?"

"Nonsense things," Bear grimaced, showing the tips of her fangs. "She says she wants to hunt. I know she lies because she never wants to hunt."

"What did she say she wanted to hunt?"

Her nose wrinkled. "Feral pigs."

"Good choice. They're delicious and best of all, humans like it when we kill them. I can let you hunt one."

She lowered her head and glared at him through a curtain of disheveled hair. "What will I have to do for it?"

"Let me have Feather for a day without interference."

Her answer was immediate and firm. "No."

"Okay." Disappointment burned, but he drowned it with a summoned bloody Mary, then produced a large salmon and laid it on a tray. "This is for you if you're hungry."

"I want the pig you promised."

"I made an offer. A pig in exchange for time with Feather. You refused, so you don't get it."

Shaking her head, she frowned. "It is too long. She will try to kill us again."

"She won't. You have my word."

"You lie like she does."

"If that was true, I would have let you fall earlier." He ate the shrimp garnish from his glass, then strode to the entrance, intending to work off his irritation with a short flight over the coast of Antarctica. "I'll let you think about it. Make yourself comfortable."

"Wait."

Rizan turned and arched a brow as she scratched at her chest, leaving long red gouges in the delicate skin. "Did you have something to add?"

"Only one day?"

"One day. Do you agree?"

Anger, followed by mistrust and indecision flickered over her pretty face and he realized she wasn't purposely being disagreeable. Her trust had been broken, both by Feather and by Vyron. He doubted Feather had purposely done it, but Bear had no positive experience with either of them. Although he had no frame of reference for her situation, he empathized with her.

Then again, perhaps he did have a similar experience. Hadn't he been trapped in a prison himself? He hadn't thought of that hellish time in years, and while it wasn't quite the same, he might be able to use it.

Knowing Feather was listening, he added, "Feather won't interfere with your hunt, but if she wants to help, will you let her?"

She let out a soft snort. "How could she possibly help me? She's useless."

"As you say," he murmured, holding out a hand. "Shall we?"

Tentatively, she touched him and he twined his fingers with hers to keep her from escaping. With barely a thought, he transported them to an atoll he knew in the south Pacific. It was tiny and remote, but perfect for his purposes.

Letting go of her, he waved a hand to summon a boar for her hunt, then changed his form in preparation for a relaxing flight. "I'll be back at sunset. Have fun."

"You're leaving me here?"

"I'd planned to. I'm sure you're capable of taking down a feral hog."

In truth, he wasn't quite certain of that. As a black bear, she was one of the smaller ursine species, but maybe it would force her to work with Feather. Either way, he didn't plan to go far.

"Aren't you worried I'll escape?"

"Not really," he replied, stretching his wings. "The nearest land mass is a six-hour flight, even for me. There's a decent riptide off shore, plus a healthy population of tiger sharks."

"Another cage, then."

Lowering his head, he peered at her, making sure she was listening to him. "Think of it more as protection. Vyron isn't the only thing in this world that wants you dead."

She pressed her lips together and changed her form before wandering into the tangled undergrowth. Chuckling softly, he launched himself into the air, then circled the island a few times to ensure she wouldn't be disturbed.

Fates, the bear was exhausting. It was no wonder Feather was so snappish. He let out a puff of flame, knowing he wasn't being entirely fair. No one could have known she'd get targeted by someone bent only on making her kill instead of socializing her. Hell, the Feather he remembered would have asked for clothes at the very least. The thought reminded him to stock his caves before their return. The bear might not want them, but Feather would, and he needed to make everything perfect for their day together.

Veering away from the island in ever-widening circles, he made sure no container ship or sailing craft was around to distract her, then returned, changing his form as he settled to the beach far away from her. Allowing himself to fade into mist, he tracked her, intent on watching.

Bear was surprisingly stealthy, but he could smell her. She hadn't yet found the hog. Leaning against a tree, he settled in to watch the show. The boar he'd chosen was roughly eight hundred pounds of muscle and gleaming tusks.

If she wanted a hunt, he'd give her one.

CHAPTER
SIXTEEN

BEAR

"Don't you dare go rushing in there," Feather hissed.

"Shut up. It's a pig with plenty of meat. You know nothing."

Bear could almost see Feather roll her eyes, but was too intent on her prey to bother arguing. It smelled so good, much better than the rabbits Vyron gave her. Carefully inching forward, she waited until scant few feet separated her from the boar, then pounced.

Tough hide turned her teeth and claws, and the boar squealed in anger. Spinning, he tossed her away, then charged, his tusks opening a deep gash in her side.

"Run, you idiot!" Feather shouted.

Panting harshly, she did something she'd never once done before. She obeyed and took off through the underbrush, the boar nipping at her heels.

"Where do I go?" she asked, roaring in pain when the beast took a chunk out of her haunch.

"Tree! Climb a fates-damned tree!"

Her hip aching, Bear scrambled up the thin trunk, snarling when the boar flung himself against it to jar her loose. "What now?" she asked, wishing she could lick her wounds. "I should have known not to trust the dragon."

"Don't you dare put this on him. You wanted the damned pig, and I tried to warn you."

She couldn't stand asking for help, but she'd be stuck in this tree until the dragon came, and that was untenable. "Fine! How do we kill it?"

"A dozen pig dogs and a thirty-caliber rifle."

"Not helpful."

Feather chuckled softly, sounding almost gleeful. "Don't you remember? Daddy used to do it all the time. He wouldn't let us join because we couldn't change our form, but he let us watch."

"Get to the point." Bear didn't remember that and wondered what purpose Feather would have for lying.

"Two-natured bears work in teams. One will distract it while the other tries to get it on its back. Their bellies and the underside of their throat is where you can bite to kill."

"You're saying I can't do it." Disappointment welled inside her and she growled softly. "I want to kill it."

"No, I'm saying you have to be smarter about it. This isn't hunting a human or a live rabbit tossed at you. It's a wild animal that would like nothing more than to eat you."

"Eat... me?"

"Yep. Boars eat everything, just like bears. I'm not interested in dying like that, so I'll help you."

She risked a look down at the enraged animal glaring balefully at her. "What do I do?"

"It's easy. When he moves directly under you, jump."

"Crazy. You're crazy."

"Probably. Living with a stubborn bear will do that to a girl. You'll land on top of him, and hopefully knock him down so you can get a good shot at his throat.

"Hopefully." It didn't sound like a good plan, but Bear had nothing else. Never once had Vyron sent her to hunt something that would hunt her back. It was terrifying, but strangely thrilling.

It was also confusing. Why was Feather helping her? She could have stayed silent and let the boar take them both, yet she'd offered advice. Maybe the dragon was right and she should listen.

"Get ready. He's moving. Remember, when he exposes his throat, bite like your life depends on it, because it does."

Tightening her muscles, she eased her claws free of the slippery bark, then pushed off the tree when the boar looked down to paw at the ground. Falling heavily, she landed hard on the boar, knocking it down.

It lashed out, opening a gaping wound across her chest, but she twisted to avoid a killing bite.

"Jerk like you're moving to his underbelly!" Feather shouted. "He'll try to protect it and you'll get a clear shot at his throat!"

Snarling, the boar rammed a tusk into her face, stunning her. Her head swam and loss of blood made her weak. She faltered, letting the boar tear into her side. Had Feather planned this, knowing the boar would kill her?

No, Feather had wanted to hunt the boar, and only argued when... For the first time in many seasons, Bear let the mage free. "Help me," she whispered. "I can't do it."

Feather moved forward, not pushing, yet insistent. Strength and purpose filled her and Bear faded into the background, content to watch. To her surprise, Feather didn't try to confine her. Then again, she never had.

Ignoring the deep wound in her chest, Feather swiped bared claws at the boar's face, tearing out its eyes. She rolled, twisting under the boar, then sank her fangs deep into the animal's throat. Hot blood filled her mouth, delicious and rich.

His struggles weakening, the boar's breaths rasped in its throat for a few moments, then ceased. It collapsed, burying her under several hundred pounds of meat. Wriggling free, Feather climbed atop the dead beast and let out a delighted roar, her happiness and pride palpable.

She had only one wish, a sharp pang that dug deep. Feather wished the male Vyron sent Bear to kill had seen it. Images flashed through her mind of the male holding a young Feather, teaching her to hunt, not with claw and fang, but with a gun. The male was Feather's sire.

Their sire. Why had Vyron asked her to kill him when it served no purpose?

Vyron could no longer be trusted. Feather had tried to tell her, but she didn't want to hear. That changed now. "I'm sorry I didn't listen," Bear said. "You killed it without me."

Still bouncing off the walls of their head, Feather didn't hear her. "I did it! All by myself! Fates, it's like..." She spun, whirling like a cub after its first meal of fruit. "Whoo hoo!"

Without another word, she hunkered down and opened the boar's belly, then buried her muzzle into soft viscera. Bear relished the sweet taste of it, and the even sweeter taste of cooperation.

FEATHER

"Congratulations," Rizan said, crouching next to her. "You did well."

Feather grunted, rolling to her back. She was full of good meat and wanted nothing more than a long nap. Bear hovered in the background, quiet and pensive. It was pleasant to not have to fight with her for a change. She still couldn't believe Bear had backed off. Then again, it had saved their life.

She toyed with the idea of attempting to lock Bear into the tiny cage. Let her spend years voiceless and powerless. Yet she couldn't do it. If there was to be trust between them, she had to take the first step. Letting go, she faded into the background and pushed Bear forward.

"I promised a day," Bear said, resisting.

"It's okay. We'll start my day when Rizan takes us back to his hoard."

"Why do you want to wait? And why do you not cage me?"

"I want a bath and pretty clothes, and…" She let out a soft laugh. "Anyway, I'm not going to cage you, ever. It's wrong, and one of us has to start trusting the other if we have any hope of surviving."

"What if I want to hunt again?" Bear asked, obviously not quite ready to embrace Feather's wishes.

"If it's another hog, I'm totally down with it. If you still want to return to Vyron and hunt humans, we're going to fight."

"That beast almost killed us!"

"I know." Feather smiled and stretched, still too delighted with herself for words. "It was awesome, wasn't it?"

"You're crazy."

Feather sat up, enjoying the sensation of freedom. "C'mon. Admit it. You had fun. It was way better than hunting a human, right?"

Bear grunted, then said, "We should shift to heal our wounds."

"Knock yourself out, babe. I'm gonna take a nap."

"No, the dragon will want to talk. What do I do?"

"Tell him..." She pressed her lips together, then decided to go for broke. "Tell him I love him and look forward to teaching him to use a condom again." Bear's horror filled their shared mind and Feather laughed.

"I can't tell him that! He is not my mate."

"No, he's *our* mate. You wanted freedom from me? Figure it out."

"Two days if you don't make me do this. A month if I never have to hunt a boar again."

"Forget it. I like boar hunting." Feather closed her eyes and smiled.

RIZAN

He tried to stop the laughter bubbling up from his throat. Rizan couldn't tell for sure without hearing their conversation, but he got the impression Feather was schooling Bear on relative levels of crazy. It was entertaining as fuck and he wished he could hear what they discussed.

It was still disconcerting though, and he wanted to ask Morgaine to research it before he went further. Dissociative personality disorder was a new concept for him, but he was sure that would be the human analogy for what Feather was going through.

"Baby, you need to change your form," he advised. "That boar nailed you hard."

Nothing happened at first, making him wonder if he'd have to use Morgaine's collar to force them. Slowly, Bear misted into a human form, then shuddered and fingered the edge of a closing wound. "I don't want to hunt another boar."

"You did very well though."

"No. Feather did it. I... I was not helpful."

"What do you think about that?" he asked gently.

She walked around the partially-eaten corpse. "I don't know."

"Do you plan to hunt humans again?"

"No." She turned to face him, her face pale. "Vyron asked us to kill our sire. That is wrong and I don't want to."

He resisted the urge to pump his fist in the air. "What about your mother?"

"The mage." She went silent for several seconds. "She used to hold us on her lap and read us stories. She smelled good."

"She and your sire both love you very much."

"Nobody loves me." She looked down and nudged the boar with a bare toe.

"You're wrong." He strode to her and cupped her chin. "I love you. I have since the day you kicked me in the chest almost five years ago."

She jerked away and he let her go. "You love Feather."

"Let me ask you something. Did you ever think Feather would want to hunt or that she might be good at it?"

"No. She never wanted us to hunt."

"Feather wanted to hunt the boar because you've

always been a part of her. And some of her is in you. You said yourself that killing your parents was wrong."

Using his thumb, he wiped a smear of blood from her cheek. "You're each aspects of the same woman, sweetheart. Someday soon, you'll find each other again."

For a scant few seconds, she leaned into his touch then pulled back. "Maybe. I'm... I'm going to go away for a little while."

The scent of wildflowers and rain filled his nose and Feather blinked. "That went well," she murmured.

Laughing softly, he pulled her into his arms, trying to ignore her unclothed body. "Are you all right? Do you need to change your form again?"

"No, I'm okay." Her eyes sparkling, she smiled, baring elongated canines he wanted buried in his shoulder. "Did you see? I killed that boar all by myself!"

"I did, morsel. You were wonderful." He stroked her disheveled hair away from her face and kissed the tip of her nose. "I'm very proud of you."

"Do you have your phone? I want to send a picture to my dad. He'll be so..." Her happy expression faded. "Yeah, let's not and say we did."

"Would you like to talk to them?" he asked, holding out his phone.

She leaned against his chest. "No. I don't want to get their hopes up." Lifting her head, she met his eyes. "You bargained with Grandmother for me, but I didn't hear it all. How long do I have?"

Refusing to insult her with a lie, he said, "Two months."

"Okay." Sighing, she straightened and tried to smile. "Do you want the rest of the boar? I'm pretty full."

Rizan hated the sadness in her eyes. He kissed her softly, relishing the taste of her before pulling away. "I'm not going to let anything happen to you," he promised. "You're going to make peace with Bear, and we're going to be okay."

"I wish I had your faith," she whispered.

"I have enough for both of us." He snapped his fingers, moving the boar to the beach so he'd have room to eat it as a dragon. "Waste not, want not, right?"

"Maybe next time pick a smaller boar," she countered. "What possessed you to choose Pigzilla?"

"Two reasons." He produced a blue cotton dress resembling one she used to wear and helped her pull it over her head. "I wanted to show Bear that hunting could be both a positive experience and challenging, and also to force her to work with you."

"How did you know I could do it?"

When they reached the beach, he stretched and resumed his dragon form, then snapped up the boar in a single mouthful. After swallowing, he burped out a small plume of flame. "You mentioned it specifically, and I've hunted them before. It seemed the correct choice."

"You definitely gave her a healthy dose of humility." She sobered, then added, "It almost killed us."

Nosing at her hair, he delighted in her sweet perfume. "You were in no danger. I was watching the whole time."

Bopping his nose, she laughed fondly. "Change your form and take me home. I want a bath."

"Your wish is my command." He pulled her close and let his flame carry them back to his hoard, then held her steady until she regained her equilibrium.

She flushed as he walked her deeper into his caverns. "I'm sorry I destroyed all your stuff earlier."

"Don't worry. It was easily mended."

She moved to the sideboard, tracing a finger over a cut

crystal decanter of hundred-year-old scotch. "You're set up well here. I see you've decided to embrace modern conveniences."

He opened the wooden door dividing his bedroom from the bathing chamber. "It's certainly made things more comfortable. I also have several cars now. I've found I enjoy driving."

"Where are they?" she asked, looking longingly at the steaming pool.

"Scattered about for when I need them." He sat on a stone bench, keeping his gaze averted.

"Thanks." Her dress fell to the floor and she stepped down into the pool. "Are you going to join me?" She peered at him from under her lashes, her gaze hopeful, yet filled with trepidation.

"Do you want me to?"

"More than anything."

SEVENTEEN

FEATHER

Rizan was even more beautiful than she remembered. He'd filled out in the time since she'd seen him last, with ridged slabs of muscle covering his chest. Although she missed his hair, its absence revealed chiseled cheekbones and wide, intelligent brown eyes. Half-hard and thick, his cock rose from a nest of dark curls, making Feather remember her prom night.

She shivered with longing, wishing things could be different.

And man, did he know how to live or what? The main chamber was gorgeous, but this bathroom was... Damn.

Fed by a waterfall, a pond easily twenty feet across rested under a soaring skylight. Shards of glittering quartz reflected the light, casting rainbows across the surface of the steaming water. Plush towels were folded on low shelves next to bottles of soap and shampoo waiting to be used.

Ducking her head underwater, she swam across the pool, feeling the temperature grow warmer as she approached the waterfall. She tried to stand, but couldn't find the bottom with her feet. Treading water for a moment, she stared up into the bright skylight for a moment before returning to the shallows and the benches cut into the sides of the pond.

Feather nearly moaned as he stepped down into the warm water. He was so gorgeous and looked at her like he still loved her. She didn't know what to do. So many things had changed between them. He wasn't a half-feral dragon with an attitude anymore, and she was...

Fouled with the blood of her victims on her hands and an order of execution hanging over her head. There wasn't enough water in the world to wash her clean. Ugh. She wasn't even worth polishing Rizan's shoes. She pulled her knees to her chest and lowered her head, trying not to cry.

Five years. A blink of time to an immortal, yet she felt like she'd suffered an eternity. She was broken inside and nothing would be right again.

Then again, considering the time remaining to her was measured in a scant few months, maybe she ought to stop thinking about it. She had Rizan now and was determined to make the most of the time she had left. Shockingly enough, he still seemed to care what happened to her.

He snapped his fingers in front of her face, making her jump and let out a squeak of surprise.

"You went away from me," he growled softly, pulling her into his lap. "I get little enough time to spend with you as it is, and I won't have you listening to whatever is going on in your head right now."

"How do you know that?" She squirmed a bit, unsurprised when he didn't let her go. Thankfully, Bear stayed quiet, but Feather sensed her rapt attention. Having him hold her in his arms like this was almost worth all she'd gone through. The feel of his hard body cradling hers so gently was indescribably wonderful.

"Because you started to cry." He settled her between his knees on a lower bench and tilted her head back, then grabbed a bottle from the edge of the tub. Pouring a dollop of shampoo into his palm, he soaped her hair, washing weeks' worth of grime and filth from the brittle strands.

His long fingers massaging her scalp felt like heaven and she hummed her appreciation. Bear didn't bathe unless Vyron forced her, and certainly not with decadent soap smelling of white ginger and spices she couldn't name.

"Let's get you rinsed."

Feather nodded and ducked under again, letting the water carry the soap and dirt away. Resurfacing, she tried to give him a smile. "Too bad it's not as easy to wash away my sins."

"Vyron's sins, you mean," he countered. "You were forced—"

"Duress doesn't make my victims less dead, or me less culpable."

He gritted his teeth, throwing the planes of his face into sharp relief. "You're arguing over semantics when I'm trying to please you?"

Leaning over, she rested her head against his muscular thigh and sighed. "You're right. Let's just enjoy the time we have together and forget about the rest."

"We'll discuss it later," he said, the warning clear in his voice. "I'm not letting you go so easily, morsel."

"Stubborn lizard." She petted his leg, the crisp dark hair tickling her palm. "You can't stop what will happen."

"You... Never mind. Stand up and let me finish bathing you."

He grabbed a sponge and filled it with soap smelling of fresh citrus and flowers, then washed every inch of her body. He wasn't purposely trying to arouse her, but the touch of his hands made her want more. She tried to stifle her body's uncontrollable response, yet she knew he could smell her need when his lips pulled back over gleaming teeth and he inhaled.

Is this what it would be like?

Eyes closing, Feather tried to focus on Bear's soft words, but it was so damned hard when all she wanted was the dragon kneeling at her feet.

"What are you talking about? I don't understand the question."

Will he pet us and bathe us always?

"Probably, yes. Why?"

I... like it. It's good. How do I make him do it again?

"Ask him."

I'm asking you. Tell me what to do.

"No. Ask him to bathe us again and he will."

"Interesting," Rizan murmured, carrying her from the water. "What were you discussing with Bear?"

"How did you know?" Feather turned to face him and reached for a towel.

He took it from her and wrapped it around the sodden length of her hair, then used another to pat her skin dry. "I can smell her when she comes out," he replied, crouching to dry her legs. "You smell like wildflowers and she smells like dried blood, yet it was very faint."

"Gross." She grimaced, then shrugged. "Sorry about that. She wanted to know if you would bathe us again."

"What did you tell her?"

"I told her you would if we ask."

"Ah." He wrapped the towel around her, then urged her to sit on a stone bench. Working a comb through her hair, he added, "I will, of course. You don't even need to ask."

"If we force her to bathe, maybe she won't stink anymore."

He tipped her chin up with a gentle fingertip. "I'm a dragon, morsel. I rather like the smell of blood. But I'd like to propose a hypothesis, if I may."

"About what?"

Leaving her seated, he held out a hand and summoned a thick, fur lined robe, then settled it over her shoulders. She pushed her arms into the sleeves, delighting at the cozy warmth.

"Bear's scent was faint, as I mentioned, but it struck me odd."

"How so?"

"I'm not sure." He swung her into his arms and carried her back to the main chamber, then placed her on a sumptuous leather couch across from his massive television. "Are either you or Bear hungry?"

"I wouldn't mind a mimosa, or just the orange juice if you don't think alcohol is a good idea."

A snap of his fingers produced a tall champagne flute and he presented it to her with a flourish. Sitting next to her, he rested his elbows on his knees. "It was rather odd. I smell one of you at a time. It's either your scent of flowers, or Bear's scent of blood."

"Go on." Feather took a sip of her drink, relishing the sweet, crisp taste of good champagne. It was delicious, but she didn't plan to have a second. There was no telling what Bear would do.

"I smelled both of you in the bathing chamber, yet..." He scratched at his jaw and cocked his head. "Her scent wasn't the same. It was softer, more like the scent of a healthy bear."

Feather frowned and tucked her feet under her robe. "I don't know what that means," she replied. "I can't exactly smell myself, and I have nothing to compare it to."

"I think Bear is starting to listen." He took her hand and kissed her knuckles. "If she is, I can conduct experiments to see if we can replicate the phenomenon, and if the same thing happens when you're in Bear's body."

"What do you hope to gain from this?" Still holding her drink, Feather got up, too filled with nervous energy to sit still. Part of it was from Bear, but they were both uncomfortable with the conversation. "Why can't you just let things be?"

Our mate is confusing and not simple, but we should listen. I don't want to die.

The glass fell from her fingers and landed on thick carpet without breaking. "Since when is he *our* mate?"

Since before Vyron. I want peace between us, so you will mate the dragon and everything will be right. I will even learn to hunt boar if you do this.

"I am not mating Rizan!"

~

RIZAN

"Yes, you will be mating me, Feather." Rizan wasn't sure how successful he was at keeping the hurt and anger from his tone. Had he already lost her without being given a chance? He should have never made that fates-damned vow to wait.

She spun to face him, eyes wide with surprise. "What? No, I..." Her face fell and she lowered her head. "I said that out loud, didn't I?"

Jaw tight, he nodded. "I will hold you to your promise on this," he said, forcing the words out between clenched teeth. "You will bond with me, either by force or by your own free will, and then we will mate as we should have done almost five years ago."

Tears welled in her eyes, making them glisten. "Rizan, we can't. If we—"

Attempting to ignore the maddening scent of her crying, he pinched her chin between two fingers and held the mage collar up in his free hand. "I'm not giving you a choice."

Jerking her head, she broke his hold on her jaw and darted away. Roaring in anger, he chased her and caught her around the waist, then forced her down to the floor of his cave. Without a word, he twisted a fist in her hair and snapped the collar around her slim neck.

Her hands flew to the collar and she stilled, her lips parted on a panicked breath. In a quiet voice, she said, "This is Morgaine's collar, isn't it? You took my magic from me."

"No, my love." Lifting her carefully, he carried her back to the couch and sat, settling her on his lap. "I won't deny your magic, but you will be bonding with me."

The scent of her tears stung his nose, and she rested her head against his chest and sighed. "Please don't make me do this. I'll be okay if I know you'll be alive after... after I'm gone. But if you force me to give you a bond, you'll die when I do, and I'll never forgive myself."

Fates. He petted her hair, trying to soothe her tears, and realized he was no better than Muir. They both sought to make Feather act against her will. "A life without you is no life at all," he said softly, still stroking her silky tresses. "I would rather die with you than live without you."

She lifted her head and smiled through her tears. "I bet you say that to all the girls." Nestling against him, she added, "Bonding with you and giving you my bite is my fondest wish, but I can't."

He kissed her softly, tasting the bitter salt dripping down her cheeks. "There is no other for me. I will do everything in my power to help you make peace with Bear, and we'll have the rest of eternity together in this life and the next." He tipped her chin up and wiped the tears away with a gentle thumb. "Will you trust me?"

She looked away and was silent for several moments. He smelled the faint scent of Bear, yet it was muted and faded quickly, telling him their internal conversation had been brief. He'd be able to hear what they discussed soon enough.

Sitting up, she wiped her face and held out a hand, her palm filling with amorphous purple. "Bear says we're trading one master for another," she murmured softly. "I think she's probably right."

His hand shook as he laid his palm over her magic, accepting the priceless gift of her trust. This was but the first step in tethering her soul to his forever. The collar opened and fell away at a touch, leaving her free. "I will never cage you, my heart."

"I don't think you'll like what you see."

Without warning, Feather's power dragged him into the darkened core of her being. It was a cold, bitter place, full of shadow and pain and the stench of abject misery. He bared his teeth at the tiny cage in the center of the physical representation of her psyche, knowing she'd been locked inside for too long. The bars were bent and jagged, evidence of her struggle toward freedom.

Bear hid in a corner, staring at him with glittering eyes. She didn't approach, but he sensed something akin to relief in her posture and attitude. He wasn't sure what to do with the separate and distinct aspect of Feather's personality, but knew they were as individual as he and his brother were. Would she be considered his mate now too?

It wasn't unheard of for supernatural creatures to embrace polyamory, yet the situation didn't sit well with him, and he doubted Bear would accept it. There was no chemistry between them. No bond of friendship or love. The only thing they had in common was Feather, and it seemed, a desire to keep her safe.

Broken rubble littered the floor and streaks of sooty black streaked bare stone walls, emanating the stench of dark Sidhe magic. This prison was Muir's creation; he was sure of it. It was a psychic abattoir designed for the sole purpose of Feather's eventual destruction. Hands clenched with fury, Rizan watched her memories unfold and swore to avenge her.

There were so many deaths and Feather mourned all of them.

The dark Sidhe had tortured her endlessly. Locked away in darkness, suffering unimaginable pain for years. How had she survived with her will intact? He'd had friends, comrades, and a duty to his brethren in the hell realm he'd been trapped in for centuries beyond counting, yet she had nothing except overwhelming guilt and loneliness. Consumed by regret for her suffering, flame rose inside him, illuminating the recesses of her soul with healing warmth.

"It's a real fixer-upper, isn't it?" She turned away and faced the cage, her small hand hovering over the bars. "I didn't want you to see."

"It's not you," he replied, wrapping Feather in his arms. "It's simply a construct you now have the strength to change."

"I tried," she whispered miserably. "Can we go?"

"Try again. You have me now, remember?" Leaning down, he inhaled her sweet perfume, then added, "Don't let him stay in your head any longer. Use me and erase every last trace of the bastard."

"Then what?"

"When you're well, we'll erase him for real."

"I want that," she hissed, purple magic lifting her hair in a nimbus cloud around her head. She tugged on the thread binding them together, drawing strength he happily gave her.

Rizan hid the twinge of regret from her, tucking it carefully away. She should never have known such pain. Her inner thoughts were a morass of self-blame and sorrow, and she saw only the blood coating her hands. She'd forgotten her kindness to her badger friend, all the sacrifices she'd made for the Arizona wolves, and every generous act she'd ever done.

He'd happily remind her. She was his now. Nothing else would touch her, and in time, he'd help her recover, but he should have never let her out of his sight in the first place. The guilt wasn't hers to carry. It was his.

Spinning, she glared at him and raised a shaking hand. "Don't you dare," she growled. "Don't you fucking dare blame yourself."

"Feather, I—"

"No!" She strode to him and took his hands, softening her tone. "I had several chances to leave before I was taken. Your brother, my mother, and even my friend Hannah warned me, but I didn't listen. I thought I could protect myself. If I hadn't been so damned stubborn, I'd have bonded with you five years ago and commuted to school."

"It was what you dreamed of," he said, tugging her gently into his embrace. "I wanted you to have it."

"Yeah, and I hated every second of it." She sighed brokenly and laid her head on his shoulder. "I should have bailed after the first week. I'd be graduated by now if I had."

"Why didn't you?"

"Stupidly stubborn, remember?"

Laughing softly, he kissed her forehead. "You fight for what you believe. I—"

The reeking stench of mold and damp rock filtered through the air and Bear let out a low whimper as Feather's lips pulled back from lengthening fangs.

"Get out," she growled.

Her only answer was a low male chuckle. Rizan's flame built in his throat, but there was nothing for him to burn. No adversary appeared, and he was infuriated Muir still had access to Feather's consciousness.

Taking her hand, he squeezed tight. "Together, beloved. We'll banish him together."

"Together." Her strength blossomed and welled, twisting with his flame into an unbreakable thread of power binding them together forever.

Letting out a furious shriek, she sent her magic flying into the low ceiling, bursting it apart like a grape. Sunlight poured inside, chasing the shadows. Another surge of magic removed the walls. The cage and broken rubble disappeared and the smell of wildflowers and rain poured in, cleansing and fresh as it forced Vyron Muir's filth away.

Nothing would separate them again—not Grand-mother, Vyron Muir, or anyone else.

EIGHTEEN

FEATHER

Vyron Muir, AKA Tweedle Dee, AKA the asshole from Hell, was gone, pure dragon flame disinfecting her brain until nothing remained but what she fucking put there. For now, her inner self was white walls, floors, and ceiling, just waiting for her to fill it.

The crushing weight of magical possession was gone, and for the first time in years, Feather felt like she could breathe without the threat of pain looming over her head.

It was almost as if the last five years never happened, yet something was missing.

"Bear?" Feather scanned the empty space, panicking when she didn't see her. There had been more than a few times she'd wanted Bear to be gone, but it felt as if she'd had a limb amputated and tears pricked her eyes.

"Here," a soft voice said. Huddled in a corner, Bear was curled into a tight ball.

Leaving Rizan behind, Feather went to her and

crouched. "We're safe now," she murmured. "Vyron is gone and can't hurt us anymore."

"I'm frightened. I don't know what to do."

"Come with us," Feather replied, her heart sinking when Bear leaned away from her outstretched hand. "Let Rizan help us get back to—"

"No. Leave me alone."

"Give her time," Rizan said, helping her to her feet. "She'll come to us when she's ready."

Eyes burning with unshed tears, Feather nodded. Why had she expected things to fall back into place so quickly? She should have known it wouldn't be that easy. Bear knew nothing except pain. She'd never been asked to think for herself, and the unexpected autonomy must be terrifying for her.

She tried to make her fangs grow, praying for the ability to give Rizan the mating bite she so wanted to deliver, but nothing happened. It was as if she'd never been two-natured at all.

"What do I do now?" Wrapping her arms around his waist, she leaned against him, desperate for comfort. Bear wasn't the only one struggling with their sudden freedom.

"Make something new," Rizan murmured, stepping away to give her space. "Create beauty that will burn Vyron's eyes if he tries to slither inside."

He fed her a tiny trickle of flame, building the thread between them into a stream of power. Instead of pushing, he let her take what she wanted.

Letting out a slow breath, Feather resisted the urge to delve into his memories and allowed their combined magic to surface. His taste and scent filled her with indescribable joy, making her wish Bear could share it.

A beach appeared, with crashing surf and a bright sun

overhead. The scent of sea grass and distant pine woods filled her lungs. Everything was the antithesis of Vyron's prison.

It wasn't quite right though. Bear wouldn't be comfortable on a beach. Removing the new construct, she started over and created a temperate forest with towering trees. Rich with life and the perfume of clean rain, such an environment was a black bear's ancestral refuge.

Feather had the faintest impression of Bear's surprised gratitude before she disappeared, leaving her completely alone for the first time in years. Maybe her choice would help improve their relationship. Crossing her fingers, she prayed to the fates Bear would find her way home.

Yet she wasn't by herself. Rizan whirled her away and back into the reality of his hoard cavern. Lifting her off her feet, he pressed her against the cool stone wall and kissed her, then untied the sash of her robe and slid it from her shoulders.

Kissing his way down her bare chest, he took a plump nipple into his mouth and suckled. A pulse of heated desire coursed down her spine like lava and pooled between her thighs.

She had a split second to contemplate the vast weight of his years. There were a few fuzzy images of creatures she'd only seen in books, but the door to his memories shut firmly when she spotted a blonde woman wearing a uniform.

"No fair," she muttered against his lips, desperately tamping down her jealousy. "I want to see."

"Another time, morsel. We have better things to do." He grabbed her thigh, pulling her leg up to wrap around his hip.

"But I—" She gasped and her head fell back when he snaked a hand between their bodies to find her clit. "Fates."

"That's it," he crooned, rubbing the sensitive bundle of nerves with his thumb. "Take your pleasure."

It had been so long. He'd been her first and only lover, but the memory of her prom night had kept her sane. Although he'd changed and embraced the modern world, his touch and scent were the same, still her Rizan.

So much more than a familiar, he was her mate. They were bound forever, in this life and the next.

Cupping the back of his head, she pulled him down for another kiss, feeling the soft prickles of stubble under her hands. The familiar scent and taste of cinnamon and vanilla rum consumed her senses, making her whimper. "Please," she whispered. "I need more."

He obliged, pushing a finger into her wet core, followed by a second. The delicious, stinging stretch made her head spin and she bucked against his hand.

"Do you remember our first time?" he asked, curling his finger to rub a spot deep inside. The sensation made her eyes cross with desire and she choked back a cry of pleasure. "Do you remember how fucking incendiary we were? Your passion shattered the windows."

"I've never forgotten." Desperate to touch him, she stroked his back, feeling the velvet over steel of his mahogany skin. "I've dreamt of that night for years."

"As have I, morsel." Smiling softly, he pushed his hands into her hair and breathed a stream of hot air over the damp strands, drying them instantly. His flame didn't burn, but instead coursed down her body, massaging away every last bit of tension.

His presence surrounded her with warmth and love, despite the mess Vyron had left in her brain. Rizan saw all of her, every awful thing she'd done, and didn't shy away. It didn't matter that she couldn't see his inner thoughts yet.

"Make love to me, Rizan." She bit her lip, then met his eyes, hardly daring to believe she was in his arms once more. "Please."

He picked her up and she wrapped her legs around his hips, desperate for more contact between them. The thought of letting him go was untenable. It wasn't enough to have him tethered to her soul; she needed his touch, needed him inside her.

Muscular arms holding her tight, he carried her into another chamber. Sumptuous and plush, his bedroom invited sex. Linens in saturated shades of red and orange decorated a massive bed, and his delectable scent filled the air.

Laying her down, he traced the line of her jaw with a gentle finger. "I've missed you so fucking much," he murmured, moving his hand to pet her shoulder, then down her arm. He took her hand and lifted it to his mouth, then kissed her fingertips.

"Me too." Cupping his head, she pulled him down for a kiss. Rizan might be able to hide his memories, but he couldn't hide his emotions. Joy, pain, love, guilt, and most importantly, hope, swirled through their bond. Tears popped in her eyes at the overwhelming surfeit of love pulsing between them.

He traced the lower curve of her lip with the tip of his tongue, teasing and enticing, yet refused to go further. Instead, he nibbled a path down her throat, sending a shock of desire into her core. Settling against the pillows, she whimpered.

"Shh, my heart," he said softly, moving down to

shoulder her thighs apart. "I want to taste you before I give you what you most desire."

Keeping his eyes fixed on her, Rizan licked her center and let out a low growl before burying his face between her legs to feast. His fingers dug into her thighs, keeping them open as he sucked her clit into his mouth and lashed it with the tip of his tongue.

She bucked under him and cried out in pleasure, desperate for more. His teasing licks drove her mindless with need. Moving further down, he stabbed his tongue into her channel, then let go of her thigh and teased her asshole with a slick finger.

"Rizan!"

Growling softly, he pushed his hands under her bottom and lifted her hips off the bed, then circled her back opening with his tongue. "You taste delicious, sweet Feather," he whispered against her wet flesh. "I could eat you all day."

It was dirty and debauched, but so, so good. She'd never known how many nerve endings were in that dark place, and every one of them was firing randomly in response to the touch of his wicked tongue. Turning his hand, he pushed two fingers into her core, then rubbed her clit with his thumb, all the while keeping his attention on her bottom.

Flame mixed with magic roiled inside her, coalescing into a tight ball of need deep within her womb. She tried to hold it back, desperate for more, yet the scourging conflagration wouldn't be denied.

Arousal echoed across their bond, driving her to the edge of the abyss.

She exploded, screaming in a mixture of pain and delight. Careening shards of purple flame set tapestries to blaze and tiny embers fell to the sheets smoldering around her.

Her body twitched with spent passion and she moaned softly, not quite able to speak, much less put out the fires she'd started.

Chuckling softly, Rizan tugged gently on the thread of magic connecting them to extinguish the flames and repair the damage.

"S—sorry," she choked, still unable to speak. She wanted to thank him, but couldn't manage the words. Their first time had been astonishingly good, but this was... incomparable. Maybe it was because she was feeling his passion through their bond. Whatever it was, she never wanted to let it go.

Still laughing, he moved up her body and positioned himself between her legs, his thick cock rubbing against her core. "On the contrary, morsel. I'm dying to make you do it again."

RIZAN

Eyes glazed with pleasure, Feather was the most beautiful thing he'd ever seen. He wanted to taste her, cover himself with her perfume so she was the only thing he ever smelled, yet he couldn't deny himself any longer. He needed to sink himself into her welcoming body more than he needed to breathe.

Lowering his head, he kissed her, a gentle brush of his lips across hers. How had he lived so long without her? Five years was a scant moment to an immortal, yet had seemed like forever despite his work with his team.

She let out a pleased whimper, moving her hand to caress the back of his head as a small smile played across her plump lips. "I—"

Without warning, her eyes widened and she pushed on his chest. "Stop!"

Abject fear filled their bond and he rolled off her without question, then scooped her into his arms. "What is it? Did I hurt you?"

Tears filled her eyes and she buried her face against his chest. He resisted the urge to delve into her mind, unwilling to intrude into her thoughts, but her distress froze him like unholy ice.

Had Muir violated more than her mind?

"We need condoms," she whispered. "I can't..." Swallowing hard, she looked up at him. "I won't risk getting pregnant until Vyron Muir is dead, and I'm sure Bear won't kill anyone else."

Once again, she refused his seed, yet when she pushed the reminder of her impending execution toward him, his anger faded and he sighed heavily. As much as he wanted to give her reassurance, their future depended on Grandmother's whims. He'd happily follow her into death, but she was right.

Mages didn't become pregnant easily, yet Feather's mother had, as had Morgaine. Aside from that, Feather wasn't entirely mage. The risk was too great.

"I'm sorry." Misery wafted from her like a cloud, palpable and choking.

"No," he said firmly, wrapping her in a tight embrace. "You're right. It's enough to have you in my arms again. We don't need anything else."

"I wish things were different. I wish I wasn't broken inside."

"Do you remember what Gandalf told Frodo about wishing?" he asked, hoping to cheer her. He'd been wrong about knowing all the stories already, but wasn't about to admit that to Feather.

Lifting her head, she blinked in surprise. "You learned to read," she said softly, cupping his cheek in a gentle hand. "I loved those books."

"I did, and many other things."

"I'm proud of you, Rizan." Resettling herself on his lap, she wrapped her arms around him. "What else did you learn?"

He traced a path down her spine with a gentle finger, needing to get her mind off their troubles. More than anything, he wanted to give her joy and make hope grow between them. "I learned there are other ways to share pleasure."

When he sent a few selected images into her mind, a fresh pulse of arousal welled, gathering strength as it coursed across their bond. Her scent thickened, deepening into the heady perfume of need.

"Someone has been a naughty boy." She turned in his arms to straddle his lap. "Butt stuff?"

He snapped his fingers, using her magic to produce a large box of condoms. "Making love," he corrected. "That's just one way to do it without risking you."

"I bet we can think of more, but that'll do for a start," she murmured, rubbing against him.

Rizan hadn't seriously considered the idea of taking Feather's lovely bottom, but the idea got stuck in his head and he wanted to share that dark intimacy with her. Judging by the decadently wicked thoughts she shared, she was more than interested as well.

"Such a bad girl."

"Oooh, maybe Daddy should spank me." Her lovely brown eyes twinkling with mirth, she leaned toward him and nipped his ear.

"Naughty," he growled, rolling her to her stomach. He swatted her bottom once, stilling at her shriek of surprised laughter.

He hadn't heard that wonderful, joyous sound in much too long. Rizan wanted the music of her laughter back almost more than he wanted to give her sexual delight.

First things first though. Grasping her hips, he lifted her to her knees, exposing her center to his greedy gaze. His mouth watering for another taste, he settled between her spread thighs and licked her succulent flesh.

"Rizan! Fates!"

She shuddered, her pussy quivering. Moving up her body, he played with her ass, the rich, earthy taste of her sweet on his tongue. He wanted her too aroused to think about anything but him. Slowly, he pushed a finger into her core, slicking it with her juices, then moved it to the tight rosebud.

"Fuck," she slurred, her shoulders falling to the bed.

"Do you like that?" he asked, easing his finger past the spasming muscle guarding her back passage.

Instead of answering, she pushed backward against him, driving him deeper inside her. He chuckled softly, then carefully added a second finger to make sure she was ready for him.

"Lube," she choked. "Then I want you to fuck me."

"So greedy." He nipped the lower curve of her bottom, kissing the spot to ease the sting, then pushed his free hand between her thighs to play with her clit. He ached with the need to be inside her, yet it was divine torment to hold off and make her come again. He'd never tire of watching her pleasure.

"Please!"

"Come for me, morsel," he ordered. "Show me your joy."

"I can't. I——" Stiffening, she bucked against him, fucking herself on his hand, then let out a sharp scream as her inner muscles clamped down on his fingers and a gush of fluid delight spilled from her channel.

"Good girl." Kissing the base of her spine, he waved his hand, summoning lubricant, then poured a generous dollop into his palm.

Biting his lip against a groan, he coated his cock with the cool gel, then rubbed more into her pulsing opening. Whimpering, she rocked her hips against him, her desire filling their bond until there was no room for anything else but their shared passion.

He rose to his knees and positioned his cock at her back entrance, praying to the fates he had enough control left to go slowly.

"Relax," he said, lowering himself to kiss the knobs of her spine. "Let me in."

She obeyed, opening not just her body, but her soul. Everything she dreamed, all she wanted. Children with his dark skin and her silky black hair. Books and sunlight, a tiny house on a beach. Flying. So many things, but all her wishes included him.

"I love you," he whispered hoarsely, humbled by what she showed him.

"I love you too." Her body relaxed and he eased his way into her as the need to come sent an electric tingle up and down his spine. Almost too soon, he was balls deep inside her and could no longer resist the urge to move. The tight ring of muscle clamped down like a fist, making him hiss in pleasure.

He started slowly, giving her a chance to get used to him, then reached for her clit. Being inside her was his every dream come true. Sparks of illicit delight rebounded between them, driving their shared joy to soaring heights.

"Fates, yes. More." Rocking against him, she picked up the pace.

"I'm going to make you come so hard you set fire to the room," he growled, rubbing her clit harder. "Then I'm going to lick you clean and start all over."

"Rizan!"

Heat blossomed, lifting her sweat-dampened hair in flowing tendrils around her head. He grabbed a handful and pulled, making her back arch as he thrust into her. Still working her clit between two fingers, he said, "Come for me, Feather."

The wall behind the bed exploded outward and she screamed as the frigid air off the Southern Ocean streamed inside. Ignoring the cold, he fucked her, dragging her into another screaming climax before the tingle in his balls wouldn't be denied any longer.

Roaring, he shot a burst of flame into the ceiling and exploded inside her. Their shared passion flared, twisting and turning into an unbreakable knot.

Falling to his side, he pulled her into his arms, his breaths sounding like a bellows as he tried to put his thoughts back into order.

"Cold." Whimpering softly, Feather burrowed into his arms.

Rizan chuckled, then waved a hand to repair the damage and summon a fur to cover her. "I believe we'll have to start making love outside, morsel."

CHAPTER
NINETEEN

FEATHER

S he buried her face into Rizan's chest, too embarrassed to look at him. "I am so, so sorry."

He pulled a fur around her, then rolled to his back, taking her with him. "It's nothing," he replied, stroking her hair. "Easily mended. Besides, I loved it." Putting a finger under her chin to make her look at him, he added, "Almost as much as I love you."

The bond between them thrummed with love, both hers and his. Like a placid river, it stretched between them, connecting her with him in a way she'd never thought she'd experience. It was everything she thought it would be, but better than she'd dreamed.

"I love you too." Smiling wryly, she glanced around at the shambles of his bedroom, then stretched up to kiss him. "I really have to stop wrecking the furnishings though. What a mess."

He turned his head away, letting out a faint puff of reddish steam. Within seconds, the room was just as it had been, including the destroyed wall. He'd even warmed the air. "As I said, easily mended."

"Nice trick." She snuggled closer, relishing the feel of his chest against her cheek. "Still embarrassing. Aunt Yan probably felt it in Arizona."

"And I'm sure she's delighted."

She let out a soft laugh and nodded. Rizan was probably right about that. "We probably ought to get up and try to find Bear," she murmured.

"Leave her be for a few days." Sitting up, he tucked her into his lap. "I have you all to myself for now, and I don't wish to share."

"More butt stuff?" she asked archly. In truth, she was a little sore, but it had been so, so good. She couldn't wait to do it again.

"Greedy girl." He tipped up her chin and kissed her gently. "I know you have a bit of discomfort though, and I'd like to just sit here and talk."

Snapping his fingers, he produced a pitcher of wine beaded with condensation, along with a charcuterie board laden with snacks. After pouring their glasses, he handed one to her, then took an olive from the board and ate it.

"What about?"

"Everything," he said, taking a cracker and a piece of ham from the tray. "What do you want to study when you start university in the fall?"

Her mouth fell open and she blinked. "What are you talking about? I'm not—"

He pushed the cracker into her mouth, silencing her. Still smiling, he said, "Well, perhaps in December, but I hope it doesn't take that long to dispose of Muir. Do you plan to go back into biochemistry again?"

She swallowed the cracker, nearly choking on it. "Rizan,

I'm probably not going to live long enough to see autumn, much less December."

Worse, he would die when she did. She didn't want to think about it though. Maybe he was right and they would stay together, and their souls would soar through the cosmos.

"You most certainly will." He ate a piece of cheese, the bond between them filled with his absolute and uncompromising faith. "We both will. So, tell me. Biochemistry again? Or something else?"

"I have no idea," she replied faintly. "It hasn't even crossed my mind."

"You should think on it." He fed her an olive, then added, "I considered going myself for engineering. I like the idea of building things."

"Um...wow. Okay." She tried to smile, then said, "What have you been up to for the last five years?"

"You have the pleasure of addressing Sergeant Rizan Carter, United States Army, Second Shifter Division." He took a sip of wine, peering at her over the rim of his glass.

"You took my last name?"

He gave her a shy, boyish smile, then ducked his head and ate a section of Mandarin orange. "Well, since we're to be mated, and I didn't have one... I hope you don't mind."

"No," she said faintly, feeling absurdly pleased. "It's okay. So, you joined the Army?"

"Yes. It seemed like a good idea at the time," he murmured. "But now you're back, so I believe I'll resign."

"What did you do?"

"I joined one of the two-natured Ranger units." Frowning, he looked down, then grabbed a handful of almonds from the board. "We fix things."

Discomfort trickled through the bond between them,

telling her he wasn't interested in talking about it. "The world could use some fixers sometimes," she murmured, deciding not to press.

She caught another glimpse of the blonde woman in uniform, this one much clearer. His feelings about her were conflicted. Fondness mixed with irritation, mixed with duty.

"Indeed."

"Who is she?" Feather asked. "The blonde with blue eyes?"

"My CO, Kali. She's a tiger. Actually, she helped me find you."

"Kali?"

Rizan smiled briefly, then moved a piece of hair behind her ear. "Colonel Theodora Andreyev. Kali is her code name."

"What's yours?"

He cocked his head to the side and was silent for several seconds. "Reaper."

Taking his hand, she kissed his fingers. Rizan's kill count likely topped hers, but there was one significant difference. His targets deserved to die, judging by the few images he let slip through into their bond.

"I hope you took some time and fixed the situation with the mages in the UK."

"Ah, I was in basic training when that happened." He held her glass to her lips, letting her take a sip.

"What happened to them?"

"Yanaha took the magic from several of them, leaving them human. They'll die in due time. The UK is safe now."

"What about the rest?"

He fed her a bite of prosciutto wrapped around a piece of fresh mozzarella. "Morgaine and Myrddin took care of it. The surviving two-natured emigrated to the states."

"Do you know what happened to my friend Hannah?"

"She's living in New Hampshire with her family. I understand she had a baby recently."

It was stupid and petty, but Feather couldn't help the sharp surge of jealousy. "That's wonderful. I'm so happy for her."

"Hey," he said, tugging on her hair. "You'll be the one with a mate and babies soon. We have just a few tiny details to take care of, then we can go on with our future."

"Tiny details like my execution?"

The smile left his face and he cupped her chin firmly, making her meet his eyes. "You will not be executed," he growled. "I won't permit it."

"But I—"

"Shh." Lowering his head, he kissed her. "I have faith in us. In our strength and our love. There isn't anything we can't overcome if we work together."

Holding back a sob, Feather nodded. "I'm sorry. I just..." She straightened and tried to smile.

Tried to believe.

The Feather Carter that used to be had never once backed down from a challenge. She'd gone into battle against a psychotic dark Sidhe king before her eighteenth birthday, for fuck's sake!

She might not be able to convince Grandmother to let her live, but there was one thing she could do. One, very necessary, thing.

"You're right." She straightened her spine and grabbed her lady balls. "We're going to stuff ourselves on this amazing charcuterie and finish our wine, have a good night's sleep, and in the morning, I'm going to York."

"What's in York?" Rizan asked, a small surge of his approval flaring through their bond.

After taking a few seconds to enjoy the sensation, she said, "A dead man walking." She ate another olive, then a piece of Stilton with a wheat cracker. "His name is Vyron Muir."

RIZAN

"We'll both be going," he murmured, kissing her. Feather tasted of wine, sweet and heady. Although she still expected to die, she was moving forward. Proactively taking charge of the days remaining to her. She might not believe it, but Rizan planned to make sure there were many.

Grimacing, she shook her head. "I'm scared shitless, Rizan. What if he tries to hurt you?"

He stared at her for a moment, tipping her chin up when she tried to look away. The silly woman truly thought she'd leave him behind to go haring off after Muir by herself.

As if.

"You're not going alone," he repeated, his voice quietly firm.

"Yes, I am!" She sat up and took his hands, squeezing them. "You heard Bear. He's after you."

"And?" He pulled her into his lap and hugged her. "Even if you go by yourself, we're bound. All he has to do is kill you to destroy me as well. Aside from that, I think I can get us some help."

"Who would help me? I'm—"

"You're my mate." He kissed her temple, then pushed her hair out of her eyes. "My team will help us."

"Absolutely not." She wriggled off his lap, then retrieved her robe. Tightening the sash, she glared at him. "I will not risk innocents."

Arching a brow, he retrieved his phone from the nightstand and replaced the chip. Tapping Kali's contact, he waited for her to answer, ignoring the vibrating message alerts. Most of them were from her anyway.

The call connected and he tapped the speaker icon. "Good evening, Kali. You're on speaker."

"It's about time you returned your calls," she groused. "Are you alone?"

"No. Feather is with me. Congratulate us on our bonding."

She went silent for several seconds, then sighed. "I hope you know what you're doing."

"Best thing that ever happened to me," he replied, holding Feather's gaze. "I've never been happier."

Biting her lip, Feather gazed at him, her eyes sparkling with unshed tears. "Me too," she whispered.

"I'm glad for you both. Also, Feather, if you hurt him, I will personally kick your ass."

"Then maybe you'll help me convince him to stay behind and let me take care of Muir myself," Feather retorted, scowling at the phone. "Worse, he thinks he's going to ask his team to help, and I refuse to put innocent people at risk."

Kali burst out laughing. "Did she just call us innocent, Reaper? Fates! Wait until I tell the rest of the team."

"Feather, I'd like to introduce you to my commanding officer, Colonel Theodora Andreyev, otherwise known as Kali. Kali, my mate, Feather Carter."

"A pleasure," Feather said, leaning toward the phone. "If you're his CO, then you can tell him—"

"Ms. Carter, you have to know how difficult it is to tell a dragon much of anything," Kali interrupted. "The best I can offer is additional support to make sure he keeps his scaled ass in one piece."

"I'm right here, you know."

Truly, Rizan wasn't irritated at all. Feather was doing as a mate ought to and attempting to protect him. He couldn't chide her for it, and it felt nice to have someone think of him as more than an asset.

"We know," Kali said. "That brings me to the reason I left so many messages, which you obviously didn't listen to."

"What's going on?" Rizan asked.

"Someone made an attempt at a bonded mage and dragon late last night in Barcelona. The dragon says it was a dark Sidhe, but we don't have a corpse to identify him."

"Did he escape?" Feather asked, her face ashen. Fear and anger surged through their bond, making him pull her into his arms.

He filled their bond with peace and comfort in an attempt to calm her. "Shh," he whispered. "It's going to be okay."

"No, she ate him and took her mage back to her hoard. They refuse to leave."

Rizan nodded. He would have done the same. "I wish she'd left the head so we could identify him."

"So do I. Her mage didn't see him at all."

"Which dragon was it? I can try to talk to her."

"She isn't the one you need to talk to," Kali retorted. "I have two hundred adult dragons swarming over Barcelona right now. They're threatening to burn the city if they don't produce Muir for punishment."

"So?"

Feather elbowed him in the gut and glared. "Rizan, you can't possibly be suggesting—"

"I'm afraid your mate is right," Kali said. "Troops are already in place to shoot them down the minute they see a spark. You need to make them go home."

"Ask Davryn. He's their king."

"Your asshole brother is leading them."

Rizan sighed and rolled his eyes. "Of course, he is. According to Feather, Muir isn't in Barcelona anyway. He's in York."

"I'm not really surprised by that," Kali replied. "The UK has been a thorn in my side for years. I'll tell the dragons, and—"

"Not the dragons. I need you, Tank, Vision, Techno, and Lady Luck. A small team will be able to get in and out without destroying the city around him."

"You'll be taking Myrddin and Morgaine too."

"No. I—"

"Are you just about to refuse a direct order, Sergeant?" He heard paper rustle in the background before Kali continued. "No offense, but Feather Carter is a few cards shy of a full deck. I need someone strong enough to control her if she goes crazy again."

"How dare you?"

"She's right, Rizan." Feather touched his arm, then leaned against his chest. "I would have been okay if you'd agreed to let me go by myself, but I will not risk other people. Morgaine and Myrddin are strong enough to keep me from hurting anyone if Bear comes back and decides to return to Muir."

"I can take care of Bear." Setting Feather down, he stood, then paced across the room in a desperate attempt to control his anger. Forgetting all about Kali, he spun to face her. "Do you not trust your mate? Is that what this is? You don't believe I'll keep you safe."

"This has nothing to do with you. I have to fix things before anyone else gets hurt!"

"Ms. Carter," Kali interrupted. "While I admire your willingness to go after Muir on your own, you have to know how stupid it is."

"I'm not being stupid." Feather rubbed her face, then sighed. "Okay, yeah, I'm being stupid, but you're right. I'm crazy, and I'm going to be executed for it. I have to make this right and kill Vyron Muir before Bear comes back and takes the choice away from me."

"For what it's worth, I don't think you're crazy," Kali said. "Your bear on the other hand..." She left the sentence unfinished.

"Yeah. Tell me about it. Anyway, as much as I don't want anyone else involved, I'll take the people Rizan mentioned, plus Morgaine and Myrddin if you make Rizan stay home."

"Is your bear still causing trouble or has Rizan confined her?"

"She's... Well, she's not exactly speaking to me at the moment," Feather replied. "Bear is hiding."

Her voice softening with sympathy, Kali said, "I can't begin to understand what you're going through, but I urge you to make peace with her. According to what I've been reading, the separation between you and your bear is going to get worse unless you can merge with her again."

"I don't think I can. She doesn't want to give up her autonomy."

"That's going to be a problem. You also have to take Rizan."

"No. I—"

"You're stronger with him," Kali interrupted. "Aside from that, you have to know he isn't going to stay behind."

"Enough," Rizan said, trying to hide his rage from Feather. "Bear will have no choice but to agree once we take care of Muir. We'll meet you and the team in Leeds at dawn local time. Have Morgaine take care of transport."

CHAPTER
TWENTY

FEATHER

Rizan ended the call without a word and spun to face her, his expression turning darkly furious. Worrying her lower lip with her teeth, Feather tried to meet his angry gaze.

"I'm sorry. I—"

"Not another word," he said softly, the force of his disapproval thickening their bond into a heavy weight. "I understand and appreciate why you want me to stay behind, but it isn't happening."

"I know." She chewed her lip for a moment, then looked up. "All I ask is that you do whatever it takes to make sure Bear doesn't hurt anyone. I don't trust her and I'm afraid she'll try to go back to Muir."

He sat next to her and pulled her into his arms, his anger fading. "Do you trust me, morsel?"

"Yes." She nestled into his embrace, knowing that better than she knew her own name. "I trust you."

"Then why are you so worried?"

"It's like I have a bomb in my head, and everyone I love will die when it goes off." She turned in his arms to face him, then cupped his cheeks and allowed herself one small kiss. "I'm afraid you won't do what's necessary and kill me when it happens."

Rizan went silent and studied her for a moment. "No, that's one thing I won't do," he finally said.

"Your team will though."

The air around them warmed with his anger. "That won't happen. I—"

Laying her fingers over his lips, Feather shook her head. "It's bad enough knowing I'll take you with me when I die. I can't bear the idea of killing anyone else. Please, let me have that."

He tightened his arms around her, determination rising over his fury. "It won't become necessary. We'll have the rest of eternity together, I promise. All you need is a little faith in us."

"You can't promise me that."

"Yes, I can." He put a finger under her chin, making her lift her head to look at him. "Even if we die, we'll be together always and nothing can separate us again."

She nodded and lowered her head to his shoulder, trying to hold back her tears. "I know. It's just..." Scrubbing a hand over her eyes, she went silent.

"Come," he said, helping her to her feet. "Let's get you dressed."

"We should probably get some sleep. Aren't we supposed to be in England tomorrow?"

"Yes, but we're going to do something we haven't done before." Snapping his fingers, he produced a red dress and matching undergarments, plus a tiny handbag and high-heeled sandals.

"Pretty," she replied, petting the luxurious silk. "It's too fancy for staying here though."

Another snap of his fingers produced a dark grey suit. "We're going on a date."

A... what?

"Rizan, we can't leave. What if—"

"Get dressed, morsel." His eyes twinkled as he stripped out of his jeans and tugged the trousers over his hips.

The words thrust her back five years to her prom night. He'd said the exact same thing. Trying to hide a pleased smile, she took off her robe and obeyed, loving the way the silk slid over her body.

"It's been a long time since I've worn something pretty," she murmured. "But we really ought to stay here. What happens if Bear tries to escape?"

"If she does, I'll catch you." He finished with his cufflinks, then kissed her forehead. "We're bound now. As long as you don't let her obscure the bond between us, I will always find you."

It was more likely Bear would want to lead him straight to Vyron. Hiding a shiver, Feather pushed the thought away before Rizan found it. A date didn't sound like the wisest idea, but she couldn't help the happy anticipation rising up to replace her misgivings.

"So," she said, smiling at him. "Where are we going?"

"It's a surprise." He held up a silk scarf and moved behind her. "Close your eyes."

Still grinning, she did as he asked. He wrapped the silk around her head, tying it carefully. "Do I get a hint?"

"No, but I think we'll have fun." He wrapped an arm around her waist and his flame carried them away.

They landed a few seconds later and Rizan held her steady until the slight nausea passed. "Where are we?" she asked, turning her head toward the sounds of heavy traffic. A warm breeze caressed her skin, smelling of car exhaust and the faint hint of a river.

Rizan tightened his arm around her. "We have a short distance to walk, and then I'll show you."

Still holding her, he walked her forward several dozen steps, then stopped. "Keep your eyes closed."

"Okay." Although she was almost too excited to manage it, she waited until he took the scarf off her eyes, then said, "Can I open them yet?"

He took a step behind her, then laid his hands on her shoulders. "Yes."

Twitching with excitement, she opened her eyes and gasped. The Pyramide du Louvre rose above them, illuminated with golden light.

"Fates," she breathed. "I've always wanted to visit Paris."

"You've been here before though." Taking her hand, he walked her toward the massive steel and glass structure, allowing a thread of knowledge into their bond. He knew about many of Bear's kills already, and she had to push away the immediate pinch of shame.

"Don't remind me." She grimaced and tried to shake away the sudden image of the poor falcon who had been one of the first to fall.

Stopping, he turned to face her. "It wasn't you," he said firmly, tucking a piece of hair behind her ear. "I see what's in your heart, love. Those things weren't you and it's not who you are."

"Bear is part of me."

"She was until Muir broke her. I don't believe she would have done all those things if she hadn't been driven to it." He wrapped an arm around her, squeezing her tightly. "Anyway, I wanted to give you a better memory of the City of Lights. Does it please you?"

Feather rested her head on his shoulder and tried to let go of the crushing guilt and sorrow. Rizan was right, and with his love bolstering her, maybe she could be whole again. All she needed was a little faith.

"It's beautiful." Lifting her head, she kissed his jaw, the scruff of his beard tickling her. "Thank you."

Holding hands, they strolled through Jardin des Tuileries. Everything was just as she'd imagined Paris would be—romantic, beautiful, and a dream come true.

"May I ask you something?"

"Anything, *ma chérie.*"

His accent was perfect, of course, making her feel even more provincial. "Why is your hoard so... well, un-hoardlike?"

"I'm not sure what you mean."

"Well, I guess I was expecting piles of treasure like King Davryn has. Yours is more like someone's vacation cottage."

He laughed softly, then bought her a lemon ice from a vendor. After helping her sit near the Grand Bassin Rond, he said, "My brother is a pack rat. He collects all sorts of useless things, but Morgaine likes to study his trinkets. I've come to appreciate the value of a more diversified portfolio."

"A..." She looked up at him, then burst out laughing. "Are you telling me you invested in the stock market?"

"Why shouldn't I? Instead of having to polish my treasures, they're earning interest and dividends. It's like a self-replicating hoard."

"Wow. I can honestly say I've never met a dragon who would give up his treasure like that."

"Many of us have. There's just something about passive income that makes even the most possessive of us take notice." He tangled his hand in her hair, then pulled her in for a kiss. "Besides, I didn't invest all of it. A dragon needs a bit of gold and platinum around to stay healthy."

"I didn't know that. Does it hurt you to be away from it?"

"No." He kissed the tip of her nose, still smiling. "I'm teasing you. We collect treasure because we're greedy and acquisitive, but we're perfectly fine reading portfolio statements."

"I'm almost afraid to ask who convinced you to invest. I can't imagine any dragon taking that well."

"It was Lily Archer. She'd been investing for decades before we were set free. Truly, it's a much better situation because we don't have to worry about protecting physical treasure anymore."

Rizan had grown so much, whereas she'd been left behind, both emotionally and intellectually. It was hard not to be a little jealous, but she was proud of him. Had he not worked so hard, he'd have never been able to find her. She wouldn't have the faintest thread of hope.

Enjoying his scent and the warmth of his body, Feather leaned against him and let herself live in the perfection of the moment. She didn't want to think about the possibility of them dying, or of Vyron Muir, or of anything else but her mate and the placid river of power binding them together.

Sudden pressure in her head made her vision bleary, and the empty cup fell from her fingers as dread crept into her belly. She couldn't stop the icy tendrils of fear when Bear pushed forward and reached for control.

I've killed here. This is my hunting ground.

"No, please," she whimpered. "Don't do this."

RIZAN

"You've interrupted my time with my mate," Rizan said, sending a small puff of steam over Feather's head. "You are most welcome to come out later, but I suggest you return to your rest now."

The bear growled and flexed against his hold, fangs erupting between her lips as Feather tried to wrestle her back.

"She wants to kill someone, Rizan! Please, you have to—"

"Stop fighting. Now."

His barked order made them both still, leaving only Bear's wariness and Feather's relieved gratitude. Although he didn't want to force either of them into compliance, he wasn't going to risk Bear causing harm to someone.

Bear broke away, wrenching free of his command, then reached for the bond between them. Smirking, he let her have it, then laughed outright when Feather sent a surge of her magic flowing between them.

Howling, she tumbled away, but attacked again. Spasming in his arms, Feather's body shimmered, growing indistinct and ephemeral as Bear tried to force her to shift.

Blowing out a hissed curse, he let his flame carry them home to his hoard. Feather dropped to her knees and growled, then bared her teeth.

"Go on, then," he said irritably, wrinkling his nose at the copper penny stench. Even in his largest chamber, the only one big enough for him to change his form, the scent overpowered everything else. "You've gotten control like you wanted, so shift."

"Take me back."

"You're joking, right?"

"Take me back!" Her shout echoed and he rolled his eyes.

"No." He turned his back on her and walked away, disappointed and frustrated. Even with the bond between them, Feather wasn't strong enough to contain her bear.

He'd promised to protect her though. Even from herself. When he felt the brush of air signaling her shift, he flowed into his dragon form, then sent his tail crashing to the floor inches from her nose.

Turning, he reached down and wrapped a claw around her, then lifted her into the air, ignoring her low, terrified whines.

"This is not the way to go about gaining your freedom," he said softly, baring his fangs. Wriggling, she sank her teeth into the base of his paw. With a sigh, he shook her, making her lose her grip and tear a chunk of hide away.

A burst of Feather's magic drove Bear back, allowing her to return to her human form. Gently, he set her on her feet, holding her up when her legs collapsed under her.

Without warning, her eyes rolled back and she fainted. He smelled a faint whiff of stone and mold, making him jerk his head up and tuck Feather under one wing.

"Show yourself, Muir!" he roared.

A vaguely human shape formed in front of him, coalescing into a dark Sidhe wearing a gray suit. Rizan sent a blue stream of flame at him, but the Sidhe only laughed.

"Did you think it would be so easy, lizard?"

Instead of a physical body, Muir had sent a projection. Rizan couldn't harm him, but it might be possible to trick him into revealing himself. Tapping into Feather's strength, he tried to use her magic, but Bear actively fought back.

"Let them go. We know you now, and Feather can be of no possible use to you anymore."

"Ah, but she's been quite a useful experiment. I'm afraid I'm not ready to let her go quite yet."

"I will hunt you—"

"Yes, yes, I know you and your filthy little band of shifters plan to go to York at dawn. The bear has told me all about it. Imagine what I could do with all of you."

A ball of black smoke built in Muir's hand, obscuring his features with malevolence. Grinning, he tossed the missile at Rizan.

Rizan swept Feather into his paws and let his flame carry them to Arizona. He was more than willing to fight Muir, but not when Feather was unconscious and vulnerable. He could barely feel the bond between them. It was as if something had covered it with a thick blanket of nothing.

"Yanaha!" he yelled, laying Feather on the porch swing before changing back to his human body. "I need help!"

The thunderbird wasn't fond of dark Sidhe on a good day. She was the one being he could count on to keep Feather safe. Then again, Grandmother was here too. If he'd had a choice, he wouldn't have put Feather within a thousand miles of the old woman.

The door opened, revealing Omer. Yanaha nudged him out of the way and crossed the porch. Dropping to her knees, she used a thumb to open one of Feather's eyes.

"What happened?"

"Muir attacked her. I thought we'd driven him away, but..." Rizan rubbed his face, pain from their missing bond like a phantom limb. "I took her to Paris to celebrate our bonding. He must have been waiting for us to get close enough, and now I can't feel her at all."

"Hmm." Yanaha opened Feather's mouth, revealing massive fangs, then tapped her cheeks in an effort to wake her up. "What happened?"

"We were sitting near the Grand Bassin Rond. She was perfectly fine, and then she..." He swallowed hard, then added, "And then she wasn't."

"And?" Yanaha sat back on her heels and peered up at him.

"I took her back to my hoard, but Bear took control, then Muir sent a projection, and—"

"I get the picture." Yanaha tapped Feather's cheeks harder.

Although her eyes didn't open, Feather moaned softly, her face contorting as her body shimmered into her bear's form. Her head jerked up and she scrambled from the swing, then swiped at Yanaha.

A bolt of electricity shot her in the side, making her roar and dart down the stairs. Her lumbering run was surprisingly fast, taking her across the desert several hundred feet before she slammed into a flickering blue barrier of Omer's magic.

"Omer, will you fetch me a cage, please?"

"What the hell are you talking about?" Rizan demanded. "I will not allow you to lock her up."

He'd promised them both that would never happen.

"I wish you hadn't brought her here," she murmured. "I cannot help her."

"Why the fuck not?"

She straightened and nodded at Omer. A silvery cage formed around Feather, trapping her. "Because she's not there anymore. That," she said, pointing at Feather, "is an ordinary bear, but with a two-way radio in her head direct to Vyron Muir."

"That's impossible. Feather is two-natured. She can no sooner separate from her bear than I could from my dragon."

Yet that wasn't entirely true. Feather and her bear were already separated, despite sharing a body.

"Magic is infinitely powerful," Yanaha replied softly. "With will and intent, anything is possible." She sighed heavily and rubbed her face. "I promise, we'll make it quick and humane. I am very sorry, but since your bond is broken, we won't have to worry about losing you too."

"No, I'd rather die with her. You have the power to repair our bond."

Sighing, she shook her head. "You forget what I am. I have no intrinsic magic, Rizan. I'm an elemental, and all I do is make sure everything stays in balance. You know that."

He turned abruptly, staring across the desert at Feather. He'd let her down so badly. Not just now, but five years ago too.

"I might be in a position to help," Omer said.

"What are you doing, garden gnome?" Yanaha asked, glaring at her husband.

Ignoring her, Rizan rushed to the king and clasped his arm. "Tell me."

"I'm going to give you balance," Omer said softly, his blue eyes glowing. "Come closer."

Rizan obliged, taking a step forward. When he was close enough, the Sidhe king cupped his jaw, then kissed him. A sudden rush of alien magic filled his body, making his spasm and fall to his knees. Shuddering, he tried to catch his breath and keep himself in his human form.

"What the fuck..." He coughed, trying to clear his throat of the thick mass of power choking him. Feather's magic was a cool river in the desert, but Omer's was a punch to the balls. "What did you do?"

"I gave you a gift, dragon prince. For the next three sunrises, you have the magic of the light Sidhe. If you allow it, it will guide you and protect you from the dark."

Straightening, he tried to stand without throwing up. "Take it away. Now."

"No." Omer glanced fondly at Yanaha. "My wife says I need to help her maintain balance in the world's magic. I can think of nothing better than allowing a dragon to use fae magic to rescue a mixed-breed mage from a dark Sidhe."

"And you had to kiss me?"

"It was the only way to give it to you and keep it hidden from Muir." Cocking his head, he gave Rizan a half smile. "I could have fucked you instead, but I think my wife might have protested."

Yanaha scowled, then turned to him, her face filled with sadness. "Go, Rizan, but remember she will be given peace after sunrise on the third day."

CHAPTER
TWENTY-ONE

FEATHER

"You are a very naughty girl," Vyron murmured, tapping the crystal hanging from a chain around his neck.

Feather said nothing. What was the point when she didn't exactly exist anymore? He probably couldn't hear her anyway.

It happened so fast. One minute, she was in Rizan's arms, and the next she was bodiless and shoved into a piece of obsidian like a genie in a bottle.

Her bond with Rizan was severed, gone like it had never been. And, oh, it ached. She felt empty, like her insides had been scoured with a wire brush to scrape away every last bit of happiness. In a way, it was worse than being dead, especially since she had no idea what had happened to her body or to Bear.

One gleaming shard of hope remained. With their bond broken, Vyron wouldn't be able to harm Rizan. Hopefully,

Rizan would cut his losses and not come to find her. All that mattered to her was his safety.

"Nothing to say?" Vyron asked, holding her prison up to the light. He laughed softly, then added, "You're just a bit of energy now. Not as much as you could have been had I been able to trap the dragon as well, but I suppose we'll have to make do until I find a better candidate. Perhaps one of the Archer brats."

She screamed, hammering ineffectively at the crystal surrounding her, the mix of terror and anger roiling until she thought it might shatter the crystalline walls around her. Lily Archer's children would be starting kindergarten by now, and the thought of Muir getting his hands on one of those precious babies...

"My distant cousin, Teran, tried this with Lily, but he failed to understand or account for the mixture of dragon and mage." He tapped the crystal with a fingertip, sending it swinging. "He thought he could lock her magic in a null-stone and use it as he pleased, but he knew nothing about dragons."

Feather calmed herself, and tried to listen, but he went silent for several seconds.

"Dragons cannot be imprisoned against their will unless they're in stasis," he murmured softly. "It's a strange bit of old magic, older even than the Sidhe. Quite problematic, don't you think? Well, I'm sure Teran thought so when the dragons tore him to pieces."

The tug started deep under where her heart might have been if she'd had a body. So gentle, she barely felt it at first, but it grew, dragging magic from her in a flood of uncontrolled power.

Although she tried to stop it, she was helpless against

the onslaught of wild magic spilling from her being, sucked away from her until she was left crying tears of impotent rage.

He tore her open, the psychic rape devouring everything she had until her consciousness wavered and she saw nothing but darkness.

～

RIZAN

"So, this is how the other half lives," Angel said drily. "Must be nice to be an ancient dragon with a hoard."

"Expedient. You all refused to let me use my flame to get us to England, and I wasn't willing to wait for mundane methods." Baring his teeth, Rizan turned to her. "Of course, if you're uncomfortable, I can transport us now, although I'm not sure how that will end up, considering we're over the Atlantic."

She shuddered and closed her mouth with a snap.

All he wanted to hear was Feather's location. He wasn't the slightest bit interested in anything else. Their bond might be broken, but he wouldn't rest until he brought her home safely.

The missing bond fucking hurt. It was a deep pain, like something had ripped his heart away, and he was desperate to get it back.

"Quit complaining, Angel," Zeke said, stretching out on the couch. "It's not like any of us are going to be flying in a private jet again."

"And the bar is excellent." Dennis filled a tumbler with hundred-year-old scotch, then sprawled lazily in a club chair.

"Knock it off," Kali barked. "We're less than an hour out, so we need to focus on the mission. Guinevere, are we close enough for you to sense anything?"

"Not yet. I—" Without warning, she doubled over and scrambled for an airsick bag.

Dennis and Angel were on her in a second to help, reminding him why he hadn't yet eaten this ragtag band of two-natured. Rising to his feet, he went to the lavatory and dampened a washcloth with cold water, then returned.

Helping her clean up, he asked, "What's wrong? Was the meal bad?"

"No." She coughed and wiped her mouth with the washcloth. "I just felt a massive surge of magic."

"Where?" Kali demanded.

"Lisbon, maybe. I can't tell. Whatever it was didn't come from anywhere near the UK."

Rizan didn't question her and went straight to the cockpit to order the change in flight plan. On his way back, he grabbed a bottle of ginger ale from the galley. "Do you know if it was Sidhe or mage?" he asked, handing it to her.

Inside him, King Omer's magic pulsed, but he ignored it. He hadn't yet told his teammates about the unwelcome power filling his body. If... when he brought Feather home, he was going to punch the disreputable elf in the face.

Sidhe magic wasn't something to trifle with, and Omer threw it around like candy tossed from a parade float. It was primeval, wild energy, creeping and insidious with dark promise. If he let it free, he could control the environment. Deserts could be turned to oases. He could bring the Aral Sea back from its manmade destruction or regrow forests lost to wildfires in California.

Oh, he would be mighty indeed, with enough power to exterminate the dark Sidhe race. He could overthrow his brother and set himself up as king—the king of all, not just the dragons. The thought was dangerously tempting, but a dragon didn't need such magic. It was only through five years of learning patience and self-control that he didn't succumb to its enticement.

Unfortunately, the longer he was separated from Feather, the harder it became to resist the urge.

Her face pale and damp with sweat, Guinevere took the bottle, then bit her lip. "Dark Sidhe, but I haven't felt anything that powerful since Teran. It's... not natural."

"Muir," Dennis said, opening his laptop. "Due south or southeast?"

Guinevere took a drink of her ginger ale, then closed her eyes and rested her head in Angel's lap. "Southeast, I think. Maybe even into Tunisia."

"We'll land in Lisbon," Kali said. "It'll give us a chance to refuel and get a better idea of where the little asshole is hiding."

"Let's just hope he hasn't gone into Libya or Egypt," Angel muttered. "They don't like supernaturals much."

"He probably won't," Dennis said, still typing. "I'm actually thinking he might have gone to southern Greece. Look at this."

Turning the laptop so the team could see, he pointed at an island in the Aegean, about halfway between Greece and Turkey. "This is surveying software that compiles satellite images looking for spatial and topographical anomalies over time. That island was recently purchased by a corporate buyer, and it's almost doubled in size in the last five months."

"Who owns it?" Rizan asked. His head pounded as the elven magic surged, nearly forcing him to shift into his dragon form. The sudden urge to break free of the aircraft and get to Greece was overwhelming.

Scales rippled over his arms and he drew in a calming breath. With some effort, he pushed it down, but wondered if that was what Omer had meant by the magic being a guide. Maybe it was trying to lead him to his Feather. If that was the case, he'd consider not punching Omer.

"No idea. Every time I think I'm getting close, I find another shell company. It might take me a few days to untangle it."

"It's hard for dark Sidhe to maintain their magic if they're not on contiguous land," Guinevere murmured. "If you're suggesting it as Muir's lair, I'm not seeing it."

"Yes, but the Aegean is really shallow there. If he managed to grow the island..." Kali didn't finish her sentence.

Feather didn't have a few days. Rizan got to his feet and strode to the cockpit, then slid the door open. "Athens instead of Lisbon," he barked.

"Sir, I can't just change a flight plan twice like that," the pilot protested.

"Do it. Tell them it's military business or something."

"I'm afraid I—"

Scales erupted and his muzzle elongated, bone and muscle shifting under his skin. Baring his fangs, he blew a puff of steam over the hapless woman's head.

"I said, change your flight plan before I change it for you." Without waiting for an answer, he shut the door.

Arching a blonde brow, Kali shook her head. "Can't take you anywhere. Fix your face before we land so you don't scare off the natives."

He hissed at her, but tried to do as she asked, forcing his

dragon form back. Logically, he knew changing into his dragon in this tiny aircraft would kill his team, yet every second without his mate made it harder to keep his control.

She was getting closer though. He could feel it.

Unsurprisingly, there was a contingent of armed police waiting for them when the plane landed. Pushing his way forward, he met them on the tarmac.

Bowing from the waist, he smiled at the tall woman in front, then said, "My most humble apologies. I'm afraid this is an emergency landing."

"I'm Captain Anfisa Raptis. Why are you here?"

"It's private business," Rizan replied.

She arched a dark brow. "Two attempted flight path changes, plus a dragon accompanied by two-natured with military training. Is this an invasion?"

He straightened, then tried to school his features into placidity. "I'd like nothing more than to invade the nearest restaurant for a plateful of spanakopita and a glass of ouzo, but as I said, I'm here on business."

"And what business is that, Prince Rizan?"

He didn't bother with feigned surprise at the address. Humans knew him on sight. "I have reason to believe my mate is being held against her will on one of the islands." Lowering his head, he allowed scales to shadow his face. "Dragons don't like being separated from their mates," he said mildly. "I'm sure you understand."

Scowling at him, she said a naughty word in Greek. "I can't allow you to—"

"I'd be despondent if anything happened to destroy this beautiful city," he murmured. "So much history would be lost."

Her brown eyes narrowed and she frowned. "Are you threatening me, Your Highness?"

He looked up and smiled, baring fangs. "You, personally? No."

Her throat worked and she swallowed hard. Giving him an abrupt nod, she said, "I want you out of my city in twenty-four hours. Can you do that without killing anyone?"

"Yes, he can," Kali said, pulling on his arm. "We're just passing through on our way somewhere else."

"Very well." Captain Raptis brought her heels together, then spun and strode to a police vehicle, followed by her team.

"We need a boat," Guinevere said. "Dennis, can you find us a rental?

After finding a boat captain willing to take them, Rizan and his team were on their way. It hadn't even taken an hour, but he begrudged every second. He stood at the rail, looking out over the Aegean pensively as he considered what he knew.

How had Muir broken their bond? He'd never heard of such a thing happening, and had always believed it to be impossible without losing the bonded pair. Of course, he knew very little about mates in general, aside from what he'd learned about the two-natured, and what he'd witnessed with his brother and Morgaine.

Nothing made sense, and there was no one to whom he might direct his questions. The only thing he knew for certain was that Feather wasn't dead.

He felt a whoosh of dragon flame at his back and turned, trying to dredge up a smile for his niece, Lily, and her husbands. Judging by the expression on her face, he hadn't managed it. Morgaine and Davryn arrived a few seconds later.

"Any news?" Davryn asked.

"No. Guinevere suspects he's on an island about twenty minutes west. You left the children with a nanny, I assume?"

Myrddin frowned and shared a glance with his husbands at the mention of Guinevere's name, but said nothing.

"Yanaha and Grandmother have them," Morgaine replied, smiling grimly. "I doubt even Muir is crazy enough to go there."

"Teran was," Lily muttered, leaning against Liam's chest.

"Point taken." Rizan straightened, meeting his friends' eyes. "Thank you for helping us."

"I, for one, am tired of being jacked around by hopped-up elves," Moses replied, a ball of blue magic forming in his palm. "I plan to make an example of him."

"Same," Liam said, laying his hand over the magic balanced in his husband's palm. "Then Lily will eat him."

Grimacing, Lily said, "Ew. No, thank you. Well, maybe if he's cooked first."

Rizan laughed softly. "I'm sure he'll be delicious if you take the time to roast him." Taking a step away from the rail, he added, "Come. We should make some plans."

They followed him to the middle deck where his team waited, and took their seats. Guinevere was pale and sat close to Zeke, resting her head on his shoulder. He doubted her distress was from motion sickness. Even he could feel the pressure of fae magic growing stronger as they approached Muir's lair.

Kali straightened, then stood and crossed her hands behind her back. "I doubt we'll be able to approach with any secrecy," she said. "Muir probably already knows we're coming, but he might not know how many we are, or our strengths.

"I can swim in as long as it isn't too far. Nobody ever notices coyotes," Angel said.

"We'll hold that in reserve," Kali replied. "It's not a bad idea, but judging by the satellite imaging, there isn't a lot of cover."

"I just need a few bushes and maybe a divot in the rocks here and there."

"Lily and I should just fly overhead and nuke the site from orbit," Davryn muttered irritably.

"You've been watching too many movies, Grandfather," Lily replied. "Unfortunately, we don't know where Feather is, and we can't risk harming her."

"We can use the tactic to herd him though," Rizan mused. "There isn't much to burn, but I'm strong enough to turn the stone into lava if necessary."

"It's not a bad plan," Kali said. "If nothing else, it will cut off his escape routes."

Lily stood and paced back and forth, her brow furrowed. "If he's anything like Teran, he won't try to escape. Do we have any intel on his personality?"

"Not really," Rizan replied. "King Brand says Muir has been living as a human for almost a thousand years, and that he doesn't personally know him."

"Well, stealing magic seems to be a Sidhe thing to do, so I think it's probably safe to assume they share some of the same qualities," Morgaine said drily. "Where is Brand, anyway? Shouldn't he be here?"

"I asked," Lily replied. "The bastard didn't answer."

"And spoil the surprise?" a voice said behind her. The dark Sidhe king materialized into solidity, then gave her a faint smile. "I'm also tired of my subjects thinking they can upset the natural order of things. Rest assured, Muir won't do it again."

Brand wore his customary black leather armor, but also carried a long sword with a jeweled hilt in a scabbard on his back. His dark hair was pulled back into a braid, revealing alabaster skin and high cheekbones.

The elven magic gifted to him by King Omer flared and pulsed in response to Brand's presence. In a desperate attempt to tamp it down, he walked to the railing and tightened his hands on the weathered metal.

"Something wrong, brother?" Davryn asked, touching his shoulder.

Morgaine joined him and took Rizan's hand. "We'll get her back," she promised. "Try not to worry."

"No, it's..." He swallowed and grimaced. "That disreputable idiot Omer gave me light Sidhe magic to help me find Feather. It's... disconcerting."

"Oh, I hate when he does that," Morgaine replied. "It's so alien."

"That's a good word for it." Rizan turned to face her. "How did you cope?"

"Well, I had Davryn's help, and it seemed easier to bear after I used it to free the dragons." She pursed her lips, squeezing his hand gently. "It seems to want to be let loose."

"It's wild magic," Davryn said. "Perhaps..." He stared off into the distance, gazing at the rocky shoreline of an island as they passed by. "I don't know if this will work, but you might consider setting it free."

"That sounds like a remarkably bad idea," Rizan retorted. At the same time, Morgaine shook her head, protesting the suggestion.

"Hear me out. Dark elves like unrelieved stone. Their

magic is less powerful in green spaces. I'd say let the magic go and turn the island into a forest."

"It can be directed somewhat," Morgaine added. "You could fix your mind on Feather and see if it will lead you to her. What's the worst that could happen?"

"I could sink the island into the sea," Rizan muttered. Focusing his attention on the strange magic inside him, he tried to direct it outward toward Muir's island, yet it didn't seem to want to obey.

"Relax into it," Morgaine said softly. "It's going to fight you at every turn unless you give it freedom."

"Ask for what you want," Davryn added. "It responds to need."

Rizan let his shoulders drop, forcing himself to do as they suggested. He thought of rain in a parched desert bringing wildflowers to life, and the sweet taste of her lips. The copper penny scent of her bear mingled with floral perfume, and he felt as if she was standing next to him. Rizan missed his mate with an ache that burned deep, nearly bringing tears to his eyes.

"Make that island green," he whispered, "and find my mate."

The alien magic left him in a rush of energy, dropping him to his knees as it expanded above him. The sky turned an impossible green and shards of lightning flared, brightening the sky. It arrowed to the island ahead of them, and as they got closer, he heard the rocks tearing themselves apart as fully grown trees and vegetation erupted from the ground.

Within moments, he staggered to his feet, his friends and colleagues surrounding him.

"Talk about terraforming," Zeke murmured. "You're

going to have to explain this soon, but we have company coming."

He pointed at the shore, and Rizan narrowed his eyes. "Let them come," he growled, glaring at the dark Sidhe army waiting for them.

TWENTY-TWO

FEATHER

"Your mate is coming," Muir whispered, holding the black crystal up to peer inside. He sounded positively gleeful.

"Sir, the boat carrying the dragon will arrive in about fifteen minutes," someone said. The male voice was soft and diffident, but Feather couldn't see who had spoken. Likely, it was one of Muir's toadies. He'd had dozens over the years, and they never lasted long. Feather could only see vague shadows and a hint of movement as the gem containing her spirit swung back and forth.

Damn Rizan for being so bloody stubborn. All he'd had to do was kill Bear and forget about her. Without the bond between them, he could have gone on to live a long and fulfilling life. Yet that tiny shard of hope persisted. It was the dream of a young girl who was absolutely certain her prince would rescue her.

Except this time, the dragon would be attempting a rescue, and the prince was an amoral psychopath.

"Does he have anyone with him?" Muir asked.

"Yes, sir. There are twelve others. We won't be able to tell who they are until they get closer."

"Very well. Hopefully, he's brought Morgaine and Myrddin, but I—" The earth rumbled under their feet, cutting off what he'd been about to say. "Find out what's happening," Muir snapped.

"Could it be an earthquake, sir?"

"Don't be a dolt. Only a dark Sidhe could do that, and none would dare." He jostled the crystal again, then tightened his fist around it, cutting off the faint light that managed to penetrate the obsidian. "We'll meet them at the beach."

She tried to press herself against the walls of her prison, hoping for some small crack or seam through which she could escape. Although Muir had given her magic a chance to replenish itself, she absolutely refused to let him use it against Rizan or anyone else.

Without warning, the ground rumbled again, and Feather heard a loud crack, followed by several more until it seemed as if the island was exploding around her. The tug on her magic wasn't gentle this time. Muir tore it away like a terrier pulling a rat from a drainpipe. She let out a soundless scream, trying desperately to keep it away from him.

"It doesn't matter how much you fight, mage," Muir said, his voice a low, angry hiss. "Your mate might have brought an army of light Sidhe to weaken me, but I stand on the deepest, most ancient part of the planet."

That was utter bullshit. No Sidhe of either caste would enter into battle against the other without a very good reason, and she doubted one rogue dark Sidhe was enough. Unlike Teran, Muir didn't seek to change the face of the planet. All he cared about were his trophies and the accumulation of personal wealth. Yet it didn't explain what was happening or who was causing the disruption.

If only she could see. Muir cursed again, shaking his fist at something. "Trees?" he demanded. "You think to defeat me with vegetation?"

He pulled harder on her magic, nearly making her lose consciousness. It barely even hurt anymore. He'd drawn too much, too fast, and there was almost nothing left. Without a body to tether her, she would soon fade into true death.

There was something different though. Muir scrabbled to maintain his grip on her, as if his own strength was weakening. Although she couldn't completely evade him, it became easier to keep the tiny spark of being that kept her alive. Unfortunately, she didn't have the power to hold out for long, but maybe she could take him with her. Instead of trying to hold it back, she reached for Muir and tangled their magic together, wresting control from him.

Knowing she had scant seconds left before he wrenched it away, Feather sent her dwindling magic outward along with Muir's. With it, went all the love she carried for her dragon.

~

RIZAN

"I'm going to have a chat with my light Sidhe counterpart," Brand murmured, gazing at the thick hardwood forest that had grown up in response to Omer's magic.

"The garden gnome passes his power around like a

borrowed cup of sugar," Morgaine replied, her lips pursed in distaste. "Did you get rid of it all, Prince Rizan?"

He shook his head, trying to calm the ringing in his ears. All but a faint twinge of Sidhe magic had left his body, leaving him weak and lightheaded, but the sensation passed quickly.

"I'm fine." Turning, he went to help Guinevere from her perch on the railing, but she let go and jumped into the surf by herself. The rest of his team followed, splashing through the shallows until they reached the narrow beach.

"Angel, I need recon," Kali said.

"He's actually coming this way. I smell the stink of dark Sidhe," Dennis said, wrinkling his nose. When Brand arched a brow and cleared his throat, Dennis flushed, then said, "Sorry, Your Majesty."

"Don't think on it," Brand replied. "The earth and cold metal do have a particular odor, especially when a dark Sidhe is using more magic than he ought to."

When Angel crouched in preparation for her shift, Rizan laid a hand on her arm. "Wait," he murmured softly. "Don't reveal yourself yet."

A man stepped from behind the trees. Dressed in a charcoal suit, he looked plain and unassuming, with smooth hands and a receding hairline. He was neither young, nor old, and had the bland, forgettable features of a human businessman. As he approached, the weight of magic was almost suffocating, and it wasn't only dark Sidhe. Feather's rain and wildflower magic was tangled in, making Rizan want to tear him apart.

Instead of stealing Feather's will and future, Muir took the very essence of her, using her spirit to augment his power. Rizan didn't know how such a thing was possible, but he made a silent promise to her and himself to fix it.

"Vyron Muir, you have something that belongs to me," Rizan called out. "I've come to get it back."

His friends and comrades spread out, surrounding Muir in a loose circle. To his surprise, Morgaine vanished, her footsteps in the sand disappearing between one step and the next. Davryn gritted his teeth, his face reddening with irritation, but said nothing as his mate traveled the spectral flames in the way of dragons.

"Rizan Carter," the man murmured. "How touching for you to take Feather's surname. Or should I call you Prince?" Dozens of people emerged from the woods behind him, carrying a variety of weapons, but none approached.

"You could call me your executioner," Rizan retorted.

Laughing, Muir shook his head. "Do you dare when I still hold Feather's soul in my palm?"

Rizan kept his face impassive, not revealing his lack of understanding. He didn't know how Muir had separated Feather's consciousness from her body, but it was the least of his worries. All he had to do was find her, kill Muir, and return her to Bear.

And pray to all the gods he could reunite them.

"Vyron, you must know you won't be allowed to succeed in whatever plan you're concocting," Brand said, stepping forward.

"Ah, Brand. I'd say it's a pleasure, but as I was exiled centuries ago, I'm afraid your words are meaningless." He smirked and pushed a hand into his pocket, then frowned as he lifted a broken chain with a black stone dangling from it.

"You utter bastard," Lily hissed. "You trapped a mage in a nullstone? How dare you?"

"Ah, yes. You're the stunted dragon, aren't you?" Muir stepped forward, holding the stone in one fist. "The late, unlamented King Teran tried to capture you with one, I believe, but they simply don't function that way with dragons. Pity for him he didn't do a little more research, but you've done me the great service of bringing both Morgaine le Fay and Myrddin to me."

Growling, Lily shifted and lumbered forward, putting herself between her husbands and Muir. A blast of blackened magic threaded with Feather's purple hit her in the chest, knocking her backward into the sea.

"Do you cretins not understand?" he shouted. "The two most powerful mages to ever exist are within my reach! They are—"

Without warning, he paled and dropped to his knees, then let out a keening wail as purple magic erupted from his eyes and mouth. Shooting upward, it arched above them in a roiling cloud of lightning-struck energy.

Feather's essence washed over him, wild and untamed as a storm burst overhead. Giant balls of hail fell, sending Muir's men running for the dubious cover of the forest. Screaming in pain and rage, Muir threw the black stone into the newly-grown woods.

Reappearing behind Muir, Morgaine lifted her arm and stared at Brand. The sword he carried disappeared from its scabbard on his back and materialized in her hand. Her expression remote, she grabbed Muir's thin hair and brought the blade down, severing his head from his body.

"Lily!" she shouted, drawing her arm back. "Catch!" Dripping blood, the head sailed across the beach.

Snaking her neck out, Lily snapped the offering from the air and bit down with a resounding crack of teeth on bone. When she finished chewing, she burped out a bubble of flame and spat a wad of wet hair tangled around part of a jawbone on the sand.

She reached down for the rest of Muir's body, but Rizan blocked her path. "We have to find Feather. Look for that nullstone."

"Morgaine le Fay," Brand said, his face thunderous with anger. "I censure you for—"

"With all due respect, stow it, Your Majesty." She handed his sword back, hilt first. "I have exhaustive experience with what happens when a rogue Sidhe isn't properly dealt with. It hasn't been a decade since the last one started a war that nearly destroyed the planet."

"You only survive because the dark Sidhe showed you mercy."

"And I came back like a bad penny too."

"I'll not forgive you for this," he replied, sheathing his sword. "You took away the justice that rightfully belongs to the dark Sidhe."

"Really?" She rounded on him, her fists balled. "Was it your mate he stole? Your family? Hmm?"

"You overstep, mage."

"I didn't steal justice from you, idiot. I stole it from Rizan, and for that I am truly sorry."

"She's right," Myrddin said. "The Sidhe way is beneficial and I admire your desire to preserve all life, but no one can be allowed to destroy so much without paying the price."

Brand grunted in acknowledgement, then nodded. "For what it's worth, he would have been tortured to death to allow the earth to recapture his magic, as Queen Sena was, and as we'd intended for Teran."

Morgaine nudged Muir's body with the toe of her boot. "This was faster, and now I'm sure of him."

Rizan let their conversation wash over him as he searched for the nullstone containing his Feather's essence.

He didn't care who killed Muir, as long as he was well and truly dead. No one came back from having their head eaten by a dragon.

In their animal forms, Angel, Dennis, and Kali disappeared into the woods searching for survivors. He soon heard faint screams in the distance, but focused only on finding the stone.

His search stretched on, making his desperation grow. How the hell was he supposed to find a black stone smaller than his pinky nail in the thick underbrush? On his knees, he kept digging, crawling a few inches at a time as he tore away the thick vegetation.

"Let me help," Guinevere said, kneeling next to him. "I can feel her, but she's very weak and I can't pinpoint her exact location."

A thousand years ago, Rizan would have refused her offer. The mighty dragon prince showed no weakness. As the oldest of his kind, he'd had none. The last five years had shown him there was no weakness in accepting help. Saving Feather was more important than his ego. It was the most important thing of all.

He crept forward another scant few inches as Guinevere searched her own patch of vegetation.

"I think we're getting closer," she said, carefully picking through the plants. "Can you try to call her? Maybe she can answer."

TWENTY-THREE

FEATHER

S he let herself float in the empty space. Muir was dead and the immense weight of his magic no longer pressed down on her. It felt as if she was light and song and poignant joy. It had been so long since she'd felt so... Good.

She couldn't even be sad about dying.

Muir had taken so much from her, leaving only a scant, dim spark of being that would flicker out soon. Yet she had everything she'd dreamed of for half a decade. Muir was dead and Rizan was free of their bond. Maybe Bear could even go on being a perfectly mundane bear, but Feather didn't know if that would happen.

She wished for it anyway.

"Feather, please, come to me," Rizan said, his voice sounding remarkably close.

She allowed her dwindling magic to spark in response, knowing it was the only way left to show him how much she loved him.

"Got her! I saw a purple light about two meters in front of you!" The strange voice belonged to a woman, but not one Feather knew.

"Thank the Fates!"

Feather felt movement and warmth, but saw nothing. Strangely, it seemed as if the gentle touch on the stone encasing her soul gave her a tiny surge of power. She wasn't sure she wanted it though. It would only prolong the inevitable.

"I have you now, darling," Rizan whispered. The warmth increased, becoming almost uncomfortably hot.

She wanted to evade the sensation, but she was so tired.

"Keep her against your skin, Rizan. The more you touch her, the more I feel her."

"I will never let her go again."

Okay, maybe there was one more thing she'd dreamed of. Comforted in her dragon's embrace, she let herself soar away on wings of love.

RIZAN

"I have no idea if this will work," Morgaine said. "Null-stones aren't meant to be broken, and I know of no mage to have survived one."

"Would it be better if her mother assisted you?" Myrddin asked, his magic buoying Feather's stone above their clasped hands.

"Perhaps." Morgaine focused her attention on the stone and allowed a thin trickle of green magic to mix with Myrddin's. "A familial connection might sustain her a bit better, but I think this will be enough to keep her alive for now."

Their combined magic solidified into a delicate web around Feather's prison, then raced up the length of the chain and repaired the broken links with pure rose gold.

Guinevere and Zeke watched with fascination, then glanced at each other. "Do you feel like an infant in comparison?" she asked.

"A fetus," Zeke replied.

Myrddin arched a brow and gave Guinevere a faint smile. "You really want to go there, Your Majesty? Have to admit, you hid very well."

"There's never been much to hide." Guinevere lowered her head and flushed. "I can barely light a candle. It was just enough to have me burned at the stake, but not enough to survive it. My one claim to competence is the ability to sense magic stronger than mine."

"What's he talking about?" Zeke asked.

"She's Guinevere. Does the name not ring a bell?" Myrddin touched her chin, making her look up. "Some of the period art actually did capture your likeness."

"Like, Arthur's Guinevere?" Zeke asked.

"I was never his! That disgusting oaf—" Calming herself, she gave Zeke a smile that didn't reach her eyes, then stood. "Excuse me."

She strode away and into the surf, then climbed the aluminum ladder to the deck of their boat.

Myrddin stared after, his expression calmly assessing as he passed the nullstone to Rizan. "Wear it against your skin," he said. "We think touch will help keep her connected to you."

"Gladly." Rizan put the chain around his neck, then

tucked the nullstone inside his shirt. It laid quiescent against his chest, but he felt the pulse of life from it. Feather was still with him, but hanging by a scant thread. "I'm taking her home now."

"No!" Myrddin grabbed his arm and shook his head. "Mundane travel only. We have no idea how dragon flame will affect her."

Hiding a grimace, Rizan nodded. "Fine." Turning to his brother and Morgaine, he asked, "Will you go ahead of us and make sure Grandmother doesn't harm Feather's bear?"

"Of course." He gathered Morgaine in his arms and they vanished without another word.

As much as he wanted Feather reunited with her bear, he'd do nothing that might harm her. He'd been patient for almost five years, but despised having to wait a single day longer. Forcibly calming himself, he reached under his shirt and stroked the nullstone.

She was safe. The rest would come.

"I will take Muir's remains home," King Brand said, covering the body in a silvery cloud that coalesced into a shroud. "There may be residual magic we can return to the earth."

A giant Siberian tiger padded from the woods, shifting between one step and the next into Kali. She wiped a trickle of blood from her chin, then said, "We're leaving in five minutes. Get on the boat or get left behind."

By the time his chartered jet landed on Kayenta's single scrubby airstrip, Rizan was desperate to reunite Feather with her bear. Knowing it was a human gesture of faith, he crossed his fingers, hoping Grandmother hadn't made good on her threat to kill the only body Feather had left.

He didn't care if she was a bear or human. He loved what was inside. Feather's brilliant, kind spirit. Her inner beauty and strength. That was all that mattered to him. Leaving his colleagues behind, he shifted, then spread his wings and launched himself from the hard-packed earth.

She was still caged, and he was desperate to free her.

Moments later, he landed a few hundred yards away from Yanaha's trailer, then returned to his human form and stalked to the cage containing his mate.

To his surprise, Feather's bear was surrounded by baby dragons. Pearlescent scales gleaming, Amelie Archer lifted her head, small horns budding atop her skull.

"Back off, asshole." She hissed, baring her fangs.

"Where's your mother, child?" he asked, hiding his amusement. Amelie had inherited Lily's command of profanity, it seemed.

"I set her on fire. Go away."

"You can't set a dragon on fire." Ignoring the ball of flame she spat at his feet, he crouched. "Thank you for keeping my mate safe."

"You're not here to kill Feather?" Amelie straightened, but kept a clawed paw on the bear's shoulder through the bars of her cage.

The bear didn't move, but to his relief, her chest rose and fell with her breathing.

"No. Never. I'm here to try to save her." The babies roused themselves, peering at him with distrustful eyes. "What happened?"

"Grandmother tried to kill her twice." A puff of steam escaped Amelie's nostrils and she wrinkled her muzzle into a grin. "We convinced her not to."

"Good. Thank you all for your help." Rising to his feet, he twisted the lock and broke it, then opened the door and stepped inside. "You may return to your mothers."

"Forget it." Amelie flared her wings and retreated, but

didn't go far. "Bring Feather back and we'll consider not killing you."

"So fierce," he murmured. "Your mother will be proud."

Sitting, he leaned against the walls of the cage and pulled the bear into his lap, then crooned softly in an attempt to rouse her.

"Baby girl, come back," he whispered. The stone pulsed against his chest, and he tore his shirt open, cradling the bear close to keep it in contact with both of them. "I miss you."

Rousing, the bear lifted her head and peered at him for a few seconds. Chuffing softly, she nosed the stone, then closed her eyes and moved until she was more firmly entrenched on his lap.

He let out a sigh of relief. His relationship with the bear hadn't been without problems, and her acceptance spurred fresh hope. Balancing the pendant in his palm, he held it out.

"Stop!" Grandmother approached, her footsteps sounding like thunder on the desert. She fingered a long Bowie knife, testing the edge. "This is over, Rizan. Take the babies and leave."

Wrapping an arm around Feather's bear, he returned her glare, furious she couldn't give him just a few damned minutes. "Children—"

Without warning, the young dragons swarmed Grandmother. Teeth snapping, they bore her to the ground, ignoring her angry screams as she tried to fling them aside. There were too many though, and soon they had her trapped, driving her into bleeding compliance with flame and tooth and claw.

"We're out of time, baby. Please, come back to me."

Lifting the stone above his head, he dashed it to the ground, snapping it in two.

CHAPTER
TWENTY-FOUR

FEATHER

Suddenly released, she hovered over Bear, desperately seeking a way to reunite herself with her other half. Yet Bear was somnolent, half-awake without comprehension.

"Let me in," she begged silently.

You're here?

"I am. I missed you."

No. Turning her back, Bear hunkered in a corner, her face tucked between her paws. *You left me.*

"I was taken from you. I didn't leave. I will never leave."

That is... not lie.

"No. I don't lie. Especially not to you, the other half of myself."

Bear grunted, but didn't turn.

"I said I won't leave," Feather pressed, sinking into Bear's warm fur. "Who else will hunt boar with me?"

No more boar.

"Fishing then. Delicious fat salmon, and as much as you want."

You hate salmon.

"I know, but you like it."

No cages?

"Never," Feather promised, hoping it was true. "Not ever again."

Mate?

"He holds us both, keeps us safe."

Without warning, Bear opened her consciousness to accept Feather inside. To Feather's surprise, their mind was as she'd left it, the temperate rainforest environment intact.

Yet one thing was changed. Bear huddled in an ephemeral cage of twisted magic. "Aw, hell no," she muttered.

Magic sprung to her fingertips and she let out a blast of purple flame, demolishing the construct to free her animal half. Falling to her knees, she wrapped her arms around Bear.

"I'm... free." Bear huddled in Feather's arms, shivering uncontrollably. "No more killing when I'm not hungry for prey I don't like."

"Shh." Feather crooned softly, her tuneless melody soothing and comforting. "No more. Not ever again. Vyron Muir is dead."

"Let us be human, please. Forever."

"No. Not forever. We will—"

"Human always. So I never kill again."

"We'll talk about it." Leaning down, she planted a kiss between Bear's ears. "Everything will be okay. I promise."

Bear stilled, then forcefully pushed them into an agonizing shift that left Feather gasping in pain.

"Feather?"

Opening her eyes, she looked up into Rizan's dear, beloved face. Lunging upward, she hugged him as tightly as she could, then let go and rose to her feet when she saw Grandmother prostrate on the ground, surrounded by the baby dragons.

Except they weren't babies anymore. Lily's daughter, Amelie, was the size of a large pony. Lasair, who had once been so weak and small she'd had to feed him ground beef by hand, mantled black wings and hissed, revealing six-inch fangs. He pressed a claw against Grandmother's neck, pricking her until a trickle of blood coursed down her shoulder.

"I'm back," Feather murmured, letting Rizan help her into his T-shirt. "Miss me?"

"Told you," Yanaha muttered, ignoring Lasair's irritable growls as she helped Grandmother to her feet.

"She's still part bear," Grandmother protested.

"So? She always was." Turning to Feather, she crossed her arms. "How's the ursine situation going? Sane or not sane?"

"Sane, I think." Winking slowly, she added, "Is it sane to ask for the black wrap dress you wore to that fancy restaurant in New York?"

"You're sane if you can find it," Yanaha retorted. "Knock yourself out."

"It's in..." Feather lifted her hand, focusing her magic on Aunt Yan's storage shed.

The task was an act of muscle memory. Something so simple, even the weakest mage could do it with little more than a description of an item and a faint touch of magic. Yet it had been denied to her for years. The dress appeared in her hand and she tightened her fist around the silk. One more surge of magic produced a long strand of turquoise beads, Yanaha's one vanity.

"Brat." Her gaze softening, Aunt Yan hugged her tightly and placed the beads around Feather's neck, then kissed her cheeks. "Blessings to you, child. Welcome home."

"Feather!"

She whirled at the sound of her name, then took off running. Her parents met her halfway, slamming into her as they swept her into their arms. Bursting into tears, she cried as they embraced her.

They'd aged so much in the time she'd been gone. Mages usually stopped aging in their thirties, yet Mama's hair was almost completely gray and had been cut in an unattractive bob, almost as if she'd done it herself with a kitchen knife. Her golden-brown complexion was sallow, and deep lines marred the skin under her eyes. Her father didn't look much better, and they were both too thin.

"Daddy," she finally said, almost choking the words out. "We killed a boar, just like you taught us."

"That's my good girl." His gray hair fell over his eyes, hiding his tears. "We'll hunt together. Just the two of us."

"I missed you, baby," her mother said, refusing to let go. "I can't even say how much."

Part of her wanted to stay and reconnect with her friends and family. Christopher and Andi must have had at least a few children in the time she'd been gone, and she wanted to see if Andi had gotten her wish to make the Arizona wolves strong again.

She wanted to drive Daisy, her old pickup, to West Canyon like she used to do when she was in high school, and touch the life-giving waters of the Colorado River once more.

"Missed you too, Mama." Wiping her eyes, Feather took

a step back into Rizan's waiting arms. "I'll be back soon, but I have something to do first."

"Oh, no you don't!" Her mother wrapped wiry arms around her, holding her tight before Rizan could whisk her away. "You're staying right here."

"And Rizan is welcome too, right, River?" her father said, winking at him.

Mama rolled her eyes, but smiled. "I suppose. Since he brought our baby home and all."

She rested her head against Rizan's chest, grateful for his support. "He is my mate, you know."

Except he really wasn't. Pressure built behind her eyes, and she prayed she wouldn't break down. Rizan hadn't said a word about restoring their familiar bond. She knew it was possible; Morgaine and King Davryn had done it after Morgaine was brought back to life. That didn't mean Rizan wanted it back.

Her life was a train wreck. It wouldn't surprise her in the slightest.

She was alive though, and Vyron Muir wouldn't hurt anyone ever again. Maybe she still had things to work out with Bear, but that would come in time.

"Come on," Mama said, pulling her away from Rizan, "let's get you home."

Without waiting for her to answer, they bundled her into their car for the short trip home. Rizan was almost forgotten, but smiled as he climbed into the back seat with her.

"Sorry," she whispered, scooting over to sit next to him.

"It's all right. They missed you." He kissed her temple, then hugged her. "Besides, I plan to sneak off with you once everyone is in bed. We have unfinished business."

"Oh?"

"Yes. We get to have all the fun of replacing our familiar bond, and..." He leaned close, his words only for her. "You also owe me a mating bite."

From the front seat, her father cleared his throat, reminding her he had the sensitive hearing of a two-natured. Her face as hot as dragon flame, she buried her face in Rizan's chest.

Maybe she was wrong. Maybe things would work out and she'd get everything she'd always wanted. Unfortunately, she couldn't help but wonder when the other shoe would drop.

RIZAN

Adam and River's home was unchanged, as if it was frozen at the moment Feather had gone missing. A faint hint of vinegar, the only household cleaner tolerated by most two-natured, perfumed the air, mixing with unscented laundry detergent.

Feather moved slowly through the rooms, touching things here and there as if trying to refamiliarize herself with her own home. Smiling sadly, she slowed as she approached a wall hung with several photos of her as a child. In one, she rode on the back of a large black bear, her toothless grin beaming. Another revealed her and her mother standing on either side of an unsmiling member of the Queen's Guard outside Buckingham Palace.

And, of course, her graduation photo held center stage. Rizan remembered it vividly, and wanted to kick himself for not speaking to her.

"I remember that day," she murmured, coming to stand

next to him. Reaching up, she pulled a somewhat faded gold cord with a frayed tassel from around the framed graduation photo. "I was going to give you this."

"What is it?"

"My honor cord from graduating at the top of a class of fifty." She laughed without mirth. "Big fish in a little pond."

"It was still quite an accomplishment." He took the twisted strand of gold cord from her, then hung it around his neck. "I will cherish it as the most valuable thing in my hoard."

With a gentle finger under her chin, he tilted her head up and kissed her forehead, then added, "Aside from you, of course."

She laughed, a watery sound, but he relished it. "I can't decide if you mean that, or are just being cheesy to make me laugh."

"Can't it be both?"

"I—"

"Feather, honey, I thought I'd send your father for pizza..." Her voice trailed off and her smile faded as she took a step backward. "I'm sorry, am I interrupting?"

"No, it's fine, Mama. Pizza is fine."

"Good. That's... yes, pizza. Do you still like mushrooms, pepperoni, and sausage?"

"Sounds great." Her fingers tightened around his, communicating her nerves.

"And for you, Rizan?"

"For me as well, thank you."

"Okay. That's... um, I'll send him out right now, and ask him to stop for a jar of pepperoncini, and..." She shook her head. "Never mind. I forgot you don't like salad."

"Mama, it's—"

Without warning, she reached for Feather's hand and

pulled her into a tight embrace. "Fates, I'm glad you're home."

"Me too," Feather whispered.

River let her go and wiped her eyes, giving them a smile. "Anyway, I'll let you two get back to your conversation." She returned to the kitchen, leaving them alone.

"Wow, this is awkward. It's like... they're complete strangers."

Although none of them fell, the acrid scent of her tears scratched at his nasal passages like steel wool. Rizan bit back a growl, unwilling to upset her further. "Give them time," he finally said, drawing her into his arms. "Give yourself time."

"Yeah." She sniffed back her tears, then sighed. "Hey, I just thought of something. Why didn't the Jaguar you gave me show up at Muir's like the rose did?"

"It did, but you must not have seen it. It vanished at the same time you did. I believe he hid it."

Her nose wrinkled into a scowl and she crossed her arms over her chest. "Ugh. The asshole probably drove my car. That's gross."

Or Muir had it cubed out of spite. The vehicle would eventually find its way home, but there was no way he'd allow her to touch it again. "Not to worry. You may buy another, or you can have my Viper. I get too many speeding tickets as it is."

"A Viper." She arched her brow and gave him an unwilling smile. "Of course. What else would you drive?"

"Or you may have the Veyron, but I think I'd like you to drive something newer."

"Or," she retorted, her voice tart, "why don't I just keep driving Daisy?"

Smiling inwardly, he remembered their first argument

the night of her prom. "What? I'm still not allowed to give you presents?"

"Rizan, I—" A knock sounded at the front door, interrupting her.

"Sweetie, will you get that?" her mother called.

"Sure, Mama!" She went to the door and opened it, then squealed happily. "Christopher!"

She flung herself at him, hugging him around the waist. The man, no longer a lanky teenager, held himself stiffly and didn't return the embrace or look at her. Instead, he gazed over her head, his jaw tight.

Gently, he extricated himself from her hug and stepped out of reach. "Hello, Feather. We need to talk."

Rizan's lips pulled back from his teeth, his nostrils flaring at the scent of Christopher's antagonism. Truly, it was less antagonism and more discomfort, but Rizan didn't want Feather anywhere near him.

"Sure!" She moved out of the way and held the door. "Come on in. Where's Andi? Daddy just went for pizza, and you're—"

A wave of the young wolf's alpha strength washed into the room, cutting off Feather's words. Lunging forward, Rizan pulled her away and into his arms.

"As the alpha to the Arizona wolves, it is my duty to protect them from all threats. Therefore, I must ask you to leave Arizona before sunset tonight. Do you understand?"

The sickly stench of her tears choked Rizan, and he had to forcibly resist the urge to rip the wolf's head from his body. She shuddered under the weight of Christopher's magic, forcing him to hold her steady.

"But... we're friends."

Christopher's expression softened, but he shook his

head. "That was true five years ago. Today, you are a threat to my pack."

"No! I'm not! I'm—"

"Grandmother told us what happened, Feather. Your bear has gone crazy, and you are no longer bound to Rizan. If you are still in Arizona at sundown, we will kill you and your family."

Without waiting for an answer, he left, shutting the door behind him.

The sound of shattering glass made him push Feather behind him. Turning, he growled, but the sound cut off at the sight of River.

"That slimy little bastard," she whispered, her face nearly purple with rage. Another glass hit the wall, tossed by a flare of blue magic so dark it appeared black, and she pushed past him to the door. "I'm going to set his fucking tail on fire."

He let her leave, too busy with his mate to concern himself with the very short life expectancy of the wolf alpha. The noise of their argument cut off when he slammed the door behind them.

Choking sobs wracked her slim body as she collapsed in his arms. "Shh, morsel. It will be okay."

Rizan would make sure of that—even if he had to lay waste to Arizona and everything in it.

CHAPTER
TWENTY-FIVE

FEATHER

Rizan was wrong. Nothing was okay. Her parents were frightened of her, she was being thrown out of Arizona, and Grandmother still wanted her dead.

Also, despite her physical age, her intellectual and emotional growth had stalled at eighteen. She was still an uneducated, socially stunted kid in an adult body with no job skills, no money, and no home.

Just fucking perfect.

She wriggled free of Rizan's embrace and wiped her face with the tail of his T-shirt. Fates, she hadn't even had a chance to put on pants before getting exiled from her home.

And by Christopher, of all people. He and Andi had been her friends since they were all in diapers.

Go batshit crazy one *fucking time...*

"What are you doing?" he asked, narrowing his eyes as he rose to his feet.

"I'm going to put on pants, then I'm going to pack my shit, load up Daisy, and leave." She barked out an ugly laugh, then added, "Assuming I still have shit to pack."

"You don't need any of that. We'll simply go to my—"

"Stop." She held up a hand and backed away. "*We* are not going anywhere. I'm leaving. I'm going to find a job, figure out a way to finish my degree, and maybe fucking grow up for a change. I'm absolutely done."

A muscle worked across his cheek as he tightened his jaw. "Feather, I promise, we'll—"

"There can't be a we until there's a me! Can't you understand that?" Knowing he was hurt and angry, she softened her tone. "Rizan, I'm sorry. I can't make you take on my problems. I can't allow my parents to do it either."

"Do you truly believe your problems aren't already mine?" Throwing his hands in the air, he glared at her. "Against my better judgment, I let you go. I agreed to five years, and that time has come. Are you saying you won't keep your vow to me?"

The words got stuck in her throat and she coughed to make them come out. "I can't. Not until... I have to get better first."

"Don't you know? You're perfect just as you are."

She swallowed back a sob and shook her head. "I will come back. That, I do promise you."

"All right." Although his face was impassive, she felt the pain and rage emanating from him. "Give me your hand."

Tentatively, she reached for his outstretched palm and hissed when a gold bangle bracelet engraved with hiero-glyphics appeared on her wrist. The metal was almost hot enough to burn, but she didn't complain. "What's this?" she asked.

"A gift that can't be taken from you. You will wear it so I always know where you are."

"I... okay." She couldn't exactly protest. If he'd given her a bracelet like that, maybe he'd have been able to find her five years ago.

"And this." He handed her a cell phone. "Another way to track you, albeit less reliable. You will also take this."

He closed her fingers around several folded one-hundred-dollar bills wrapped around a black Amex, then kissed her forehead. "You will be as safe as I can make you until you come back to me."

"Thank you." Unable to stop herself, she threw her arms around him, tears pricking her eyes. "I'm sorry."

"Go, morsel. I'll be waiting."

He left quietly, closing the door behind him. She could only watch as he took two steps into the yard and morphed into the shape of his dragon. Roaring, he sent a burst of flame into the air and vanished.

Tears burst free and she raced into her room. Without thought or the ability to see what she was packing, she emptied her drawers into one of her father's old hard-shell suitcases, the faded blue reminding her of all the times he'd traveled and come home.

"Feather!" Her mother burst into the room, hair in disarray. "We can fix this. I—"

"No." She put her hands on her mother's shoulders and shook her head. "It's not worth it."

"We'll go to Yanaha. She'll tell that flea-bitten whelp where he can stuff that autocratic order."

Not when Christopher had threatened her parents. He hadn't been kidding either, and she wasn't about to let anyone go to war for her. Aunt Yan had already done enough.

"I'll be okay, Mama." She tried to smile and kissed her mom's cheek, maybe for the last time. "Take care of Daddy for me, okay?"

"Please, don't do this." Tears trickled down Mama's cheeks and she put a hand over her mouth to stifle a sob. "I can't bear to lose you again."

"You won't." She held up Rizan's phone and the bracelet. "Rizan will know where I am, and I'll call when I get settled."

"You just came home to me." Putting a hand over her mouth, Mama backed from the room, leaving Feather alone.

"That went well," Feather muttered, tears still blurring her vision as she crammed the last of her things into the overstuffed suitcase.

She felt like such a bitch, but she had no intention of putting her family or Rizan at risk. Maybe she wasn't about to go crazy again, but Christopher's threat struck home. He'd meant every word too. River and Adam Carter were a formidable team, but they were no match for a determined pack of wolves.

By the time she finished loading Daisy, the sun was almost down. As she slammed the tailgate, a low growl sounded behind her. She scowled, but didn't turn around to see who it was.

"I'm going, asshole. Keep your fur on." Feather walked around the truck and got in, then started it. As she backed from the driveway, a heavy weight slammed against her door.

Obviously, her time had run out. She considered sending a bit of magic to drive them off, but truly didn't want to hurt her friends. Well, former friends anyway.

Instead, she got on the road and sped away, leaving them eating her dust.

"So, what do you think, Bear? Where are we going?" She asked the question without expecting an answer, but to her surprise, Bear responded.

South. Far south.

"There isn't anything south of Arizona except the Sonoran Desert, and it's a seven-hour drive. Christopher isn't going to let us stay that long."

South.

Bear stirred, her distress palpable. Feather had no idea why going south was so important, but it wasn't as if she had a better idea. Hell, maybe she'd turn west and just follow the Gulf of California coast and find a cheap resort until she got her head on straight.

"South it is, I guess. We'll just catch 160 to Shiprock and drive through New Mexico. Nobody's said I can't go into Texas, so Juarez is as good a place to cross the border as any."

RIZAN

He soared low above Feather's old truck, keeping his distance. As much as he wanted to swoop down and take her away, he couldn't. The betrayal of her friend had broken something in her. Something he couldn't fix.

He could only protect from a distance now. As she drove east toward the New Mexico border, several motorcycles approached, their pace quickening as they caught up to her.

"No, you don't." He growled the words between

clenched fangs. Dropping like a stone, he swept his wings across the road, scattering motorcycles and wolves everywhere. His claws touched the sun-warmed pavement and he parted his jaws, a bubble of flame boiling in his mouth as the wolves struggled to stand.

A tall man approached, limping slightly. His graying hair seemed to grow as he approached, signaling an imminent shift into his animal form. "The abomination is no longer welcome here. You will not hinder us."

"Seems to me she's leaving just fine on her own," Rizan replied.

A few of the younger ones looked away. They'd probably been Feather's friends and classmates. "You have no right—"

Rizan slammed his paw down, knocking the man back. "No, asshole. You don't have the right. She's ten minutes from the fucking border. Do you think she's going to turn around and come back? Or did you plan to chase her all the way to Maryland?"

Although he couldn't hear it, he sensed his brother landing behind him. He didn't need help dealing with this band of idiots, but he welcomed the support.

"You don't want a war with us," Davryn said softly, folding his wings. "Go home, gentlemen."

"King Davryn," the older wolf said, inclining his head. "This isn't your concern."

"I'm afraid it is. You're threatening my brother's mate." Lowering his head, Davryn blew a bit of steam across the wolf's feet. "In what universe is that not my business?"

"Our alpha told us to get rid of her."

"I'm sure he didn't mean get rid of in the permanent sense." Davryn shot out another burst of steam, melting the asphalt into sludge, then picked up one of the motorcycles in a clawed paw. "Feather is my wife's very good friend and babysat my children. Losing Feather would make my wife cry."

Slowly, he twisted the motorcycle. Metal grated as it spindled and broke apart. "Obviously, you see my position here. People die when they make my wife cry."

Although a few stood their ground, most of the wolves took a step back, knowing they'd been outmaneuvered.

"Oh, and just because I'm a generous fellow, I took the liberty of contacting the New Mexico bears. Did you know their alpha is Feather's uncle?"

"Go home," Rizan finally said. "She's across the border and out of your reach."

Spreading his wings, he launched himself into the air, meaning to follow her. To his surprise, Davryn caught up. They flew in companionable silence for several minutes before Davryn finally said something.

"Feather is a great deal like Morgaine."

"Aside from both of them being abused by the Sidhe, I don't follow."

"They both blame themselves for what happened to them. Morgaine is getting better, but..." He bobbed his head sideways, an instinctive gesture communicating camaraderie, but didn't elaborate.

"How did you make her better?"

"I didn't. She's doing it herself, but she's a few thousand years older than Feather."

"That isn't the slightest bit helpful." Rizan resisted the urge to blast his brother out of the sky. He meant well, but Rizan was too furiously angry at the wolves to pay him much heed.

Davryn moved closer, brushing against him as they flew. "Give her time," he said. "She loves you."

"She has a funny way of showing it."

"At least she didn't jump from your back, despite being afraid to fly, to let an insane dark Sidhe king stab her so she could kill him."

Wincing, Rizan nodded. "That is true. I hope you spanked her thoroughly."

"A gentleman never tells."

"In what lifetime were you ever a gentleman?"

"Well, this one. I'm trying, at least." Davryn turned and winked, his blue eyes filled with ancient sadness. "She will come back to you, brother."

"And if she doesn't?"

"Then you'll chase her down and add her to your hoard." He stalled in midair, his wings beating to keep him aloft. "I must return. Morgaine plans to meet with Feather's mother to discuss relocation."

"What? Why?"

"Didn't you ever watch *Lilo and Stitch?* The bit about ohana?"

"I have no idea what you're blathering about."

"Family is everything, Rizan. Deny one, deny us all. The wolf alpha made a very big mistake tonight. If he's lucky, he'll live long enough to regret it."

Without another word, Davryn sent a burst of flame into the air and vanished.

Davryn was right about one thing. The wolf alpha had made a mistake. Knowing his brother, Rizan was sure there wouldn't be a mage or dragon left in the state by the time he returned with Feather.

Five years of peace ruined by the rash actions of an alpha too young and frightened to consider the consequences. Then again, perhaps that was what he'd been after and Feather was a convenient scapegoat. Even as he thought the words, Rizan knew they were wrong, but the results were the same.

Pushing the wolves from his mind, Rizan flew on until he located Feather's path. She'd turned south at Farmington, and eventually stopped for the night at a roadside motel just south of Albuquerque. He flew on, unable to find a secluded spot to roost where he could watch over her.

Her rain and wildflower scent called to him, yet he gave her the space she needed. The bracelet, given to him by the daughter of some Egyptian king several thousand years past, told him her exact location. He'd even spelled it to give him a sense of her emotions.

Feather was sad, but also determined. Excited. He wasn't sure what to do with the morass of feelings pouring from his little morsel, yet for the moment, she was safe.

She continued south the next morning, crossing the border into Juarez without issue, then stopped for the night at a small motel west of town. It didn't look as safe as the last one, a perception turned into truth when she was accosted the minute she parked.

Four human men surrounded her, their smiles feral. Her back was to him, meaning he couldn't see her face as he flew down to remove them from her presence. Without warning, the men scattered and he smelled the rich scent of their terror, plus a faint hint of urine from one of them.

Dark laughter bubbled from her as she slammed the door of her truck and grabbed her suitcase. There was no fear from her—only smug satisfaction.

"That's my girl," he murmured, soaring away to watch from a distance. Maybe things would be okay. He'd give her the time she needed, let her grow her confidence, and then she'd come back to him.

CHAPTER

TWENTY-SIX

FEATHER

B y the time she reached Janos, it took everything she
had to keep heading west on México 2. She had no
idea why, but Bear was desperate to go south.

It wasn't as if she had anywhere to be, but Chihuahua
was a whole lot of northern Mexico nothing. Finally, she
pulled off into a small gas station, unable to resist Bear's
entreaties, but unwilling to continue without a damned
good reason. Using Rizan's Amex, she filled both Daisy's
fuel tanks.

There was no point in hiding her location by using
cash. The bracelet and cell phone would tell him where she
was, and she wasn't stupid enough to try to get rid of them.

She tried not to think it, but listening to Bear never
ended well. The only reason she was willing to give Bear a
chance at all was because Muir was dead. Otherwise, she'd
be headed back north so fast it would make both their
heads spin.

"Girl, you need to tell me why you want to give up

255

margaritas and gourmet resort food that neither of us have to hunt, or we're going to keep going west until we hit a beach with a cantina and umbrella drinks."

Can't you hear him? He's calling for us.

Feather threw open the door and upchucked the frybread and eggs she'd had for breakfast, palms sweating from the immediate surge of terror as she wiped her mouth. Her hands slippery on the wheel, she threw the truck into gear and burned rubber out of the parking lot.

The only thing that stopped her from going straight north cross country was knowing Christopher would kill her parents if she crossed the border back into Arizona. Hell, he'd had his pack chase her out the previous night. Thankfully, they'd stopped before she had to make them.

She tried to control her breathing, but her heart stuttered in her chest. "Who calls for us?" she asked, terrified of the answer.

I don't know. Not Muir. He is gone.

"Well, I suppose that's a relief, but honestly, unless you come up with a better reason, I'll be damned by the Fates before I start listening to mysterious voices. Haven't we learned better?"

She felt Bear considering the words, which didn't help her nerves. Still driving west, she stared straight ahead, but barely registered the road stretching out in front of her.

Hadn't this been her goal? She'd wanted to have the freedom to grow up and come to terms with her bear before bonding with Rizan. She'd wanted to be his equal—not a damaged kid who still needed someone bigger and stronger to hold her hand when things went tits up.

Slowing she pulled off the road and let out a breath, trying to steady her racing pulse. "Tell me about this voice. What does it say?"

He makes me feel good. Warm and happy. He says I am a good bear.

"You are a good bear."

No, but he makes me feel like I could be. Please, let us go south.

"Fuck." Feather slammed her head against the steering wheel, trying to talk herself out of Bear's shitall stupid idea, then made a quick U-turn. "If you get us killed, or worse, captured again, I'm going to haunt your mangy ass forever."

Bear settled, but pushed forward into their shared mind, letting Feather feel her joy. Fangs grew in her mouth, yet it wasn't uncomfortable. It was as if they belonged there. She wondered if that was how a normal two-natured felt.

For once, they were in tune with each other, sharing equally.

"This isn't going to end well," she muttered, still afraid despite Bear's obvious happiness.

You worry too much. It will be good.

"There'd better be umbrella drinks and food."

Eight hours later, they were almost to Torreón before Bear made her turn east. The narrow dirt road was littered with potholes, and Feather prayed to the Fates that Daisy would keep her innards intact. The last thing she needed was to drop a rod in the middle of nowhere.

"Do you even know where we're going?" Feather couldn't help her waspish tone. She was hangry, thirsty, and the only reason she didn't need to use the restroom was because she'd finally given up and squatted at the side of the road, Bear chafing at the delay.

Not far. Soon. Keep going.

"It better be. You didn't even let us stop in Chihuahua for food, you furry cow."

Bear didn't answer, but her overwhelming happiness made Feather's chest ache. Despite knowing she was driving straight toward sure danger, maybe it was worth it. Maybe this was what they'd needed.

Here!

The abrupt turn sent Daisy fishtailing across the narrow dirt track, almost spilling them into a ditch. Pumping the brakes, Feather got her straightened out and slowed down.

"Fates, give a girl a little warning first," she muttered, keeping a close watch through the dusty windshield.

Almost there. See?

Feather didn't see a thing except a massive stone hill directly in front of them. She'd have almost thought it was a Mesoamerican pyramid, but it wasn't quite the right shape. Slowing, she parked about a hundred yards from the hill and listened to Daisy's engine tick.

"What now?"

He's coming.

Shading her eyes to watch, Feather didn't bother asking who she was talking about. A figure resolved itself in the distance, slowly approaching them, but she couldn't be sure of a gender. Bear had called the person by a male pronoun though, so Feather would go with it.

As he got closer, she let out a sigh of relief and collapsed against Daisy's fender. The blonde hair, kilt, and jacked muscles were very familiar.

"Davryn, what the hell are you doing here? Where's Morgaine?"

Bear was desperate to go to him, but something held Feather back. Some sense of *wrong* as he stopped a few feet away and inhaled deeply, his muscular chest filling with air.

"I haven't smelled a mage in five thousand years. Such a delicious treat."

Instead of giving her a chance to answer, he morphed into the largest dragon she'd ever seen. Rizan was huge, but this pearlescent behemoth eclipsed the sun and his wings shaded acres. Curved horns crested his head, their points sharp as razors over a gaping maw full of teeth. His long, graceful neck was covered in spikes, protecting the sensitive tissue of his windpipe. The dewclaws on his forelegs were as long as she was tall.

He lied!

"Ya think?"

Feather lunged out of the way of a fireball and sprang to her feet, magic filling her palms. Screaming in anger, she aimed a writhing ball of deadly purple at his head.

He ducked, letting her magic hit the hill behind him. It exploded, sending dust and pieces of shrapnel flying. Grunting, the dragon moved to block the debris from reaching her.

"Good girl! Try again."

Parting his jaws, he reached for her, snapping his teeth closed inches from her head as she rolled out of reach. Magic sparked at her fingertips and she managed to lob another bolt of magic directly into his open maw.

He flew sideways, her magic knocking him off his feet. Bear roared, her rage and hurt palpable as she forced them into a shift between one step and the next. It was as if their bodies flowed together into a black bear easily the size of a Kodiak.

Feather wished she'd had time to marvel over their shift into an animal twice the size of a black bear. It was as if every part of her was completely merged with her bear, and it was absolutely glorious. This was how it was always supposed to have been.

Thick fur stood on end, lifted by surges of magic more powerful than anything she'd felt before. The ground rumbled under paws tipped with six-inch claws as she stalked the stunned dragon. Rousing, he shook himself, then faced her once more.

As she approached, readying another surge of magic, a black shape tumbled from the air and tore into the white dragon, fangs rending as they fought.

Rizan!

Her shout went unheard and she roared as blood sprayed from the combatants. He was barely a quarter of the white dragon's size, and she couldn't bear the thought of him being hurt. It was all her fault he was here.

She sprang forward and scrambled up the white dragon's haunch, her claws digging into his hide as she raced along his back. When she reached his shoulder, she sank her fangs deeply into the joint. Magic flared and surged, digging into the wound.

Letting out a scream, the white dragon shook in an attempt to dislodge her. Growling, she tightened her jaws, blood running over her clenched teeth. Maybe she couldn't kill him, but he wouldn't be using that shoulder joint anytime soon.

Without warning, the dragon changed his form, shrinking to human so fast she barely had time to get her feet under her for the landing. Rizan hissed and jerked away, then shifted to his human form as well.

The two men stared at each other, saying nothing. She couldn't read the expression on Rizan's face, but his scent was a mix of anger, hurt, and something she couldn't identify.

Bear pushed her into an unwilling shift, reminding her they needed human vocal cords to figure out what the hell was going on. Her T-shirt was in tatters, but she knotted it as best she could and slipped it over her head.

With careful steps, she approached Rizan and positioned herself between him and other man. "That isn't Davryn. Don't trust him."

His shoulder dislocated and bleeding, the white dragon gave them a shamefaced grin and cupped his groin. "Hey, son. Good to see you again. Are you going to introduce your dear old dad to your lovely mate?"

RIZAN

"Let's go, Feather."

Rizan wrapped his arm around her waist, then pushed her into movement toward her truck. He had no desire to talk to the dragon who had left their entire race to the mercies of a hell realm.

A man who had also not bothered to show his fucking face in the five years since the dragons had been released from their prison, and who had been responsible for putting them there in the first place.

"Wait! Are you going to leave me like this? Don't you want to stay for supper?"

"Fuck off, old man."

Feather glanced between him and his sire, then said, "Maybe we should—"

"No." He lifted her into the passenger seat, but she escaped before he could catch her.

Striding to the dragon who had adopted him after his sire's death, she sent a blast of magic into his shoulder, healing the damaged joint. "Tell me why you dragged me to the ass end of nowhere. And if it was just to lure Rizan here, I will literally kick your ass."

"I'm Madrak, sire to Davryn of Scotland and Rizan of, well, it used to be Nubia, but it's Sudan now."

His accent had even changed. He'd spoken bastardized Euskara the last time Rizan had seen him, but now the clipped syllables were softened with Latin, and hadn't come close to answering Feather's question.

Of course, Madrak had been beyond ancient when humans lived in trees and didn't have a spoken language.

"What do you want, Madrak?" Rizan asked, wanting nothing more than to take Feather far away.

"Just a nice supper with my oldest son and his new mate. Is that too much to ask?"

He resisted the urge to remind Madrak that he wasn't his son. They were not related by blood at all.

"Calling bullshit. Answer my question," Feather retorted.

"Can't it be both?" The deceitful old fuck tried for another grin, but Feather didn't seem a bit charmed.

"Considering you went behind my back and summoned a vulnerable creature who hasn't exactly had great experiences with strange voices in her head... no. What do you want?" Feather asked.

Her words struck Rizan odd for a moment, then he realized she'd been speaking of her bear. This was the woman he remembered from five years ago. Fierce, and brave enough to attack a dragon many times her size. He

262

squeezed her, then kissed her hair, suddenly so proud of her that tears blurred his vision.

Maybe she'd been right to leave. She needed to know she could make choices, and have enough courage to defend herself. If nothing else, Madrak had given her that.

"What? What happened? Did someone harm you?" To Rizan's surprise, Madrak looked almost like he cared enough to be angry, even going so far as to blow a burst of superheated steam from his nostrils.

"Long story. Are you going to answer my question, or do I walk away?"

"Your bear. I started feeling her distress maybe a week ago, and when she got closer..." Madrak shrugged and looked at his bare feet. "I just wanted to help her."

"No," Rizan replied, his anger at the older dragon growing. If he thought for a single second he'd be able to worm his way back into the family after what he'd done, he'd be sorely disappointed. "Feather doesn't need your help. After what you did, I have a hard time believing you want to help anyone."

Madrak studied him for a moment, then nodded. "Yes, that's something we need to talk about, but let's get Feather out of the sun. It looks like she could use a good meal too."

He snapped his fingers, and the hill behind them morphed into a Mesoamerican pyramid, complete with leading up all four faces. It vaguely resembled Kukulcán in Yucatán, but was smaller and less ornate. All the damage from Feather's magic disappeared as well.

Taking Feather's hand, Rizan said, "You don't have to go in there. I can take you wherever you want."

"No, I... I have questions, and it seems like he has

answers. Maybe we need to talk to him about more than just Bear."

To Madrak, she said, "Fancy. Hiding in plain sight?"

"Just a little glamour I learned from a light Sidhe," he said, leading them to the structure. "Omer's grandsire, I think, or maybe a few generations before that. I can't remember."

"How old are you? Omer has been king for millennia."

"Really? Last time I saw him, he was a babe at his mother's breast. Fascinating."

"Do you always answer questions with irrelevant information?"

Rizan hid a grin. Despite having to deal with his adoptive sire, he loved watching Feather come into her own. She might not believe it yet, but she was well on her way to healing. Well, she'd taken the first steps at any rate. He knew better than to think one meeting with a disreputable old dragon who had shirked his duty to his people would make things right for her.

"Only when I don't know the answer." He winked, then touched a stone finial shaped like a serpent. A block of stone weighing tons slid to the side, revealing a corridor lit with elegant electric wall sconces. "Welcome to Chez Madrak. Your server will be with you momentarily."

"There better be an umbrella drink and resort food," Feather muttered.

"Hold out your hand."

Giving him a distrustful glare, she obeyed, her palm sparkling with purple threads of her magic. A second later, a mojito appeared, balanced on her hand, the glass beaded with condensation. Fresh mint leaves were wrapped around the paper umbrella resting on the edge of the glass.

"Thank you." She took a sip, then licked sugar from her lip, sighing happily. "It's delicious."

"Delicious enough to make you forgive me for luring you out here?"

"No, that will require food."

Laughing, Madrak led them deeper into the pyramid. Rizan still wasn't sure he wanted Feather anywhere near the older dragon, but he had questions of his own.

The passageway suddenly opened into a massive gourmet kitchen with copper pots hanging over a massive center island containing a grill and work surface. Mahogany cabinetry gleamed with polish, and he saw every possible convenience, including a dishwasher and commercial refrigerator.

"What's your pleasure?" Madrak asked, pulling an onion and several peppers from a basket. "Empanadas, perhaps? I also have a deer harvested just this morning. I could do carnitas or carne asada, and I'll whip up some fresh tortillas."

Feather blinked, taking in the kitchen. "I didn't know dragons cooked. Why bother when you can just summon what you want?"

"I have to admit, taking the deer without roasting it on the spot was a challenge, but I've come to recognize the value of a well-prepared meal served on a plate. Cooking is relaxing."

He took a ball of dough from the fridge, and within moments, had tortillas frying on a griddle. With the grace of an experienced cook, he added vegetables to a sauté pan, along with thick slices of venison. Almost too soon, Madrak plated the food and sat across from them at an oak farm-house table.

"Eat first, then we'll share a bottle of tequila while you ask your questions."

Feather didn't wait for a second invitation and devoured everything within minutes. Without being asked, Madrak refilled her plate, his expression pained.

Although the food was delicious, Rizan picked at it, trying to settle his thoughts in preparation for their talk. He had so many questions, but he thought he'd start with asking why Madrak hadn't gone through the portal with the rest of the dragons.

"Thank you," Feather finally said, leaning back in her chair. "I haven't had food that good in..." The words trailed off and she looked down at her hands. "Anyway, it was delicious."

A puff of steam escaped Madrak's nostrils. Jaw tight, he nodded. "I have questions of my own regarding your bear, child, but they'll wait. I believe my son would like to speak."

TWENTY-SEVEN

FEATHER

Between the cocktails and a stupid overabundance of food, Feather was almost ready to curl up in a corner for a nap. Even Bear was drowsy from the food coma. The only thing that kept her conscious and alert was getting a chance to learn why Rizan looked so angry—like he was one wrong word away from attacking his father.

Rizan didn't waste any time. "First of all, I'm no offspring of yours, thank the Fates, but if you insist on calling me that, tell me, dear sire, why you thought it necessary to send us to a hell realm. Then tell me why you left us there to rot. Out of thousands, barely two hundred survived."

Madrak rubbed his face, but met Rizan's angry gaze. "It wasn't intentional. I had a beautiful realm picked out. It was a paradise with game, water, caves, and even treasure, but..." He closed his eyes and let out a dry chuckle. "That damned mage buggered it to hell and back, and mispronounced the spell. I tried to fix it, but Myrddin wasn't strong enough to hold it, and—"

"And how dare you blame Myrddin for your mistake?" Rizan interrupted.

"Let him finish." Feather rubbed his knuckles in hopes of soothing him.

"No, Rizan is right. I should have made Myrddin practice more, and I was too busy herding everyone through. It was too late by the time I recognized his mistake. And then..."

He didn't speak for several seconds, then looked up. "We were attacked by humans, and I had to make a choice. I could open the portal and bring everyone back to try again, or I could get Myrddin and Davryn to safety. I couldn't risk them because they were the only hope I had of bringing my people back. So, for my sins, I chose the latter."

"What happened to you in the meantime? Why haven't you revealed yourself?" Feather asked.

"Cowardice," Rizan muttered.

Madrak tipped a tequila bottle in his direction, acknowledging the barb. "Yes, some of that, but I was also left much in the same condition as Davryn. He had Myrddin to keep him tethered, but I..." With a smile that didn't reach his eyes, he added, "I took up residence on the shoulders of an accommodating Russian bear. I wasn't able to break free until about a year ago."

"Well, that explains how you were able to lure me here. What happened to the bear?"

Inside her, Bear whined. Her pain broke Feather's heart and tears pricked her eyes. When he didn't answer, she repeated the question.

Madrak gazed at her sadly, then rubbed his eyes. "She

passed, as did a multitude of creatures I used to keep myself alive. It is for that, that I am most sorry."

"Not for sentencing an entire race of beings to genocide in a hell realm?" Rizan snapped.

"No. I had hope, you see. Hope that your new home was suitable. The creatures I possessed... I drained them of life, Rizan, without their consent, knowing they'd last a year at best. Yet I did it anyway, still clinging to the hope that I might one day bring you back."

Rizan's pain was palpable, despite their missing bond. Rising to her feet, she took his hand. "We're leaving now. I suggest you share what you told us with King Davryn. He'll be the one to decide what to do with you. Don't think to hide either. I'm going to tell him where you are."

Without protest, Rizan let her lead him from the pyramid and back to Daisy. He didn't say a word when she opened the passenger door, and simply got in and folded his hands in his lap. It was as if he'd completely checked out emotionally.

She couldn't exactly blame him. Finding out that thousands of years of torture came about because one mage mispronounced a spell had to be rocking his world.

"Okay, then," she muttered, rounding the hood. "It's well past time to hit a beach with an open bar."

After retracing the tooth-rattling drive to Madrak's pyramid, she got on México 40 toward the coast. Rizan barely spoke, except when absolutely necessary, but that was okay. She had no idea what to say. Six hours later, her eyes burning with exhaustion, she pulled up to the valet station at some nameless Mazatlán resort, then tossed the keys to the attendant.

Dragging Rizan behind her, she trudged to the front desk. The night clerk smirked when, in halting Spanish, she asked for their best room. Rizan's Amex wiped the man's haughty expression away, and within minutes, they were escorted to a suite bigger than her parent's house.

Her gaze skimmed over the leather couches fronting expansive windows. She opened as many as she could, allowing the sounds of the surf just below to fill the suite. The rhythmic pounding of the tide soothed her, and she breathed in the perfume of salt and vibrant life.

Despite her worry for Rizan's continued silence, she was just too damned tired to deal with him. It could wait until morning—after she'd had breakfast and a mimosa or three. Thankfully, she'd had the presence of mind to request an all-inclusive, meaning someone would bring her food and booze whenever she wanted it. She had every intention of parking her ass next to the private infinity pool for every meal.

Aside from that, she still had to unpack her own baggage. Between her exile from Arizona, the continued risk presented by Grandmother, and her utter lack of skills necessary to survive her new normal, there was a lot to handle. With luck, Bear wouldn't try to convince her to hare off after strange voices again, but it was also something to consider.

"You're wrong, you know," Rizan said, still standing in the middle of the suite.

She turned to face him, thankful beyond words that he'd managed to drag himself out of his catatonia. "Oh? About what?"

He strode to her, then stopped bare inches away. Tipping her chin up, he forced her to meet his eyes. "You're not broken. You're not damaged or crazy, or whatever else you're telling yourself. And you sure as fuck aren't weak."

Lowering his head, he kissed her, his plush lips meeting

hers so painfully softly it made her heart clench and seize with longing. She wrapped her arms around his hips, feeling the ridges of muscle in his back as she pulled him close to deepen their kiss.

Giving her a gentle smile, he pulled away. "Careful, morsel. I said I'd give you time, and you shall have it for now, but don't push your luck."

Feather considered his words for a moment. She'd managed to get herself out of Arizona without killing anyone, survive a battle of wits with Rizan's father figure, extricate both of them from his presence, find peace with Bear, and still had the presence of mind to drive halfway across Mexico, again without killing anyone.

"You know what? Fuck it. I'm going to take what I want for a change." Laying a hand on his jaw, she opened herself and her magic, and invited Rizan to accept the bond she offered. Everything else would come out in the wash.

RIZAN

Feather's magic poured into him and their bond snapped into place like it had never been lost. It wasn't quite the same though. Although guilt lurked, there was no fear and the taint of darkness was almost gone. She and her bear were at peace with each other.

Gone were his conflicted feelings about his adoptive sire, and all thought about the problems his presence would create for the remaining dragons. He didn't give a single damn if Madrak and Davryn wanted to kill each other for the crown. They could fight over it with his blessing.

"Do you want to return to my hoard now, or to—"

"Three words," she replied, her fingers working the buttons on his shirt. "Private. Infinity. Pool."

Forgetting their mutual exhaustion, he swept her into his arms and carried her to the couch, too impatient to look for a bed in the opulent suite. "I also like room service. And naked."

"Room service eaten while naked in our private infinity pool."

"You're brilliant." Still kissing her, he let her slide down his body, then helped her pull her T-shirt over her head. Her desert rain and wildflower perfume washed over him, untainted by blood or anything else except the clean fragrance of warm, aroused woman.

"You're gorgeous." Sliding her hands down his chest, she reached for his belt buckle and opened his trousers. "But I see Morgaine's fascination with Davryn's kilt."

"Oh really?" Snapping his fingers, he exchanged his jeans for a garment similar to what his brother usually wore, making her giggle.

Still smiling, she dropped to her knees and ducked her head under the loose fabric. "Mmm. I definitely see the attraction."

"Feather, what are you— Oh, fuck!"

He was lost from the moment her lips closed over the head of his cock. Her need thrummed through their bond, reverberating between them, and purple magic flared, illuminating the room. Cursing under his breath, he tossed the kilt away, desperate to see her.

"If you have to ask, maybe I'm doing it wrong." She fisted his cock, squeezing until he saw stars, then caressed his balls and stroked the sensitive perineum. As she sucked him, he could feel her playing with her pussy, sensing the wet glide of her fingers over slick flesh.

Their combined arousal surged and a lamp exploded, reminding him of what always seemed to happen when he made love to Feather. With Herculean effort, he pulled back and helped her to her feet.

"Outside, morsel," he said, gasping for air. "We have to go outside. And we need condoms."

"Yes to outside," she replied, kissing his chest. "No to condoms. I'm going to give you my mating bite, and you're going to put a baby in me."

Flames of need roiled inside him, but he forced himself to stop. "What about college?"

"Distance learning. It will happen, but I'm not going anywhere." She nipped his throat, drawing a little blood. "Should have done that in the first place."

He opened his mouth to argue, but she laid a hand over his lips. "Don't. You know I'm right."

"It was your dream."

Smiling, she took his hand to lead him outside. "I have better dreams now."

Following her, Rizan searched their bond. She might say that now out of residual fear, but he had to be sure she meant it. To his surprise, he found nothing but desire for... him. He didn't even sense her bear.

Unwilling to wait a single second longer, he tossed her over his shoulder and strode through the glass door to the patio. The pool, with its own hot tub, glistened under the stars, placid and welcoming, but it wasn't his goal.

He caught the sounds of a party in the distance, but it was nearly drowned out by the pounding surf fifty yards away. It was as if they were in their own private universe filled with the scent of the sea and blooming tropical flowers carried on the balmy breeze.

Lowering her gently to a lounger strewn with plush pillows, he kissed her again, then traced his lips down her breastbone. Moonlight shimmered over her golden skin, dappling her in fairy lights.

"You're the most beautiful thing I've ever seen," he said, his voice thick with desire.

"I feel the same." Catching his shoulder, she pulled him down to her, claws digging into his flesh.

It should have hurt, yet the slight pinching pain only ramped up his desire. She moaned in response, her hips flexing unconsciously.

"Please, Rizan. I need you."

He felt her desperation grow, matching his own, but he forced himself to slow down, needing to make this good for her, but she growled deep, the sound resonating in her chest. Without warning, she lunged at him and flipped him to his back on the hard wood of the deck and straddled his hips.

Wet and slick with need, her core slid against his shaft, making him hiss out a breath. "I wanted to taste you. Let you come on my tongue so I could let your sweetness drip down my throat. Do it a million times until you're crying for me."

Her lips parted into a smile, revealing lengthening fangs. "That can be round two."

TWENTY-EIGHT

FEATHER

Whimpering, Feather fisted his cock and centered herself over him. As entertaining as his ideas sounded, she was too desperate to wait. It was as if something drove her—a need too deep to be assuaged by anything but his thick shaft inside her.

Before she could lower herself, he rose up until he sat, and in an astonishing display of upper body strength, scooted them back until he was leaning against the wall. Biting back a hysterical giggle, she wondered if he'd gotten splinters in his ass, but her mirth disappeared as quickly as it came when he surged into her.

He filled her, stretching her tight channel almost painfully, but it was a good hurt. A claiming hurt that marked her as his as surely as her bite would do to him. Grabbing her hips, he held her tightly, the tips of claws digging into her.

275

She met his gorgeous dark eyes and rocked her hips against him, taking him even deeper inside her clenching channel.

"I love you." She breathed the words like a catechism, a prayer to the Fates. She prayed they'd listen just this once and let her keep him forever.

His pupils, barely visible in his dark eyes, became vertical slits, turning red as they caught the ambient light. "I love you more than my life. You are my everything."

Their combined need ricocheted through the bond until she didn't know where she ended and he began. Every twitch of his cock inside her, every flex of her channel around him blended into a single perfect storm of sensation.

She felt the moment he reached the point of no return. The tingle of electricity racing down his spine to his groin mirrored itself in her body.

A voice, familiar, yet not, whispered, "It is time."

Her fangs ached as her orgasm bore down on her, the weight of their combined pleasure nearly crushing the breath from her lungs. Without giving herself time to think, she struck, burying her canines deep into the meat of his shoulder.

Feather felt every bit of that excruciating, perfect pain. Rizan's sudden joy tempered it into something sublime as she bound them together by more than magic.

Throwing her head back, she screamed, the sound augmented by Rizan's delighted roar of pleasure. Their climax, loosed from its fetters, drowned them in a wave of delight as her magic soared to the heavens.

Unable to hold herself up, she collapsed against him, their panting breaths loud in the sudden quiet. She couldn't even hear the surf over the pounding of her heart as she licked the bite until it closed into a ridged scar.

The taste of his blood was more intoxicating than tequila and sent another pulse of desire into her core, but she was too tired to do anything about it. Clearly, round two would have to wait until after she'd gotten a few hours of sleep.

Chuckling breathlessly, Rizan nuzzled her hair, then said, "Look up, morsel."

"Ungh."

He laughed again, then lifted her, turning her until she was curled up in his lap. "Look up."

Grunting, she brushed hair out of her face and tried to focus. To her surprise, the sea was as smooth as glass. "What the—"

He cupped her chin in a warm palm and tilted her head toward the sky. "I've been alive a very long time, but I've never seen an aurora borealis this far south."

"Holy... Aunt Yan is going to kill me."

Swirls of her magic painted the night sky, bright enough to overcome the light pollution from Mazatlán. She couldn't decide whether it was better or worse than destroying a hotel room.

Still laughing at her, Rizan helped her up and half-carried her to the lounger. They laid together, watching the sky, until the aurora faded with the light of dawn across the mirrored sea.

Fates, she loved him. He'd pulled her from the blackest despair, saved her when she couldn't save herself, and gave her the freedom to make her own choices. He was her everything, and nothing would ever part them. Not in this world or the next.

EPILOGUE

Madrak's son soared with his mate over a tumultuous sea. Her laughter rang like bells as she took a swan dive off his outstretched paw, only to be caught in gentle claws before she hit the water.

Such a tempestuous lot, the black dragons. They wore their hearts on their... well, scales. The human idiom didn't exactly fit, but they loved as deeply and as hard as they fought. The half-breed bear was a good match for him. Strong, clever, and empathetic, she would temper and soften Rizan's turbulent emotions.

Chuckling, he watched Rizan take his mate down to visit a pod of whales. One of the creatures rolled, peering at them with a liquid eye, then shot Rizan in the face with a stream of water from its blowhole.

As far as he knew, Rizan was the last of the black dragons. One infant had gone into exile, but the poor mite was likely dead. The immediate pang of guilt struck like an arrow through his chest and he lost altitude, nearly losing his concealment in the bright sunlight.

Thousands died, all because of his carelessness. Madrak

didn't blame Myrddin for his mistake, of course. The fault was solely his. Despite the danger, he should have called them back before it was too late. He'd live with the failure forever.

Thankfully, his youngest son was now king. He even had a granddaughter, a crown princess already prepared to take the throne when Davryn retired.

They didn't need him at all, but he supposed he ought to explain himself at some point. Although he wanted to see his brethren, he did not relish the confrontation.

A brush of power he hadn't felt in—fates, he had no idea how long—tickled his scales, making him bank into a turn.

Wings flared, *she* appeared, hovering in front of him. The creature had no name—at least none she cared to share—but he knew her. She was the eternal, the neverending. The guardian of realms, and the one being separating order from chaos. Female, yet neuter in a way he would never understand. Gold and bronze feathers lay smooth on her back, and she was barely larger than a harpy eagle, meaning she'd been reborn recently.

He'd already seen it twice, and did not regret missing the third. Her rebirth heralded cataclysm.

Bowing his head, he called her by the name given to her by a people long dead and forgotten, "Greetings, Storm-bringer."

"Hey, Maddy. Long time, no see. You about done with the pity party?"

Her words shocked him speechless, rendering him unable to answer. Although he'd addressed her first, he hadn't expected her to reply. He'd never heard her speak. Not once in thousands upon thousands of millennia.

"Excuse me?"

"I asked if you were done sucking the pity dick. We got things to see and people to do."

"Isn't that supposed to be the other way around?" A year obviously hadn't been enough time to familiarize himself with the modern world, and he wondered if he was missing a joke somewhere.

She winked one golden eye, a surprisingly human gesture. "Fuck no. That would be boring. Now, get a move on. If you make me late for the Army Navy game, I'll set your tail on fire."

"Army Navy? I don't understand."

Her wings mantled and she dove at his head, making him dart out of the way. "I'll catch you up on the way to Arizona."

ACKNOWLEDGMENTS

As always, my undying gratitude goes out to Engineer Hubby, Mr. Greywood, for his love, encouragement, and support. Without him, I don't think I'd be writing at all. Love you to the moon and back, baby.

Want to see what I'm up to next? Join my Renegades. You can also sign up for my newsletter to get a free Wicked Magic story delivered straight to your inbox!

About Minette Moreau

Minette is the alter-ego of USA Today bestselling author Raisa Greywood, and writes all the things that go bump in the night. Shapeshifters, aliens, vampires, and especially dragons all find their way into her stories.

www.minettemoreau.com

facebook.com/AuthorMinetteMoreau

bookbub.com/authors/minette-moreau

goodreads.com/minettemoreau

Also by Minette Moreau

Shifters' Mates

Tiger's Gambit

Leopard's Surrender

Jaguar's Initiative

Wicked Magic

Wicked Truth

Wicked Fire

Wicked Rage